"I want the truth, Slade. I deserve the truth."

"Right now, and for the foreseeable future, I am your foreman. That is the truth."

"But that's not the whole truth. Lies of omission are still lies in my book."

He quirked an eyebrow, clearly confused. "When did I—"

Amanda jabbed him in the chest with her finger. "So if you are hiding something from me, something about who you are or what's happening on this ranch or my daughter's safety or—"

Slade wrapped his hand around the finger poking his chest and hauled her closer. "I would *never* do *anything* to put your daughter at risk." His eyes blazed with conviction. "Let's get that straight from the start."

Her mouth dried, and she lost her train of thought until he said, "I'm an agent with the Wyoming Bureau of Investigation."

The Coltons of Wyoming: Stories of true love, high stakes...and family honor.

Dear Reader,

When I was asked to write the last book for The Coltons of Wyoming, the continuity was pitched to me as "Dallas meets *Downton Abbey*." I'd just finished watching the first two seasons of *Downton Abbey* on DVD and loved, loved, loved it! Write a Downton-esque continuity book? Why, yes! Write a tortured hero who's an undercover agent working as ranch foreman? Double yes. I was all in.

I had a great time working with the other authors as we hashed out intersecting plotlines, created new characters and shared the magic as this continuity came to life. In this, the final book in the continuity, oldest sister Amanda Colton gets her turn with romance. Amanda has her hands full as a single mother and ranch veterinarian, but knowing someone on the ranch is trying to kidnap her daughter raises the stakes for Amanda to a new level. When handsome and brooding Slade Kent arrives to take over as ranch foreman, Amanda finds an unexpected ally in the fight to keep her daughter, the Colton heir, safe. With Slade's help, can Amanda finally root out the traitor at Dead River Ranch and put a stop to the terror haunting the Coltons of Wyoming?

Merry Christmas and happy reading!

Beth Cornelison

COLTON CHRISTMAS RESCUE

Beth Cornelison

—

HARLEQUIN® ROMANTIC SUSPENSE

Special thanks and acknowledgment to Beth Cornelison
for her contribution to
The Coltons of Wyoming miniseries.

Recycling programs
for this product may
not exist in your area.

ISBN-13: 978-0-373-27850-3

COLTON CHRISTMAS RESCUE

Copyright © 2013 by Harlequin Books S.A.

HARLEQUIN®
www.Harlequin.com

Printed in U.S.A.

Books by Beth Cornelison

Harlequin Romantic Suspense

Special Ops Bodyguard #1668
Operation Baby Rescue #1677
^Soldier's Pregnancy Protocol #1709
^The Reunion Mission #1717
Colton's Ranch Refuge #1724
^Cowboy's Texas Rescue #1746
Colton Christmas Rescue #1780

*The Bride's Bodyguard #1630
P.I. Daddy's Personal Mission #1632
*The Prodigal Bride #1646

*The Bancroft Brides
^Black Ops Rescues

Other titles by this author
available in ebook format.

Silhouette Romantic Suspense

To Love, Honor and Defend #1362
In Protective Custody #1422
Danger at Her Door #1478
Duty to Protect #1522
Rancher's Redemption #1532
Tall Dark Defender #1566
*The Christmas Stranger #1581
Blackout at Christmas #1583
    "Stranded with the Bridesmaid"

BETH CORNELISON

started writing stories as a child when she penned a tale about the adventures of her cat, Ajax. A Georgia native, she received her bachelor's degree in public relations from the University of Georgia. After working in public relations for a little more than a year, she moved with her husband to Louisiana, where she decided to pursue her love of writing fiction.

Since that first time, Beth has written many more stories of adventure and romantic suspense and has won numerous honors for her work, including a coveted Golden Heart Award in romantic suspense from Romance Writers of America. She is active on the board of directors for the North Louisiana Storytellers and Authors of Romance (NOLA STARS) and loves reading, traveling, *Peanuts'* Snoopy and spending downtime with her family.

She writes from her home in Louisiana, where she lives with her husband, one son and two cats who think they are people. Beth loves to hear from her readers. You can write to her at P.O. Box 5418, Bossier City, LA 71171, or visit her website, www.bethcornelison.com.

To Keyren Gerlach Burgess, who created this continuity and who was my awesome-sauce editor for many books. Best of luck in your future endeavors!

Thanks to Deborah Boyd for allowing me to honor her kitty, Reyna, as Amanda's cat. Deborah won the chance to have Reyna featured in my book through Brenda Novak's Annual Auction for the Cure of Diabetes 2012.

Prologue

Ten years ago

If he were the kidnapper, how would he have made his getaway? How could someone have gotten off the ranch with a baby, unseen?

Officer Roland Kent of the Dead River, Wyoming, police department moved the beam of his flashlight across the grass and along the fence line at the employee entrance to Dead River Ranch. He mulled over the questions that had stumped the local police for the past twenty years. Intrigued by puzzles and determined to solve the cold case of Cole Colton's twenty-year-old kidnapping, Roland Kent had volunteered to work on the mystery, even if it had to be on his personal time. His boss, Chief Drucker, was not pleased with Roland's overtime investigations but couldn't give him a valid reason why he shouldn't work on the cold case. Roland had taken that as grudging consent and had begun his after-hours detective work three weeks ago. So far, he'd met nothing but resistance, silence and stone walls from the family and staff at Dead River Ranch, a mystery in its own right. Didn't the Coltons want their heir found?

Walking closer to the driveway gate, Roland examined the locking mechanism. Had the gate or locks been changed in the past twenty years? This one seemed rather old and rusty. Perhaps if—

"Stop right there or I'll shoot!" a voice shouted. A bright flashlight swung up to shine directly in Roland's eyes, blinding him. "What are you doing?"

Roland made out a dark figure, and his attention zeroed in on the weapon aimed at him. He reached for his own weapon. "Don't shoot! I'm—"

But before he could identify himself, the muzzle of the gun aimed at him flashed. A bullet punched his chest, knocking him backward. Pain exploded in his torso and he struggled to draw a breath. He tried to raise his weapon to defend himself, but his arm hung limply at his side. His legs buckled, and he sank to the grass at the foot of the entry gate.

The dark figure moved closer, and the flashlight beam stayed on his face.

"Officer Kent?" his shooter rasped, clearly frightened by the notion of having shot a cop. "I didn't realize... I didn't mean to—"

Roland clutched his chest, felt the warm seep of blood through his shirt. "Can't...breathe."

The shooter moved closer, but Roland's vision was dimming.

Dying...I'm dying. Roland struggled to suck in oxygen. The bullet must have hit his lung.

His thoughts turned to Slade, his only son… *I love you, cowboy. I'm proud of you.*

Above him, his shooter was frantic. The flashlight beam swung about wildly until it landed on the fence. The shooter stepped over Roland, offering him no comfort, no assistance. Instead, Roland watched with fading sight as the shooter scrabbled in the dirt for a loose nail and dug something out of the fence post and slipped it in a jacket pocket. The bullet. Evidence. Covering up the murder of a cop.

Roland's hand slipped weakly from his chest. Gasped for breath. Closed his eyes. Murdered…

I'm sorry, Slade.

Early the next morning, Agnes Barlow, the head cook at Dead River Ranch, drove out toward the sunrise farmers' market for fresh fruit to serve the Colton family at breakfast. When she reached the employee entrance, she climbed out of the ranch truck and lumbered up the driveway to open the gate. In the predawn darkness, the truck's headlamps shone on a dark lump by the fence.

She slowed her steps, narrowing a wary gaze on the object. A trash bag? A dead animal? Moving cautiously, she edged closer. A tingle of apprehension crawled through her. It looked like a body. Was some riffraff sleeping there, waiting to waylay an employee?

"Hello?" she called.

No response.

Shuffling closer, she approached the figure, nudged the man with her toe. "Hey, you can't sleep he—"

The body rolled onto its back. Officer Roland Kent of the local police. Why would—

Then Agnes noticed the dark bloodstain on his chest, the dead, fixed stare of the man's eyes.

And she screamed.

Chapter 1

Present day

The trill of a ringing phone woke Amanda Colton from a deep sleep, but her maternal instincts had her fully awake in seconds. She grabbed the phone before the next ring, praying the noise hadn't woken eight-month-old Cheyenne. Her daughter had been fussy last night at bedtime because of a stuffy nose, and Amanda had worked for two hours to get her to sleep.

She glanced at the alarm clock as she dragged the phone to her ear. 3:23 a.m.

Her gut tightened. Nothing good ever came of a call at three in the morning, and her family had had enough bad news and tragedy in the past several months to last a lifetime.

"Hello?" she said warily.

"Amanda, thank God! I need your help!"

Hearing the fear in her youngest sister's voice, Amanda sat up and shoved her hair from her face. "Gabby? What's wrong?"

"It's Peanut. I think he has colic, and he keeps trying to lie down!"

Dread speared her chest. "Oh, no."

Equine colic could be deadly, especially if the horse tried to roll on the ground, which could cause the intestine to become wrapped around itself.

Amanda tossed back the covers, disturbing the fuzzy orange cat sleeping beside her, and swung her feet to the floor. "Is Trevor there with you?"

Trevor Garth was head of security for the ranch. But more important, in this case, he was Gabriella's fiancé.

"Not yet." Gabby's voice cracked, and she sniffed hard, clearly trying not to cry. "He's on his way. He said to call you."

Peanut, Gabby's horse, had been a birthday present when her sister was seven and Peanut was still a foal. Gabriella and Peanut had grown up together and her soft-hearted sister loved the horse dearly. Amanda hated the idea of Gabriella losing Peanut.

"Who's going to stay with Avery?" Amanda asked, her mothering instincts again surging to the forefront when she thought of Trevor's infant daughter.

"Mathilda, I think. She— No, Peanut! Stop. Please, stop!"

"Okay, I'm on my way. Until I get there, do *not* let him lie down."

"I *know* he's supposed to stay up," Gabby said, her voice tense with frustration and panic, "but you try keeping a fourteen-hundred-pound animal on his feet when he wants to roll on the ground."

"Gabby, it's critical! Do whatever you have to." With

one hand Amanda stepped into a pair of jeans while she held the phone with her other hand. "Are any of the hands there? Do you have any help at all?"

"No. The place was deserted when I got here a little while ago."

Amanda groaned, lamenting the shortage of ranch help, thanks to the National Finals Rodeo competition taking place in Las Vegas that week. She shoved her feet in her boots without bothering with socks. "I'll make some calls, see who's around to help. Meantime, try to get Peanut to walk, even if just up and down the center aisle of the stable."

"Okay. Hurry!"

Amanda keyed off the connection to Gabby and pushed speed dial 4, ringing the land line in Tom Brooks's room. Tom was a retired Marine and former police officer who had been shot in the hip five years ago and forced to take a desk job. Trevor had hired him this summer after it became clear Cheyenne was the target of kidnappers. He answered with a crisp, "Tom Brooks."

Amanda tucked her night shirt into her jeans and grabbed a sweatshirt from a drawer. "Tom, it's Amanda. I'm so sorry to wake you, but there's been an emergency."

She heard the rustle of sheets and squeak of bed springs as Tom flew into action. "What's happened?"

"Gabriella's horse is sick."

"And you need me to guard Cheyenne while you see to the horse."

"Yes, please. I know you're supposed to be off duty, but—"

"No such thing as off-duty. My job is to protect that sweet babe of yours, whatever and whenever. I'll be there in two."

"Thank you, Tom. You're a godsend."

Amanda disconnected and stuck her cell phone in her back jeans pocket as she hurried into the adjoining room where her daughter slept. In the dim glow from the bunny-shaped night-light over the crib, Amanda peeked over the railing at her sleeping child. Her whole world. Her life.

As it always did whenever she looked at her precious baby girl, Amanda's heart swelled until she thought it might burst. How could someone so tiny and fragile stir such a deep, consuming love?

Cheyenne gave a snuffly sigh, and Amanda bit her bottom lip, concerned over the baby's congestion. Levi, Amanda's half-brother and the doctor who was caring full-time for her ill father, had assured her it was nothing but a cold, that Cheyenne would be fine in a couple days. But as a first-time mother, Amanda still fretted over every runny nose and hiccup.

Bending over the crib rail, Amanda rubbed Cheyenne's back and tucked the fuzzy pink blanket around her daughter's feet. Straightening, she whispered, "Oh, chickpea, what would I do without you?"

A soft knock heralded Tom's arrival, then he opened the door and peered into the nursery. "Miss Amanda?"

Amanda waved him in. "I don't know how long I'll be. Maybe all morning. If she wakes up all congested, Levi said to give her a dropperful of this." She handed him the decongestant bottle and backed toward the door. "Thanks again."

Tom nodded gravely. "Yes, ma'am. You go help that sick horse."

Amanda grabbed her veterinary bag from a bench at the foot of her bed and hesitated at the bedroom door. In recent months, it had become all too clear that her daughter was the target of kidnappers intending to extort money from Amanda's wealthy family. Leaving Cheyenne, even for a few minutes, even with a trained guard, always reminded Amanda how vulnerable Cheyenne was, how quickly her baby could be snatched, how devastated she'd be if anything happened to her daughter.

Tom noticed her hesitation and smiled. "Go on, Miss Amanda. I'll protect your little princess as if she were my own."

With a sigh and a smile of gratitude, Amanda ducked into the hall and hustled to the stairs. She took the steps two at a time, grabbed her work gloves and a parka from the back closet, and was practically running by the time she reached the back door. She'd just pulled her cell phone from her back pocket to start waking ranch hands when a tall dark-haired man barreled out of the employees' wing.

"Hey," she called, squinting in the darkness to determine which of the ranch hands he was. But when he raised his head, glancing her way as he strode briskly across the ranch yard, she didn't recognize him, and a tingle of apprehension crawled down her spine. In light of the recent tragedies at the ranch, a stranger wandering the grounds in the predawn hours sounded all kinds of alarms for Amanda. "Hey, stop right there, pal!"

The man stopped, shifting his weight restlessly and sending her an impatient glare as she hurried to catch up to him.

She returned a hostile stare, sizing him up as she approached him. "Who are you and what are you doing here?"

He flicked his black Stetson back from his face and frowned. The blue-white security lights cast harsh shadows across his square jaw and rugged cheeks. "Slade Kent. Word is there's a horse with colic needs tending, so I'm headed to the stable."

Somewhat mollified, Amanda hitched her chin for him to accompany her as she continued toward the stable. "So you're a new hand?"

"Who's asking?" Slade fell in step beside her, his long-legged strides outpacing her so that she was nearly jogging to keep up.

"I'm Amanda." When he sent her a look that said, *So?* she added, "Amanda *Colton.* Dead River Ranch belongs to my family. It's my sister's horse that has colic."

He gave a little nod. "I see. Well, ma'am, I promise to take good care of the horse. You can go back to the house and stay warm. I'll be sure someone keeps you posted on how the horse is doing."

His patronizing tone grated her already-stressed nerves, and she barked an ill-humored laugh. "I also happen to be a vet." She held up her medical bag. "I'll be the one treating Peanut."

He gave a dismissive scoff. "Unnecessary. Any ranch hand worth his salt has dealt with colic before. I don't need your help."

Her eyebrows shot up, and she gave him an incredulous look. "Oh, really? Who died and made you king?"

"Not king. Foreman. Which means decisions about the livestock and horses are my call."

She slowed to a stop, stunned by his audacity and his job title. "You're our new *foreman?* Since when?"

He stopped when she did and faced her. "Since Dylan Frick hired me."

"Dylan?" She cocked her head, suspicious. "Dylan moved out of town." To be precise, he'd entered Witness Security with his fiancée, but Slade didn't need to know that.

Slade gave her an impatient glance. "He made the arrangements before he left. I have an employment contract with his signature I can show you if you need proof. But later. Right now, that horse is my only concern."

He spun on his boot heel and continued up toward the stable.

Clamping her mouth in a line of frustration, Amanda ran to catch up again. "Foreman or not, I'm the one with the veterinary degree, and I'm in charge of medical issues with the animals." She panted for a breath, irritated to be winded from keeping pace with him. A white cloud formed in the frigid December air as she puffed out a deep breath. "That includes colic."

Slade reached the stable first and grabbed the large slide bolt that secured the alley doors. "A degree is no substitute for experience."

When he opened the heavy door, she scooted past him and sent him a smug grin. "Then it's a good thing I have plenty of experience, as well." Spotting Trevor and Gabby in the center alleyway walking Peanut in circles, she hustled toward them. She dug an elastic band out of her coat pocket and finger-combed her hair into a ponytail. "How long has he been symptomatic?"

Relief eased the worry in Gabby's face when she saw Amanda had arrived. "He was acting edgy when I was in here after dinner, and I couldn't sleep, worrying about him. I got up a little while ago to check on him and found him like this." She waved a hand at the sorrel gelding, who tossed his head, fighting the lead clipped to his halter and kicking at his abdomen with a rear hoof.

"Have you taken all the water and feed out of his stall?"

"Yes," Gabby answered.

Amanda set her medical bag on a bale of hay and retrieved her stethoscope. When she turned around, Slade had taken the lead from Trevor and was stroking Peanut's neck. He leaned close to the horse and made a low soft noise meant to calm Peanut.

Amanda opened her mouth to tell Slade to butt out, but she caught herself and swallowed the words. She needed his cooperation in calming Peanut while she examined him more than she needed to win a battle of wills with the new foreman. She introduced Slade to Trevor and her sister and learned Trevor had already met the new foreman earlier that night.

Peanut pawed the ground restlessly, and Amanda sent Slade a hard look. "Keep him still. I need to listen for gut sounds."

Trevor and Gabby helped Slade calm the horse while she moved the stethoscope from one spot to another on Peanut's abdomen, checking for sounds of intestinal motility. "It's pretty quiet in there, but I do hear some movement, which is good."

"Can you give him something for the pain?" Gabby asked, her eyes full of tears. "I hate to see him suffer."

Amanda moved the stethoscope to listen to Peanut's lungs and heart. "I'll need to sedate him before I insert the naso-gastric tube. That and a dose of Buscopan to suppress the intestinal spasms will help him feel better." She returned to her medical bag and dug out the case where she kept a small selection of drugs for the most common emergencies. She prepared injections of both an appropriate sedative and the anti-spasmodic. Knowing she needed to perform a rectal exam, she gave her sister an errand to keep her busy. "Gabby, can you get me a pair of long gloves? I want to check for impaction." She caught Slade's raised eyebrow as she turned back to her patient and cocked her head. "Unless you want the honor of doing that exam."

He slid a pack of peppermint gum from his pocket

and calmly stuck a piece in his mouth while he gave her a level look. "I will if you're too squeamish."

"Oh, brother," she grumbled under her breath. She refused to rise to his baiting. Now was not the time to lock horns with the new foreman.

Nickering testily, Peanut tried to lie down again, and Slade walked the horse forward a few steps, then crooned to him. "Easy, fella."

Gabriella returned with the long examination gloves. Taking them, Amanda sent her sister off on another errand, this time for the mineral oil and naso-gastric tube she'd need once Peanut responded to the sedative.

Feeling Slade's watchful gaze on her, Amanda removed her parka and snapped the long latex glove into place, covering her arm past her elbow.

Stepping to Peanut's hind end, Slade pulled the horse's tail up and held it out of her way.

She cut a side glance to him, prepared to thank him for his helpfulness, but the smug challenge in his eyes stopped her. Did he think she would balk? That the less pleasant aspects of veterinary care would stop her from doing what was best for an animal in need? Amanda gritted her back teeth. A rectal exam was not her favorite way to spend an evening, but she was no shrinking violet. She'd never shied from doing the dirty work involved in either large animal veterinary care or ranching.

She squared her shoulders and flipped her ponytail over her shoulder, silently accepting his challenge. The sooner the new foreman knew who he was dealing with the better.

Chapter 2

Amanda Colton was a piece of work. Bossy, brash, sarcastic.

Slade studied the furrow of concentration in her brow as she palpated the horse's colon and admitted silently that she also knew what she was doing. He let his gaze slide over her, from her long average-brown hair, pulled back in a messy ponytail, her rumpled Snoopy nightshirt, only half tucked in her jeans, and her makeup-free, pillow-creased cheeks. She looked like what she was—a woman called to an emergency in the middle of the night. Yet despite her disarray and the fact that she was up a horse's behind to her elbow, she was also…sexy.

When they'd reached the lighted stable and he'd gotten his first good look at her, he'd been caught off-guard by the fire in her gold eyes and the tantalizing pout of her full, if slightly chapped, lips. He might be grieving

Krista and Emily, but he wasn't dead. And a man would have to be dead not to notice Amanda Colton.

She stepped back from the gelding and pulled off the latex glove. "I don't believe he's impacted. Surgery shouldn't be necessary."

"Thank God," Amanda's redheaded sister said. *Gabriella*—he needed to start learning names around the ranch, figuring out who all the players were. Especially the ones named Colton. Until he proved otherwise, everyone was on his suspect list.

Amanda's pale brown eyes met his. "Will you help me get the tube in him so I can administer the laxatives?"

Slade jerked a tight nod. "At your service, doc."

Over the next couple of hours, Slade worked beside Amanda, feeding the horse mineral oil through a nasal tube into his stomach and waiting for the gelding to pass the obstruction.

Trevor was able to convince Gabriella to return with him to the main house around 4:00 a.m. after Amanda promised to call if there was any change for the worse.

At first, conversation between Slade and Amanda centered around their minute-by-minute progress with the task at hand. But after they removed the nasal tube and were left with the tedium of waiting for the horse to take a dump, Amanda sent Slade a curious look and said, "Tell me about yourself, Slade. Where did Dylan find you? And why hadn't I met you before tonight?"

Slade settled on the ground with his legs stretched out in front of him, and she sat across from him on a bale of hay just outside Peanut's stall. He met her gaze and considered his answer carefully. The last thing he needed was to give himself away or ring any warning bells with a Colton before he'd accomplished what he'd come to Dead River Ranch to do.

"I met Dylan through a…mutual acquaintance." The new chief of police for the Dead River Police Department, actually, not that she needed to know that detail. "And I only arrived at the ranch tonight around 11:00 p.m. My plane was late, and I was told the family had gone to bed. I'd planned to introduce myself in the morning."

She waved a hand toward the window where a thin gray light crept across the ranch property. "Well, it's morning, and we've got time on our hands. Who is Slade Kent? Where are you from?"

Slade rubbed the two-day bristle on his jaw. "I'm fully qualified for the job, if that's your concern."

Amanda tipped her head. "I don't doubt it. Dylan wouldn't have hired you if he didn't think you were top-notch. But I'd like to know more than where you've worked and what skills you bring to the job."

Slade leaned back against the stall partition and folded his arms across his chest. "I came here from Jackson. I grew up around ranches and got my first summer job working as a hand when I was sixteen. I used to ride bulls on the PRCA circuit—"

Her face brightened. "A bull rider? Me, too."

He snapped his eyebrows together in disbelief. "You rode bulls?"

She laughed. "Yep. Well, saddle bronc actually. But I gave it up when I got pregnant with my daughter, Cheyenne. Naturally. Now, since I'm a single mother, it's just too great a risk. I miss it sometimes, but…" She took a deep breath and smiled warmly. "Cheyenne's worth it."

Slade quickly squashed the flash of memory that jabbed his heart. He refused to let ancient history interfere with the job he'd come to do.

Amanda nudged his boot with her own. "You said *used to.* Why'd you give it up?"

He gave a dismissive shrug. "Life got in the way. New priorities. Didn't have the time for it anymore."

"What about family?" she asked. "Was that one of the priorities?"

His gut quickened, and he shoved to his feet, grabbing his Stetson from a tack hook where he'd hung it earlier. "Say, where can a guy get a cup of coffee around here?"

Amanda checked her watch. "The kitchen staff should be up by now. Our cook, Agnes, will have coffee ready." She looked up at him with sleep-deprived eyes. "You know where the main kitchen is?"

"I'll find it." He jammed his hat on his head, pleased his distraction tactic had worked. "Can I bring you some? You look like you could use a jolt of caffeine."

She arched a manicured eyebrow. "Such flattery."

He scowled at her. "I just mean that it's been a long, tough night, and—"

"Yes," she interrupted with a chuckle. "Cream and sugar, please." He was almost to the stable door when she called, "Oh! And socks!"

He turned. "Excuse me?"

"I was rushing when I came out here and didn't bother with socks. But now my feet are frozen. Would you have Fiona or Mathilda get a pair of thick socks from my room and bring them back with you?"

"Socks."

"Mmm-hmm. And maybe a bagel or sweet roll. I'm starved."

He hooked his thumbs in his jeans pockets and cocked his head. "Anything else, *ma'am?*" he asked, not caring if she heard the derision in his tone. He'd been hired as the foreman, not her personal butler.

"No, that should do it." She sent him a smile that was

either oblivious to his frustration or maddeningly uncaring how spoiled and bossy she came off.

He huffed a humorless laugh as he headed out in the cold gray morning, his boots crunching in the thick layer of Wyoming frost. When he reached the main house, he followed his nose, and the tempting aromas of bacon, cinnamon and coffee, to what was clearly the employee dining area. House staff and ranch hands already buzzed around a long trestle table filled with cinnamon rolls, scrambled eggs, thick sliced ham and steaming coffee. Slade's stomach growled.

"Can I help you?" A woman with short silvery-blond hair and a high-collared black maid's uniform dress approached him, giving him an appraising look.

"Yeah, maybe." Slade removed his hat and offered his hand to the woman. "I'm Slade Kent, the new foreman. Amanda and I are working with a sick horse and could use some coffee. She also asked that I send Mathilda or Fiona to her room to find a pair of warm socks."

"Well, I'm Mathilda," the woman said, shaking his hand with a welcoming smile, "but as you can see, things are rather busy for me at the moment. How soon does she need the socks?"

"About three hours ago, if you ask me."

"I'll see if Fiona has a minute to run upstairs and get them, but we're a bit understaffed at the moment."

When Dylan had hired him, he'd filled Slade in on the recent firings and staff resignations that had left the ranch short-handed. Of more concern to Slade were the murders. Something sinister was afoot at the Colton ranch, had been for many years, and he intended to get to the bottom of it.

Mathilda cast a glance around the bustling kitchen

and motioned to a brunette finishing a bowl of oatmeal at the table. "Fiona, a word?"

The maid, a woman about his own age, approached with a wary look. Mathilda explained Amanda's request, and Fiona visibly relaxed.

Man, the staff around here was tense. Although with all of the recent killing and attacks, he supposed he couldn't blame them.

As Fiona set off to retrieve Amanda's socks, Slade glanced past Mathilda and eyed the bounty of food again. "We could also use a few of those cinnamon rolls. We've been up since about three with a colicky horse."

One of the ranch hands glanced up from his plate with a worried look. "Which horse?" he asked around a full mouth of food.

Slade sized up the young hand. High on his list of duties today was a meeting with all the hands to introduce himself and lay out his ground rules for how the ranch would be run under his leadership. "I believe his name is Peanut. We could use a hand out in the stable when you finish eating."

The hand shook his head. "Sorry. Can't. George and I are headin' out to Vegas for the National Finals Rodeo in just a few minutes. Stewie's already there. He was competing in an event yesterday."

Slade frowned. "And you are…?"

The cowboy stuck his hand out. "Jared Hansen."

Slade shook the young man's hand. "Slade Kent—"

"The new foreman. Yeah, I heard." Jared turned back to his plate, shoveling in large bites of eggs and bacon.

Slade tamped his irritation with the brash kid. Jared didn't look much older than twenty, which made him a kid in Slade's book, especially when he showed so little respect for his new boss. "Who's staying here to take care of the ranch?"

The cocky ranch hand gave him a blithe look. "Cal's around somewhere. Miss Amanda helps out. And there's you, I guess."

Slade clenched his teeth. Having most of his hands disappear for the rodeo finals was not the best way to establish himself as the foreman or to get an insight on who might be behind the attacks at the ranch. But the PRCA Nationals was a big deal in the cowboy community. He'd even competed there himself before his career took another road.

Trevor walked into the dining area at that moment, a baby in his arms, and paused beside Slade. "Any news from the stable? Gabriella's a wreck waiting for a report."

"He's holding his own, resting, but we're still waiting." Slade eyed the drooly-mouthed baby in Trevor's arms, and his pulse quickened. "Is that Amanda's daughter?" *The Colton heir targeted by kidnappers.*

Trevor wiped the baby's mouth with his sleeve and shook his head. "No, this is Avery. My daughter." A fatherly pride warmed Trevor's face as he gazed at his child. "That's Cheyenne in the next room with Tom." He hitched his head toward the large kitchen just through an open doorway. He saw an older man with graying hair holding a baby with one arm while he sipped coffee from a mug in his other hand. He wondered who this *Tom* was and what his connection to Amanda and her child could be.

Mathilda nudged his arm. "It's all right for you to go in the kitchen, so long as you don't get in the way. You can ask Kate to bag up some rolls for you. Coffee is there." She pointed to an electric urn on a banquet behind them. "You'll find a thermos in the cabinet underneath. Help yourself."

Slade gave Mathilda an appreciative nod as she hurried off, gathering an armload of dirty dishes as she returned to the kitchen. The stack wobbled and rattled as she lifted them, and Slade swooped in to steady the pile of plates before one could topple off.

"Oh, thank you, young man." Mathilda gave a gracious, if somewhat embarrassed, smile. "I guess I'm not as young as I used to be. I can't carry loads as heavy as I once did."

"Can I take that for you?" he offered.

"Oh, no…I'm fine."

Mathilda bustled away, and he followed her into the kitchen. As he approached Tom, Slade eyed Amanda's daughter.

"Cute kid," he said, admitting that Cheyenne was, in fact, exceptionally cute with a cherubic face and bright eyes. Although with a mother as attractive as Amanda, how could she miss?

Tom lowered his coffee and appraised him with a wariness Slade recognized. A cop's subtle scrutiny. Tom was either on the job or used to be. "I agree."

Slade introduced himself and explained that he'd met Amanda this morning in the stable. "Why are you taking care of the baby instead of one of the maids or one of her sisters?"

"Someone else might help out after breakfast, but I'm Cheyenne's bodyguard. Amanda called me when she had to take care of the sick horse early this morning." Tom took a sip of his coffee before continuing. "I was hired after attempts were made during the summer to kidnap her. But having raised three girls of my own and currently spoiling five grandkids, I don't mind changing diapers or wiping snotty noses when my little princess here needs it. Amanda knows her girl is in good hands with me."

One of the cooks walked up and held out a small pastry to Cheyenne. "Hey, sweetie pie, do you want a yummy?"

The young woman glanced at Tom before handing a piece of the sweet to Cheyenne, and he shrugged. "Go ahead. I let my grandkids eat cookies for breakfast if they want. It's part of spoiling them."

Slade kept his opinion of the sugary diet for the baby to himself and turned to the attractive cook. "Are you Kate?"

She blinked her surprise. "I am."

"I was told you might bag up some cinnamon rolls to go for Amanda and me? We're working with a colicky horse out in the stable and have been up for a while."

Kate nodded. "Absolutely. Just cinnamon rolls? I can fix you an omelet or something if—"

Slade shook his head. "No, thanks. Just the rolls for now."

Another member of the kitchen staff approached Cheyenne, cooing over her, and Slade took his leave, returning to the dining room to fix the thermos of coffee. Soon Fiona was back with Amanda's socks, Kate had supplied him with a bag of cinnamon rolls and he had a thermos, condiments and two mugs tucked in a sack. Armed with what he'd come inside for, Slade headed back to the stable and found Amanda grinning from just outside Peanut's stall.

"We have achieved poop!" she announced cheerfully. When she smiled, Slade was struck again by her natural beauty and felt a stir of attraction low in his belly.

He arched an eyebrow and gave her a wry look, although the fact that Peanut had moved his bowels meant the crisis had passed. "Um…yay?"

Raking loose strands of hair back from her face, she laughed and shook her head. "I know. How sad is it that horse poop is the highlight of my day?" She twisted her mouth in thought, then added, "In fact, as a ranch vet and the mother of an eight-month-old, my days are pretty much filled with poop and vomit and other bodily excretions." She sighed dramatically. "I need to get a life…but where do I find the time?"

He extended the bag of pastries toward her. "I can't help with the state of your life, but I brought sugar and caffeine."

She peeked in the bag and groaned hungrily. "Bless you!"

He reached in his pocket. "And socks."

A cinnamon roll already jammed in her mouth, she mumbled, "Oh, thanks!" After taking a large bite of pastry, she put the roll back in the bag and sat down on a hay bale to pull off her boots.

Somehow the sight of her slim bare feet, red from the cold, felt awkwardly…*intimate* to his sleep-deprived brain. He set the socks down beside her and turned his back to pour their coffee. "By the way, your daughter was the center of attention in the kitchen just now when I was getting our food."

"Yeah, she's going to be spoiled if I'm not careful. The staff loves to dote on her."

An unmistakable pride filled her voice that both moved him and rubbed a raw spot in his soul. He shoved both reactions down, burying them under layers of practiced control and distance. He wasn't here to get involved in the Coltons' personal lives. He had a job to do, and he needed to keep his focus on that mission.

He doctored her coffee with cream and sugar, and when he turned to hand it to her, he was greeted with a smile that shone as much from her golden eyes as from her lips. Damn she was beautiful!

He cleared his suddenly dry throat. "Cream and sugar."

She accepted the coffee and sipped, then hummed her enjoyment, a purr of pleasure that he could easily imagine her making during sex.

"Perfect. Thanks." She retrieved her cinnamon roll and turned back to Peanut's stall. "I think it's safe to leave him for the time being. I'll check on him throughout the day, of course." She took another big bite of cinnamon roll, then licked crumbs from her lips.

Good old-fashioned lust kicked him hard, and his chest tightened. He took a sobering gulp of coffee. His reaction to Amanda had to be due in part to fatigue lowering his defenses.

She cut a glance to him. "We're short-handed today, so I'll be in the area helping feed the horses and mucking stalls."

"Yeah, I heard most of the hands are heading to Vegas today for the rodeo." He jammed his free hand in his back pocket. "I'd planned to meet with the ranch crew for introductions, getting myself up to speed on the operation." *Getting insight to who might have pertinent information about the events of recent months, who might be hiding something.*

"Cal's sticking around. I'll ask him to be sure to give you the lowdown." She popped the rest of her roll in her mouth and gave a satisfied sigh. "God, Kate makes *the best* pastries. Dangerous for a gal like me with a sweet tooth and five more pounds of baby weight to lose."

Slade let his gaze roam over Amanda's snug jeans. If

she was still carrying baby weight, he liked the way it looked on her. He drew a cleansing breath, needing to refocus his thoughts, needing to get some distance from Amanda Colton if he wanted to accomplish anything today. She was too distracting with her piercing gold eyes, sexy rumpled hair and shapely curves.

"Well," he said, topping off his mug of coffee from the thermos, then backing toward the door. "If you need me, I'll be checking the equipment down at the barn."

Of all the obstacles he'd known he'd encounter in this job, the last thing he'd expected was an inconvenient attraction to the oldest Colton daughter. He'd do well to avoid her if he wanted to find his father's murderer in a timely manner and get back to his real job.

Amanda dragged herself up the stairs toward her suite, dying for a hot shower and a nap after mucking stalls and feeding stock with Cal for three hours...on top of her stint this morning with Peanut. She made a mental note to talk with Gabby and the hands about Peanut's diet to figure out what had caused his colic. They'd need to tweak his rations or up his fiber intake to avoid problems in the future.

"Amanda!"

She turned when she heard Gabby call, and her younger sister hurried down the hall to meet her at the top of the stairs. "How's Peanut?"

Amanda smiled patiently. "The same as when you saw him an hour ago. Resting comfortably. He'll get restricted rations today, though. Okay?"

Gabriella visibly relaxed. "Thank you. So much. I don't know what I'd do if I lost Peanut."

She flashed a tired grin to her sister. "Be sure to thank the new foreman, Slade, too. He stayed up with me and assisted with administering the mineral oil. He was a real help."

"I will." Gabby grinned. "So what do you think? Our new foreman is pretty hot, don't you agree?"

Amanda shuffled past her sister, shaking her head. "Listen to you. Aren't you supposed to be getting married in three weeks?"

Gabby tossed her red hair and flashed a coy smile. "I may have ordered already, but I can still read the menu. Besides, it was clear he only had eyes for you."

Amanda grunted and spread her arms, flicking a hand toward her dirty, wrinkled clothes. "Oh, right. Because I was *so* appealing in my sleep shirt, work jeans and bed-head hair." She chuckled and continued toward her bedroom.

Gabby followed. "Say what you want. I saw him checking you out."

Amanda's pulse scampered. Slade was checking her out? She shoved the notion aside as preposterous. If he was sizing her up, he'd likely been appalled at the eldest Colton daughter's appearance. Not that she cared. She had enough in her life caring for Cheyenne, serving as ranch vet and worrying about a kidnapper lurking on the ranch, waiting to steal her daughter. She had no room for a relationship.

"Say, I've narrowed down the stack of applications to fill the empty housekeeping positions. I'd like your input before I select five to interview."

Amanda nodded, her heart heavy remembering why so many positions at Dead River Ranch were suddenly available. Murder, treachery, deceit. At least pastry chef Kate McCord, who'd be leaving all too soon with Levi, and nurse Mia Sanders, who'd resigned two months ago, had found true love amid the tumult and tragedy this past several months, so not all of the reasons for needing replacements were sad. "We need to hire new help as soon as possible. Mathilda would never complain, but I know the added work load has been difficult for her."

Gabby agreed, then her expression brightened some. "And if you have time later, I want to finalize the seating chart for the reception dinner."

Amanda's own spirits lifted when her sister smiled. Anything having to do with her impending Christmas wedding brought a well-deserved and hard-earned joy to Gabby's face. The middle Colton sister, Catherine, had recently married, as well, and was living in Cheyenne while her husband attended the police academy. As happy as she was for her younger sisters and the new men in their lives, Amanda couldn't help the twinge of jealousy that nipped at her. She might be surrounded by people on the ranch, but everyone else seemed to be moving on with their lives.

She'd thought she'd found her soul mate in Cheyenne's father, David Gill. Problem was, so had David's wife.

"I could use fresh eyes on the setup," Gabriella was saying. Amanda shook off the thoughts of two-timing David Gill and focused on what Gabby explained. "I don't need any unplanned drama at my wedding thanks to inadvertently putting Trip next to…well, any female with a pulse really."

Amanda snorted, acknowledging the trouble their skirt-chasing former stepbrother caused. "Why is he even invited?"

Gabby grimaced. "How can I avoid it? I don't want to hurt anyone's feelings."

Amanda tugged her sister's hair. "You're too nice. And yes, I'll look at the seating chart with you. But if you want fresh eyes, you'll have to wait until I've had some sleep. Right now I'm seeing double, I'm so tired."

Down the hall, Cheyenne's cranky whine wafted out of the nursery, and Amanda sighed. If Cheyenne wasn't napping, then a nap wouldn't be on the agenda for Amanda, either. She glanced back to her sister. "Have you seen Dad today? How is he doing?"

Gabriella sobered and said in a hushed tone, "He looks terrible and sounds worse. You were told that he's developed pneumonia, weren't you?"

Amanda sighed. "Levi said pneumonia was pretty common in late-stage illness when a patient is bedridden."

Gabriella's face creased with worry. "He's so pale… and more gaunt every day. Dylan's leaving hit him hard, especially since he didn't tell Dad goodbye in person. He'd just gotten his firstborn back, and then he disappeared from his life again." Gabby's shoulders drooped. "Not that I blame Dylan for being angry with him."

Mention of their half-brother brought bittersweet thoughts of Amanda's college friend, Aurora Worthington, to mind. Aurora had recently spent time at the ranch, hiding from her mob-connected ex-husband's henchmen. Amanda had relished the opportunity to renew her friendship with Aurora, and had missed her friend terribly since Aurora entered Witness Protection with Dylan. She missed their late-night chats, missed knowing her best friend had her back no matter what. She'd love to have Aurora's perspective on Slade Kent and borrow her ear to unburden her heart regarding her father's failing health.

Amanda rubbed her tired, gritty eyes, knowing she needed to visit her father before she napped. She'd put off visiting him recently because seeing the man who'd turned Dead River Ranch into a thriving business reduced to skin and bones was too difficult to bear most days. Amanda met her sister's eyes. "Levi says Dad still has moments of lucidity, but because of the pain meds, he sleeps most of the day."

Gabby took Amanda's hand, her green gaze troubled. "Levi doesn't think Dad has too much longer. He may not even make it until the wedding." The redhead, who looked just like pictures of their mother at her age, bit her bottom lip. "You should go see him today."

Amanda promised she would visit Jethro and dragged her weary bones to her suite. Cheyenne was still crying, and Tom's expression was comically relieved when she walked in the nursery.

"I don't know what's wrong with her. None of the usual stuff will calm her down." He held Cheyenne out to her mother, shaking his head.

Amanda plucked a facial tissue from a box by the changing table. "Poor baby. I think she's getting sick." She wiped Cheyenne's runny nose and tossed the tissue in the trash. "I'm going to visit my dad after I've had a shower. When I see Levi, I'll ask him to stop by and check on her." She kicked off her boots and stretched her sore back. "Will you watch her for one more hour? I need a shower, and I can't take a sick baby into Jethro's room."

Tom gave her a patient smile and squared his shoulders. "Of course, Miss Amanda. Glad to help."

Amanda read a lingering apology in his expression, as well. Tom still felt guilty that three months earlier an unknown assailant had nearly kidnapped Cheyenne on his watch. Never mind that the assailant had mounted a brutal surprise attack that could have killed Tom. Never mind that Amanda told Tom he was not to blame for the violent assault. Tom continued to feel he had failed both

Cheyenne and Amanda that day. In recent weeks, Tom's guard over Cheyenne had been hypervigilant, and he rarely took breaks.

"Thanks, Tom." Amanda carried Cheyenne into her bedroom and set her daughter on the floor to crawl while Amanda undressed. As she peeled off layers of grimy clothes, Amanda paused to stroke the soft orange fur of her Cymric Manx, Reyna. The imperious orange cat raised her head and gave Cheyenne a disdainful glare as if to say, "That one disturbs my peace and quiet."

"Sorry, Reyna, didn't mean to disturb you." Amanda laughed to herself over the haughty manner that had earned the cat the Spanish name for "Little Queen." Amanda had rescued Reyna from an animal shelter as a kitten to live in the barn with the other ranch cats, but Reyna let it be known early on that she didn't belong with the "commoners." When the hands reported fights between the cats, Amanda had brought Reyna inside to live in her suite. In the years since, Amanda had enjoyed spoiling the long-haired cat and indulging the cat's presumption she was the queen.

Cheyenne pulled herself to her feet, using the bedspread as her support, and peered across the bed at the orange cat. A grin lit Cheyenne's chubby face, and she loosed an excited squeal that sent Reyna scurrying for cover.

Amanda lifted her daughter in her arms, chuckling. "You need to work on your approach, chickpea. You scared kitty."

Cheyenne craned her head to find the spot on the floor where Reyna had stopped to lick her ruffled fur. "Kee!"

Amanda hugged her daughter tighter, savoring the warmth, the pure, sweet love that only Cheyenne stirred inside her. She'd witnessed maternal love and sacrifice in the animals she cared for, but experiencing it firsthand with her own daughter was entirely unique. No love in the world was as unconditional, as honest, as unblemished as the bond she had with Cheyenne.

And she'd do anything—even give her own life—to see that no harm came to her daughter.

Chapter 3

Slade exhaled deeply, his breath forming a white cloud in the December air. He turned slowly, taking in the property fence, the gate, the terrain, willing the scene to yield its secrets. Based on his preliminary research, his father had been here, standing where Slade stood now, when he'd taken the shot to the chest that killed him. Slade could almost imagine the blood stain spreading on the dry Wyoming soil.

He stopped when he faced the fence, narrowing his eyes on the post directly behind him. A bullet-size hole was still visible on the post, and Slade crossed the fence to examine the hole more carefully. The patina of time had turned the inside of the hole the same shade of gray as the wood surrounding it. He poked his finger in the pit, and his chest tightened.

Ten years. His father had been gone for a full decade, but the loss still sat hollowly in his soul. A senseless murder, left unsolved by crooked cops. An obvious cover-up by a family with more skeletons in their closet than in the family crypt. Slade gritted his teeth as resentment poured through him. For the next several weeks, he'd be living among the people who had, at the very least, turned their backs on his father's murder, and, more likely, had a hand in the crime.

What part, if any, did Amanda have in the cover-up? Ten years ago, she'd have been a teenager, old enough to understand the seriousness of having a murder happen on the ranch property. Did she have information she'd hidden from the police in order to protect her family?

He rubbed a spot at the center of his chest out of habit, even though the gnawing ache of his heartburn was inside him. The idea that Amanda could be part of the cover-up unsettled him more than it should. An image of her licking cinnamon sugar from her fingers flashed in his memory and he sighed. He'd known plenty of women in his life who were polished and pampered, yet none of them had triggered the gut-level response from him that rumpled, makeup-free, hardworking Amanda Colton had.

Slade pulled out his pack of gum and jammed a piece in his mouth. In the cold air, the powerful peppermint had an extra bite to it, but the gum helped soothe the fire in his chest. The heartburn had been his near constant companion since his wife, Krista, died.

Hearing the crunch of tires on gravel, Slade straightened and tugged the brim of his Stetson down.

A pickup truck pulled to a stop at the gate, headed out from the employees' wing of the ranch house. When the truck stopped, a man in faded blue jeans and a tan ranch coat emerged and walked toward the gate, casting a glance toward Slade. Behind the steering wheel, Jared

Hansen, the young hand Slade had met in the kitchen, gave a small wave.

"Howdy," the second man said as he opened the gate so that Jared could drive the truck through.

"Morning." Assuming this must be another one of the hands he'd be working with, Slade stepped forward, his hand out, and introduced himself.

"George Jeffries," the hand returned. "Jared told me the new foreman had arrived last night."

As the men shook hands, Slade sized up the ranch hand. He looked fit, capable and had the courtesy to look Slade in the eye.

"Off to Vegas, huh?" Slade asked.

George looked contrite. "Yeah, bad timing. Sorry to be leaving just when you arrive. Cal's staying, though. He'll show you the ropes."

Slade nodded.

George flicked a glance to the truck as Jared drove through the open gate, then back to Slade. "Whatcha doin' out here, if you don't mind my asking?"

"Just taking a look around."

George eyed him. "You heard the story, didn't you?"

"What story?"

"About some cop getting shot out here some years back. Before my time. I've only been here four months, but when other crazy mess started happening this summer—people getting killed and babies kidnapped—folks started talking about the other murder that happened on the ranch." George pointed to the bullet hole in the fence post. "That hole's the only evidence left. Crazy, huh?"

Slade wanted to ask the hand what exactly he'd been told about his father's murder, but Jared whistled from the truck. "C'mon, George! We're already late!"

George gave a nod as he closed the gate and hurried to the pickup. "Nice meetin' you."

Slade returned a wave. "Good luck in the competition."

He watched the pickup pull away, then turned back to the fence post and grunted. A hole on a wooden post wasn't going to give him the answers he needed. His time today would be best spent going through the cold case files at the police station. Chief Peters had promised to make all the evidence and crime-scene photos available to him, a courtesy the previous police chief had denied him. Slade now knew that the previous chief in the Dead River Police Department had been covering up a lot of dirty dealings and botched investigations. If Slade's instincts were right, the identity of his father's murderer was among the secrets the ousted chief had taken to his grave.

Shoving down a ripple of grief, Slade headed back toward the employee quarters of the ranch house. The sooner he solved his father's murder, the sooner he could end his charade as the Coltons' foreman and begin piecing his life together again.

Jethro was a mere shadow of his former self. That was Amanda's first impression when she entered the room where her father lay dying. *Dying.* A spurt of frustration and anger roiled inside her that Jethro's illness had come to this. But her father had refused treatment when it was discovered his increasing pain, frequent infections and fatigue were because of late-stage leukemia. His diagnosis had sent shock waves through the family, but none as great as when Jethro declared he would not take chemo or other treatment to slow the advance of the illness. Jethro had, for all intents and purposes, given up on life.

For Amanda, his decision had felt like an affront to the family. Jethro had long been accused of selfishness, and to her, his refusal to try treating his cancer smacked of just such self-centeredness. If he loved his family, why wouldn't he want to fight the disease and give himself the chance to attend Gabby's wedding, see Cheyenne learn to walk, be there when Catherine's baby was born, share one last Christmas with the first-born son he'd just found after thirty years? But he wasn't willing to endure the discomfort of chemo to buy himself more time with his growing family.

Pain needled Amanda as she drew close to his bedside and eyed the machines and oxygen tanks he was hooked to via a web of wires and tubes. Had Jethro ever really loved his daughters at all? She couldn't imagine giving up on any fight that would give her precious moments with Cheyenne.

"Amanda. Hi."

She glanced from her pale, sleeping father to Dr. Levi Colton, her illegitimate half-brother, who'd agreed to serve as Jethro's private physician throughout his illness. The position had given Levi and Jethro an opportunity to find a strained peace with each other. But Levi's presence on the ranch had also united him with his half-sisters, after years of only barely acknowledging each other's existence—by Jethro's design. If losing her father had a silver lining, it was the newly formed bond and promise of closer relationship she now had with her half-brother.

Levi stepped into the bedroom-turned-hospice-ward from the adjoining sitting area and flashed a warm smile at her. "I thought I heard someone come in. How are you?"

Amanda returned a grin to her brother. "Sleep-deprived. And you?"

Levi's brow wrinkled. "Sleep deprived? Has there been trouble?"

She raked her hair, which she'd left loose after her shower, back from her face with her fingers. "Sick horse. Sick baby. Nothing that isn't in the mommy-slash-veterinarian job description."

He lifted his cheek in a sympathetic grin. "Sounds a bit like when I was in med school." He sobered. "Is Cheyenne getting worse?"

"Not really. Just the stuffy nose. Low-grade fever." She tipped her head and implored him with a worried expression. "Just the same, could you stop by and check on her? I'd bring her here, but we were warned about Dad's vulnerability to germs."

"Of course." His smile softened, and his eyes warmed. "Anything for my niece."

Instinctively, Amanda analyzed Levi's tone and body language, searching for sarcasm or the subtle hostility that he had shown the family when he'd first arrived. Having been lied to last year by Cheyenne's father, Amanda kept her guard up around men. Her trust was hard-earned lately.

But she found no deception in Levi's expression or voice. She was relieved and reassured the amicability between them was genuine. In fact, his hazel eyes twinkled with the same joy she'd seen in her sisters' eyes in recent days—a happiness rooted in finding true love. In Levi's case, Kate McCord, the ranch's pastry chef and kitchen assistant, had snagged her brother's heart.

"So…" She glanced awkwardly toward the bed where Jethro slept. A nasal cannula fed oxygen into his nostrils, an IV dripped painkillers and fluids through a needle into his frail, bruised arm, and a clamp on his finger monitored his blood oxygen level. "How is he?"

Levi sighed and jammed his hands in his pockets. "I won't lie, Amanda. This pneumonia has set him back a good bit. It's hard for him to breathe at times, and his strength is failing." He twisted his mouth in regret. "He doesn't have long."

"What if he changed his mind about the bone marrow transplant? We might still find a match."

Levi shook his head. "He's beyond that point, Amanda. All we can do now is make him comfortable until…" He left the "until" unsaid but understood.

Her father was *dying*. Despite knowing the gravity of the situation before she came in, hearing Levi's grim assessment shot Amanda with an arrowlike pain in her chest. She drew a short, soft gasp and squeezed her eyes shut.

A large hand curled around her bicep, startling her from her moment of grief. "I'm sorry. I know it must be hard to see him like this."

Levi's comforting gesture touched her, and she forced a smile. "Yeah. I mean growing up, he always seemed so…indestructible. Larger than life." She covered Levi's hand with her own. "I know he's not perfect, and I know he's hurt a lot of people, including you and your mom— heck, including me—but…he's my dad, and I love him. Despite all his flaws."

Her half-brother nodded. "I understand. You can try talking to him. He might rouse some, but I've been up-ping his painkillers, so he's been real drowsy the last few days."

"I knew it," Jethro mumbled from the bed. "Knew you were…pushing me toward my grave…don't need your… stupid drugs…."

"My, my," Amanda said, turning toward her father

with the brightest smile she could muster. "So the cranky old coot is awake."

Her father opened one eye to peer at her sourly. "You're not…too old…to spank…missy."

She carefully pressed a kiss to his sunken cheek. "Maybe. But you'd have to catch me first."

"Where's…my granddaughter?" Jethro rasped.

Amanda settled on the edge of the bed. "In the nursery. She's a little sick, and I didn't want to expose you."

Jethro grunted weakly. "As if…I could get sicker."

A soft rap sounded on the bedroom door, and Levi answered the knock.

"I hope I'm not intruding," a familiar male voice said, drawing Amanda's attention to Jethro's visitor. "I just wanted to pay my respects, introduce myself to Mr. Colton."

"I'm sorry," Levi said, frowning, "But who are you?"

"Slade?" Amanda moved from the bed toward the door. Levi and Slade both glanced her way. "What are you doing here?"

Nodding a greeting to her, Slade fingered the brim of the Stetson he held. "Meeting the ranch's owner. As a courtesy." His gaze darted to Jethro, then back to her. "Unless this is a bad time."

"Who's there?" Jethro asked, his eyes fully open now and as shrewd as ever.

"Our new foreman," Amanda said, waving Slade in.

Levi stepped back to let Slade enter, then disappeared into the sitting room again to allow Amanda and Slade a private audience with Jethro.

"New foreman?" Her father's gaze slid over Slade, clearly sizing him up. "I didn't…hire you."

"No, sir. Dylan Frick did." Slade stepped forward and extended his hand to Jethro. "Slade Kent, sir."

Jethro's eyes widened at the mention of Dylan's name and, if possible, his face turned a shade paler. Only weeks earlier, Dylan, the son of the nanny who'd raised Amanda and her sisters, had been proven to be her long-lost half-brother, Cole. Clearly Jethro was still adjusting to the knowledge that his son, who'd been kidnapped as a baby, had been living under his roof for most of the thirty years the family had been searching for him. For a moment, he only stared at Slade and the proffered hand, but finally he seemed to gather himself and raised a frail and shaking hand to Slade's. "All right." Jethro's brow dented as he glared at Slade. "You can stay…on a trial basis…."

Slade blinked, but, to his credit, showed no other outward sign that would counter Jethro. "Yes, sir. I appreciate that."

Amanda bit the inside of her cheek, both covering a grin and fighting back the well of tears in her throat. Her father's paltry attempt to show he was still in control of the ranch was bittersweet. Jethro Colton had wasted away to skin and bones and barely had a breath left in him, but in his chest beat the heart of the stubborn, despotic, arrogant man who'd turned Dead River Ranch into a multi-million dollar operation.

Jethro's eyebrows drew closer together as his frown deepened. "Have we met? You look…familiar."

Amanda jerked her gaze up, startled by Jethro's question.

Slade, too, seemed shaken by the question. "No, sir. We've never met before today."

But Jethro was rarely wrong about such things. Her father had a mind like a steel trap for anything related to business and people. She leveled a curious gaze on the new foreman. Was Slade not who he claimed?

"What did you say...your name was?" Jethro asked, wheezing.

A muscle in Slade's jaw twitched, and his fingers tightened around the brim of his hat. Drawing a deep breath, he said, "Slade Kent."

Jethro's wheeze caught, and a strangled-sounding cough rattled from his chest. He gasped for air as the coughing fit wracked his weakened body.

"Dad?" Amanda hurried to his side, desperate to do something to help. If Jethro were a sick horse or cow, she'd know what to do, but her father's frail health left her feeling helpless. "Levi!"

But her half-brother was already at their father's side, having raced back in to his patient at the first rattling cough. He helped Jethro sit up, giving him firm smacks on the back until Jethro regained his breath. When Levi laid Jethro back on his pillows, a tiny trickle of blood seeped from Jethro's nose.

Amanda gasped. "He's bleeding."

"Nose bleeds are common at this stage of his illness." Levi dabbed at the blood until Jethro batted his hand away.

"I can...do that." Jethro held a tissue to his nose, but Amanda noticed the telltale tremor in his arm.

"I should go." Slade, who had backed away from the bed during the chaos, stood near the door, his hat still crushed in his hand. "I apologize if I'm responsible for—"

"No, no," Levi cut him off. "Not your fault. It's the pneumonia."

Despite Levi's exculpation, Slade seemed uneasy and eager to leave. "Just the same, I have things to tend to and an appointment to keep."

Amanda rose quickly. "I'll walk you out."

She had questions for the new foreman that wouldn't wait. Bending, she brushed a quick kiss on her father's forehead. "Bye, Dad. Don't give Levi a hard time, eh?"

"Next time," her father rasped, "bring Cheyenne...or don't bother coming."

She scoffed a short laugh. "Love you, too, Dad." Swallowing hard, she choked back the emotion that clogged her throat and followed Slade into the hall.

Though still rattled by her father's deteriorating health, she didn't miss the way Slade's shoulders visibly relaxed once the door to Jethro's room closed behind them. Maybe her father's obvious suffering had put him on edge. Plenty of people were uncomfortable around dying patients. But she couldn't forget her father's question or Slade's startled reaction to it. *Have we met?*

Amanda's nape tingled with suspicion. In recent months, she'd had her fill of deceitful men and people's secret agendas. She caught Slade's arm as he started down the narrow rear staircase toward the employees' quarters. "Have you met my father before?"

His blue gaze darkened, and his brow furrowed. "Did you not just hear me answer that question for your father?"

She raised her chin. "I heard you. But I haven't decided if I believe you."

He faced her fully and squared his feet. Standing on a lower step as he was, his eyes were nearly level with hers. From this angle, she could see the flecks of sapphire that gave his irises their bright color, and their intensity made her belly quiver. "And what proof are you looking for that I'm telling the truth?"

"I don't know. But my father is rarely wrong about whom he's met. He doesn't forget a face." Amanda crossed her arms over her chest, trying to quell the jitters Slade's stare induced.

His gaze dipped briefly to her breasts, plumped by her defiant posture, before returning to her glare. Her pulse tripped, but she held her ground.

"Well, he's wrong this time. We've never met." He firmed his mouth and turned to leave.

"I hope you're right. I don't take kindly to liars or con artists."

He sent her a cool look over his shoulder as he descended the stairs. "Then we're square, Miss Colton. Because neither do I."

Later that week, Slade took a break from ranching work to head into town. He'd been swamped with chores that the hands would normally do. Amanda had helped out, mucking stalls and riding the fence with her daughter bundled in a baby carrier on her back. Cal, the only hand who'd stayed home from the rodeo finals, was a hard worker but stayed to himself—which suited Slade just fine. He got enough questions and suspicious looks from Amanda.

He was eager to get down to the brass tacks of his investigation, maybe even be back in his own apartment by Christmas.

A young officer looked up from a computer screen when he walked into the Dead River Police Department headquarters. "Can I help you?"

"I'm here to see Chief Peters."

"Slade," the police chief said amiably, strolling in from a back room with a steaming mug before the officer could summon him. "How are things at Dead River Ranch?"

"Quiet for the most part. I thought I'd use this time to dig into those case files on my dad's murder."

Chief Peters sipped his coffee and nodded. "Follow me. I'll set you up in an interrogation room."

Slade fell in step behind the chief of police, an anxious roll in his gut. After all these years, was he finally going to know who killed his father and why the case was shelved with little investigation? He plucked his peppermint gum out of his pocket and shoved a stick in his mouth.

"You can wait here," Peters said, opening the door to a Spartan room with a rickety table and metal folding chairs. "I'll get the file. Would you like some coffee?"

Slade shook his head. "Thanks, but no."

A few minutes later, Chief Peters returned with a surprisingly slim file. The chief's brow was furrowed. "I'm afraid this is all I found. There is appallingly little here. The autopsy report states the obvious—your father was killed by a gunshot wound to the chest. No bullet or casing was found for a ballistics test. Only person who claimed to know anything was the cook who found the body."

Slade took the folder from Peters and flipped it open. He paged through the top sheets, sketchy police reports, a handwritten statement from Agnes Barlow and—

Slade froze, his gut churning, when he uncovered the first of several crime scene photos. His father's face was pale, his eyes staring sightlessly, his shirt drenched in blood....

"Slade?" Chief Peters's voice shook him from his brief stupor. "You okay?"

He cleared his throat and flipped to the next photo, digging deep for the professional detachment he needed to process the information in the file objectively. "I'm fine. Was a search warrant issued to look for the weapon on the grounds of the ranch?"

"No record of it. Supposedly they didn't have grounds for a search."

Slade scowled and glanced up at the chief. "Other than the victim being found on the ranch property, you mean?"

"I know. Lotta holes in the police work, but I don't have to tell you the former chief played fast and loose with rules and procedures. Someone on the Colton ranch knows something. I'd wager my whole paycheck on it."

Slade clenched his jaw. "And I intend to find out who."

Chapter 4

Early the next morning, Amanda finished dressing Cheyenne in a warm hooded coat and mittens and had to laugh at the puffy Eskimo bundle her daughter made. Cheyenne's wide eyes blinked at her from the small opening in the hood, and a wave of love swept through Amanda.

"Are you sure you don't mind my going, Miss Amanda?" Tom asked, rattling keys in his pocket. "Cheyenne's safety is more important than my appointment. I can reschedule if—"

"I'm sure." Amanda reassured her daughter's bodyguard with a smile. "You take care of your business in town, and we'll see you this afternoon." She pressed a kiss to her daughter's nose, winning a grin from Cheyenne. "My little Eskimo baby will be fine with me in the stable. Believe me, a kidnapper will have to come through this mama bear to lay a finger on my daughter."

Tom's face remained skeptical. "That's what worries me. Not that you won't do everything to protect Cheyenne, but that you might have to and will be hurt in the process."

Amanda pushed down the haunting memories of Faye Frick's death during the summer. The woman who'd raised her had died trying to protect Trevor's daughter from a kidnapper who'd thought he was stealing Cheyenne. Trevor's daughter was recovered safely, but if the kidnapper *had* taken Cheyenne, then or in a subsequent attempt, what would have happened to her sweet little girl?

She shuddered at the thought and forced a strained smile to her lips. What mattered was that Cheyenne was safe, and between herself and Tom, she felt confident her daughter was protected.

"You've barely taken a day for yourself since you started protecting Cheyenne months ago. Take the morning, go to your appointment. That's an order."

Tom gave a reluctant nod.

"But before you go," Amanda said, slipping the baby carrier backpack onto her shoulders, "will you load her up for me?"

Tom lifted Cheyenne off the bed and slid her into the sling seat of the backpack. "There you go, princess. All set."

Amanda and Tom walked down the back stairs together, winding up at the door to the employee wing. Tantalizing scents wafted from the kitchen where lunch was already being prepared. Amanda paused, stepping into the staff dining room to savor the aroma of chocolate that said Kate was baking one of her delicacies for dessert.

"Miss Amanda? Do you need something?" Mathilda Perkins, who'd been the head maid for as long as Amanda could remember, looked up from wiping the long trestle table where the employees ate.

"No, just savoring the smells of baking." She took another deep breath and sighed contentedly.

Mathilda flapped her rag at her. "You shouldn't be down here. It's not fitting for you to be in the staff quarters."

Amanda smiled at Mathilda, who'd repeated the same outdated concern innumerable times over the years when Amanda and her sisters came down to the kitchen to play or scavenge a snack. "Don't worry, Mathilda. I won't tell Jethro if you don't."

"Won't tell Mr. Jethro what?" Another of the family's maids, Hilda Zimmerman, hustled in from the front of the house, a feather duster in one hand and a broad smile spreading her lips when she spotted Cheyenne. "Oh, look at you, Cheyenne! How's our little girl?"

"Mathilda was just reminding me of the impropriety of the family mingling with the staff." Amanda waited while Hilda cooed over Cheyenne.

"Phooey. Old-fashioned rubbish." Hilda placed a hand on Amanda's cheek. "You come see me anytime you want, especially if you have your darling girl with you."

Mathilda huffed a frustrated sigh. "Have you finished cleaning the main living room, Hilda?"

The older woman cut Mathilda a disgruntled side glance. "Nearly."

"Well, when you're done, I need your help changing sheets on all the upstairs beds."

The door out to the ranch yard opened, and a dour woman with long gray hair pulled back in a ponytail strode in carrying a large basket. Without acknowledging anyone, she retrieved the bundle of dirty kitchen towels and aprons that sat in the corner on the floor. As she turned and started toward the door to the basement laundry room, the stern-faced woman eyed Amanda and Cheyenne with a dark look.

Amanda flashed a weak smile of greeting. "Good morning, Mrs. Black."

The laundress, who lived on the property in an old shack with her husband, the handyman, ignored Amanda's greeting and shuffled past her. As it often did, the contrast between Hilda's warmth and cheerfulness and Mrs. Black's sullen silence made Amanda shake her head. Quirky as they were, from Mathilda's outdated insistence the staff remain separate from the family to head cook Agnes's bossy rule of the kitchen, the ranch staff was her family as much as Cath and Gabby were.

Kate breezed in, a hot pan in her hands, and Amanda called to her, "What smells so good, Kate?"

"Chocolate torte." Kate sent Amanda a sad smile. "I was hoping one of my desserts would tempt your dad to eat something. He's getting so thin."

"Well, if anything will tempt him, it's one of your treats." Amanda stepped out of the way as another maid, Fiona Cudge, hurried through the dining room, apparently oblivious to Amanda's presence.

"Fiona!" Mathilda scolded. "You nearly knocked Miss Amanda over."

Fiona glanced up, her cheeks flushing. "So sorry. I'm just in hurry. Mr. Colton is asking for a fresh blanket."

No doubt her father had been berating Fiona for not having an endless supply of whatever he randomly demanded at the ready. As much as she tried to treat the staff like family, her father treated the staff like slaves. Like dirt.

The impulse to apologize for her father—again—swelled inside her, but Mathilda cut her off.

"So get the blanket. Shoo! Hurry." Facing Amanda, Mathilda gave the baby a curious look. "Why do you have Cheyenne? Where did Tom go?"

Amanda explained to Mathilda about Tom's errand while watching Kate bring another torte pan in to the buffet to cool. The staff dining room felt a bit like Grand Central Station at the moment, and Amanda started backing toward the door.

"Shall I ask someone on the staff to watch the baby for you?" Mathilda asked.

"No, we're fine. I'll just be in the stable feeding the horses and mucking stalls."

Mathilda looked offended. "That's not your job. Leave that for Mr. Kent or Cal."

"I don't mind helping out until the hands get back from Las Vegas, and chickpea and I enjoy being around the horses. Right, sweetie?" she asked, glancing over her shoulder. All she could see of her daughter was the back of her hood-encased head, but Cheyenne kicked her legs and gurgled at Hilda, who was still admiring the baby.

Mathilda gave a disapproving shake of her head, and Amanda headed out into the frigid morning.

Cal was loading tools in one of the ATVs when she reached the stable. Bingo and Betsy, the ranch's two English Shepherds, were milling about his feet, looking for attention. He paused long enough to ruffle Bingo's fur as Amanda entered. "Morning, Miss Amanda."

"Morning, Cal. Where are you off to?"

"Repairing fence in the upper pasture."

Cal was known for being more reserved than the other hands, spending much of his time by himself, disappearing for long periods. They'd recently learned he was responsible for an ailing grandfather, which explained some of his time away from the ranch and his reason for not going with the other hands to Nevada, but Amanda remained cautious around him, despite his courtesy and hard work.

David Gill, Cheyenne's father, had been personable and ambitious, but he'd proven to be a two-timing jerk with a family in Boston. That experience had taught her to be more cautious about who she trusted. And Cal still had shaky alibis for several of the attacks on her family and the staff the past few months.

He climbed on the ATV and whistled for Bingo to join him. Tail wagging, the black-and-white dog jumped onto the all-terrain vehicle behind Cal. "I'll take care of mucking the horse stalls when I get back, but I don't want any cows getting loose in the foothills through that downed fence."

"Where's Slade? What's he doing?"

"Finishing his breakfast, last I saw him. But that was an hour ago."

Amanda waved to Cal as he cranked the engine. "I can handle cleaning the stalls. You don't have to do everything while the rest of the guys are gone."

"Thank you, Miss Amanda. Back as soon as I can." With that, he rumbled away on the ATV and Betsy whined at being left behind.

"Come on, Betsy. You can hang with us girls." She patted her leg, and the brown-and-white dog followed her farther into the stable.

Amanda tugged on the straps of Cheyenne's carrier, readjusting the load as she found the feed bucket and checked that the heaters in the watering troughs were working. Having Cheyenne in the stable while she worked was inconvenient, but with the threat of kidnapping still hovering over her, Amanda didn't dare let her daughter out of her sight unless Cheyenne was with Tom.

She was still feeding the horses and making sure they each had ample water when Slade strode into the stable. Spotting her, he crossed the alley and leaned against the gate of the stall where she worked. "How's Peanut?"

"Better. I put him back on full rations last night." She moved into another stall to feed Prince William, the horse she'd gotten at the height of her teenage crush on Great Britain's royal hunk.

Slade nodded and glanced down the row of stalls. "I thought I'd ride out on the property and get a feel for the land and the herd, maybe check the equipment. Is there a horse you prefer I ride?"

"You don't want to take one of the four-wheelers?" Amanda motioned toward the back of the stable.

"Naw. I prefer a saddle to an engine most any day, but especially when I'm out in the pastures." He adjusted his hat and returned his gaze to her. "I plan to bring my own horse down next weekend, but I wanted to make sure things were going to work out here before making the transfer."

She dumped the bucket of feed in PW's trough, rubbed his nose then moved out of his stall as he started his breakfast. "While Jared and the others are in Vegas, you can pretty much take your pick of the hands' horses." She pointed to a stall near the back where a black horse tossed his mane. "But Midnight needs exercise. He's Jethro's stallion and can be temperamental, so be careful. Cal just left for the upper pasture to repair a fence. He may need a hand."

Slade jerked a nod. "All right." He eyed her as she fixed a bucket of grain for the next horse. "You always tote your kid on your back while you work out here?"

"Not always, but often. She enjoys it." Amanda freed her hair from Cheyenne's grip before continuing her work.

"I'd have thought you'd have your pick of babysitters, what with your sister, stepmother and a half-dozen staff in the house."

"The staff wasn't hired to take care of my daughter. They have plenty of other things to do." She lugged the feed bucket into the next stall. "My stepmother and her lazy spawn couldn't be bothered to do anything as helpful or nurturing as babysitting. Not that I'd ever leave Cheyenne in Darla's care. All you have to do is look at how Trip and Tawny turned out to see why that's a bad idea."

Slade stepped into the stall with her and took the handle of the bucket. "Let me do that."

"I can handle it."

"I'm sure you can," he replied but still nudged her out of the way to finish the task. "So Darla and her kids don't help out on the ranch?"

Amanda gave an indelicate snort. "Puh-lease. They have freeloading down to a science. I really don't know why my dad lets them stay. Gabby helps with Cheyenne sometimes, and Tom guards her almost around the clock. But he has to sleep sometime. I gave him this morning off because he had some kind of personal business in town."

Cheyenne kicked and whined, the first signs that she was getting restless.

Slade poured the grain in the feed trough and shot her an annoyed look. "Which leaves you hauling a kid on your back while you pick up the slack for the hands who are off in Vegas."

Amanda straightened her spine and cocked her head. "First off, that *kid* on my back is my daughter. Carrying her with me while I work is not a burden, it's a joy. She loves the animals, and I love having her with me. I don't need a babysitter, because taking care of her is my job. I'm her mother, and she is safest with me.

"Second, our hands work hard all year. They've earned their week off, and December is the best month for them to take time away. I'm perfectly capable of feeding the horses and mucking the stalls for a few days while the guys are at nationals."

Cheyenne sneezed and gave another cranky whimper.

Slade raised a hand, palm forward. "Hey, don't shoot. If you want to bust your butt doing grunt work, be my guest. But I think Cal and I can hold the fort down a couple more days until the rest of the hands get back. And for what it's worth, your daughter's nose is running. You don't need to have her out in this cold air."

Amanda fished a tissue from her coat pocket, then twisted, trying to reach Cheyenne's face. Finally she held the tissue out to Slade. "Will you? I can't reach her."

He looked at the tissue as if it were a rattlesnake. "Me?"

"Why not?"

He scowled. "I don't think wiping snotty noses for the owners' kids was in the job description. How about I stick to looking after the animals, and you stick to wiping noses? After all, you are her mother and taking care of her is your job."

She grimaced, hearing him toss her words back at her, then lifted her chin. "What's wrong, cowboy? Scared of a little baby snot? I thought tough guy wranglers like you would be used to a little messiness." She shoved the tissue toward him again and softened her expression. "Please?"

Pulling a face, he took the tissue and cleaned Cheyenne's face. When he was done, he jammed the dirty tissue back in her hand. "There. But if I were you, I'd take her to a doctor. She could be sick."

She arched an eyebrow. "Aren't you full of parenting advice? Levi already examined her. He says it's just a cold." She tossed the tissue in a trash barrel and sent Slade a sweet smile as he strode away. "But your concern is duly noted. Thank you."

Amanda continued working in the stable for the next hour, singing silly songs to her daughter when Cheyenne fussed. Eventually, she hung Cheyenne's backpack-style baby carrier on a tack hook when her back started to ache. She kissed her daughter's forehead, tucked her blanket more snugly around her and, within minutes, Cheyenne's head lolled to the side, resting on the rolled head pillow in the carrier. Amanda hurried to finish mucking stalls before her daughter woke up.

As she finished her last stall, the sound of hooves and jingle of reins called her attention to the holding pen next to the stable. She stepped to the stable door in time to see Slade leading a cow into the small corral. He dismounted from Midnight and headed toward her.

"Problem?" she asked.

"Cow versus barbed wire. Looks infected."

She nodded. "I'll get my bag and take a look. Put her in a squeeze chute, will you?"

Amanda put Cheyenne's carrier on her back again and retrieved her veterinary bag from the storage room where she'd left it after caring for Peanut a couple of days before. By the time she'd returned to the holding pen, Slade had moved the squeeze chute, a narrow steel cage that was only big enough for one cow to stand in, and was coaxing the injured cow inside. Once in the chute, the cow would have severely limited ability to move while Amanda treated the injury on its shoulder.

She did a preliminary exam of the wound and saw that it was, indeed, infected.

"Well?" Slade said, coming to stand behind her.

"I'll need to clean out the infected tissue for starters."

Kneeling beside the chute, she opened her bag and began preparing a sterile wash. "I'm almost out of Betadine." She glanced over her shoulder at Slade. "If there's not more in the cabinet inside, I keep vet supplies in the storage room at the back of the barn, as well."

He scoffed a humorless laugh. "Is that your way of asking me to bring you more, princess?"

She paused from pulling on latex gloves from her bag. "Must you call me princess?"

"It fits. You've done nothing but hand out orders since we met. I'm not your butler."

Amanda raised her chin as she snapped her gloves in place. "Have I? I'm sorry. When I work, I get in a zone. I'm focused on my task, on my patient. Not on manners." She twisted her mouth as she thought. "Although my sisters say I'm bossy, too. Hazard of being the first-born?" She sent him an apologetic look. "I don't mean to be demanding." She squared her shoulders. "If I make an effort to be less imperial, will you call me Amanda instead of princess?"

He jerked a nod and extended his hand. "Deal."

She pulled her hands back. "Can't. Sterile gloves." She showed him the nearly empty bottle of Betadine. "Will you please find another bottle of this?"

"I will." He pulled a clean rag from her vet supplies and wiped Cheyenne's face. "And when you finish with the cow, will you please take that kid inside out of this cold air?"

She wavered between irritation that he would tell her how to care for her own daughter and being touched that he'd bothered to wipe Cheyenne's nose without prompting. "Cold air doesn't make you sick. Germs make you sick. And it isn't that cold in the stable where I was working." When he scowled, she added, "But I do plan to take her inside when I finish here—" she flashed a sassy grin "—*Dr.* Kent."

He gave a low growl as he strode across the half-frozen dirt in the pen. Patches of ice lurked in spots where the sun hadn't yet sent its melting rays, and by the fence Midnight stood impatiently waiting to either be unsaddled or ridden back out into the fields. The horse shook his head, rattling his reins.

"Easy does it, Midnight," Amanda called to the horse before turning back to the ailing cow and refocusing her attention for the task at hand. "Okay, Cheyenne, let's fix this girl's booboo, huh?"

Amanda stroked the cow's side and crooned calming words as she set to work opening the wound and draining the infection. She started irrigating the gash, but quickly ran out of the sterile wash. While she waited for Slade to return, she gently probed the wound, making sure it was free of debris and estimating the extent of tissue damage. Later, much longer than she'd have thought it would take him to do his errand, she heard footsteps. She decided not to say anything about the delay, cutting him slack for being new to the ranch and unfamiliar with where things were stored.

Using the bars of the chute to help pull herself up, Amanda climbed to her feet and turned toward...

Not Slade. The person who crossed the holding pen toward her was dressed from head to toe in winter garb—bulky coveralls and a heavy coat, gloves and ski mask. Overkill in Amanda's view.

"Can I help—?" Amanda swallowed the rest of her question as the heavily dressed figure withdrew a handgun from his coat pocket and aimed it at her.

Chapter 5

Amanda gasped and stumbled back a step, an icy fear for Cheyenne sinking to her bones.

In the next second, a loud blast rent the air, ringing in her ears and reverberating in her chest. Her daughter loosed a frightened wail.

Cheyenne! The instinct to protect her daughter overrode the numbing disbelief that threatened to paralyze her.

Rallying, Amanda scrambled for cover, first behind the cow in the squeeze chute, then toward the stable. She jogged backward keeping her body between the attacker and Cheyenne, shielding her daughter from the gunfire. But her foot hit a patch of ice as she scurried backward and Amanda fell, landing butt first with a jarring impact.

As Amanda clambered stiffly to her knees, her attacker descended on her like a black wraith and grabbed Cheyenne by the arms.

"No!" Amanda screamed, her tone so full of panic and anguish she didn't recognize her own voice. Cheyenne cried, her sobs full of terror. The assailant grunted as he tried to free the baby from her carrier.

Amanda gritted her teeth, resolved to give her life if needed to protect her child. She grabbed desperately for her daughter's foot, battling her attacker for possession of her child. "Slade! Help me!"

When the assailant raised the gun again, Amanda swung her arm in a powerful upward arc. She knocked the heavily garbed man's arm away. The gun flew from his grip. Her counterattack startled the attacker, giving her precious seconds to shove to her feet. But the assailant came at her again, fighting hand-to-hand and still reaching for Cheyenne.

"Get away from her!" Amanda raised her arms defensively. She met each swing with a defensive block. With Cheyenne still in the pack on her back, Amanda struggled for balance as she battled, but she quickly realized she would lose the fight if she stayed on defense.

Amanda had never been a fighter, had never so much as attended a kickboxing class. But working the ranch had given her strength, and for her daughter's life, she would batter and claw her opponent to her last breath. She swiped at her attacker's head and landed a weak glancing blow. Her attacker grabbed Amanda's hair and yanked hard, dragging her forward. Pinpricks of fire blazed through her scalp, and Amanda yelped in pain.

Cheyenne's heart-wrenching cries soared through the frozen air.

Enough!

Rage fueled her fight. This person, or his puppet master, had terrorized her and the rest of the ranch for months. The mastermind behind all of the tragedy had remained safely anonymous by delegating his dirty work. But no more! Amanda was determined to stop the reign of terror, to unmask the person behind the horrors.

Unmask... The word replayed in her head. Shouted.

Lunging, Amanda reached for the person's ski mask. The assailant ducked, grabbed for Amanda's hand, ripping off her latex glove.

Another swing. Another blocked punch. Another attempt to snatch Cheyenne.

Amanda kept moving, sidling left, backing up, turning. Keeping the backpack carrier and her daughter as far from the attacker's reach as possible.

"Slade!" she shouted again. Where was he?

Finally backed to the fence, cornered at the far end of the holding pen, Amanda made a final effort to either incapacitate her attacker or snatch off the ski mask. She braced on one leg and kicked, aiming for the assailant's kidney. More mobile than Amanda, the attacker shifted out of range, avoiding the strike...then landed a stunning punch to Amanda's jaw.

She saw spots and felt her knees tremble. *Cheyenne!*

When the attacker reached for Cheyenne, Amanda growled her fury and frustration, her fear and determination. She swung for the ski mask, her fingers curled like claws, and she raked her bared hand down the side of her attacker's neck. The ski mask shifted. Amanda met flesh.

And a male voice shouted, "Amanda!"

Her assailant's head jerked up. He backpedaled, swinging his gaze toward the source of the shout. And he ran.

Shaking to her core, Amanda slumped to the dirt.

"Stop him!" she yelled to Slade as he charged out of the stable. "Don't let him get away!"

Scooping up the gun as he fled, the attacker took advantage of his head start. Took advantage of Midnight, standing there saddled and ready. Took advantage of Slade's detour by Amanda. And got away.

"Are you hurt?" Slade asked, skidding to a stop beside her, his eyes wide and worried.

"I'm fine! Get him!" she shouted again, pointing at the escaping assailant. *Not again!*

Slade hesitated only a moment, clearly torn, before racing after the attacker. He cranked one of the ATVs and roared into the surrounding woods where the man had disappeared on Midnight.

Fumbling weakly to her feet, Amanda reached for the straps of the backpack, eager to pull Cheyenne into her arms and soothe her sobbing daughter. But she stopped.

She glanced at her hands—one still wearing a latex glove, the other covered in mud from her fall, both likely contaminated by the cow's infected wound.

Cold doesn't make you sick. Germs make you sick.

"It's okay, sweetie. We're safe now," she cooed to Cheyenne breathlessly as she rushed into the stable. "The bad man is gone. You're okay, sweetheart." She raced to the sink in the back of the stable, tossed out the glove and scrubbed her hands with hot water and antibacterial soap. She washed away the holding pen mud and the lingering germs from the cow's wound and dried them on fresh paper towels.

Hands now clean, she pulled her daughter from the carrier and held Cheyenne against her chest. She swayed and crooned and fought to gather her own composure.

The rumble of an ATV engine filtered in from outside, and she moved to a window to look out. Slade was alone on the ATV and held a riderless Midnight's reins, leading the stallion back to the holding pen. Frustration punched Amanda in the gut.

"He got away?" she groaned when Slade entered the stable. "Again?"

"We can set up a search of the property, starting from where I found Midnight, but chances are he's long gone." His gaze narrowed on Cheyenne, his brow puckering. He raised a hand toward Cheyenne's head before balking and shoving it back in his pocket. "Is she all right?"

"I think so. Just scared mostly." She released a pent-up breath. "Oh, God. He had his hands on her, pulling her out of the carrier…." A shiver rippled through her, and her stomach soured. "If he'd managed to get her out, if he'd—"

"Don't play the 'what-if' game." Slade slid a hand along her cheek, cupping her face.

Pain skittered along her jaw, and she hissed, winced.

His worried expression darkened further. "You *are* hurt." He angled her head toward the light and brushed her messy hair behind her ear. His warm fingers skimmed her cheek and sent an unnerving rush of sensual tingles to her core. "Your jaw's already bruising."

"I'll be fine." Pulse scampering, she pulled away from his touch and tested her mouth by opening, closing and wiggling it sideways slowly. Cheyenne's crying had made her nose run again, and Slade pulled the rag he'd used before on her from his back pocket and offered it to Amanda. "Why don't you walk me through what happened?"

"Okay." Amanda accepted the rag and moved to a bale of hay to sit down. She wiped Cheyenne's face as she gathered her composure and recalled the frightening events. "I heard someone walking up behind me and assumed it was you. But it wasn't, and then the guy pulled out a gun and fired at me—"

"I heard the gunshot. That's why I headed back this

way." He hitched his head toward the holding pen. "Show me where you were, where the shooter was. If I can estimate the trajectory, we might be able to find the bullet so the police can run ballistics on it."

In the aftermath of her fight with the assailant and with her adrenaline receding, Amanda had little energy for reenacting the attack. But she struggled to her feet, cradling a much calmer Cheyenne to her chest, and headed outside.

Slade stood where she told him the shooter had been, squinting in the direction the gun had been aimed, then crossed the pen to begin his search. While he scoured the area, looking for the bullet, she described the brawl, knocking the gun from the attacker's hand, her attempts to unmask the man, the way she'd scratched him...

Slade straightened suddenly and spun to face her. "You scratched him? His skin, not his clothes?"

Amanda blinked, working to remember exactly what happened. "I think so. On the cheek or neck, maybe. It all happened so fast and—"

He marched over to her and grabbed her wrist, lifting her hand near his face, his expression energized. "You could have the assailant's DNA under your nails. They can do a scraping and compared it to other evidence...." He stopped when he saw her frown. "What?"

"I washed my hands."

Chapter 6

Slade's eyebrows rose, and his mouth tightened. "You *what?*"

She jerked her hand free of his grip. "Cheyenne was crying. I was only thinking about her and needing to comfort her—"

"So you washed critical physical evidence down the drain!"

"I had mud and God-knows-what bacteria on my hands from working on that cow's infected wound!" She stabbed a finger toward the cow, still trapped in the squeeze chute. "I was not going to touch my child with contaminated hands!"

Grumbling a curse, he huffed angrily and turned to glare at the ground, clearly battling his temper. His expression shifted abruptly, and he took a few steps and squatted to stare at something in the dirt.

"What is it?" She moved closer to see what he'd found.

He pointed to a shiny cylinder glinting in the sun. "Bullet casing." He pulled out his cell phone and called someone on his speed dial. "We need to preserve the scene until it can be photographed and all the forensic evidence collected by the crime scene unit."

Amanda frowned and tipped her head skeptically. "Forensic evidence? Ballistics? Fingernail scrapings and bullet trajectories? Someone fancies himself an amateur detective."

He opened his mouth as if to counter her assertion but turned his attention instead to the person who answered his call. "Chief? Slade Kent. There's been another attack at Dead River Ranch. An attempted kidnapping. Shots fired. Can you send a crime scene team out here?"

Slade had the chief of police on speed dial?

Amanda studied Slade curiously as he made arrangements to meet the chief and go over the crime scene with him. She shifted her daughter to her hip as Cheyenne started wiggling to get down. *What's wrong with this picture?*

Slade disconnected his call and waved her back. "Let's go inside to wait. The more we tromp around here, the more we contaminate the scene."

Amanda squared her shoulders. "Who are you?"

He snapped her a puzzled look. "What do you mean?"

"It's a simple question. Who *are* you? Why do you have Chief Peters on speed dial, and why do you sound like a cop when you talk about the attack instead of a ranch foreman?"

He braced his hands on his hips and inhaled slowly. "And what is a ranch foreman supposed to sound like?"

She waved a hand. "Well, a little less like an episode of *CSI* and a little more like *Bonanza*."

A muscle jumped in his cheek as he clenched his teeth. Turning, he started back into the stable.

Amanda followed him. "Well?"

He stalked over to Midnight and started unsaddling him. "I'm who I said I am. If you have complaints about my job performance, fire me."

"Your job performance is not in question. Your honesty is. And frankly, Slade, I've had about all I can take of lies and secrets and double identities." Amanda seized his arm, and dug her fingers into his arm. "I want the truth, Slade. I deserve the truth."

He stopped working on the saddle and met her gaze. His eyes were a deeper shade of blue in the shadows of the stable, but no less intense as he drilled her with a hard stare. "Right now, and for the foreseeable future, I am your foreman. That is the truth."

But she could see more lurking in his gaze, an uneasiness that belied his claim. She shook her head slowly. "But that's not the whole truth. Lies of omission are still lies in my book." She snatched her hand away from his arm and fisted her fingers. "Omissions like not telling me you're married."

He quirked an eyebrow, clearly confused. "When did I—"

"Not you. Cheyenne's father." She huffed her frustration with herself. Why had she brought *him* up? "The point is lies *hurt*. And I know my family has been guilty of its share of deception, but I, for one, am sick of it." She jabbed him in the chest with her finger. "So if you are hiding something from me, something about who you are or what's happening on this ranch or my daughter's safety or—"

Slade wrapped his hand around the finger poking his chest and hauled her closer. "I would *never* do *anything* to put your daughter at risk." His eyes blazed with conviction. "Let's get that straight from the start."

Standing this close to him, she could feel his body heat, smell his peppermint gum and the remnant soap from his morning shower, count the eyelashes that framed his sapphire blues. Her mouth dried, and she lost her train of thought until he said, "I'm an agent with the Wyoming Bureau of Investigation. Chief Peters is the only person who knows. I came here to work undercover, to find answers to a lot of troubling questions."

Clutching Cheyenne close, she staggered back a step, glaring at him in shock. "You're a *cop?*"

His deception caused an unexplained ache in her chest.

He pressed his mouth in a taut line and nodded once tightly. "A WBI agent, yes."

While she had reason to be angry with him for his deceit, she couldn't explain the stab of pain, the slice of betrayal she felt. For his dishonesty to hurt her this way, she'd have to…*care* about him. Care *for* him. She shoved that thought aside to examine later, focusing now on his revelation.

"What questions? And how does being a WBI agent qualify you for being our foreman?"

He drew a slow breath and bumped his Stetson back to scratch his forehead. "Amanda, I know you have a lot you want to ask me, and I will explain everything for you. I promise. But I think our priority now needs to be helping Chief Peters and his officers process the scene and find your assailant."

Cheyenne squirmed harder and whined, now thoroughly tired of being held. Amanda patted her back and bounced her daughter on her hip as she regarded Slade levelly. "Cheyenne's restless. I need to take her inside. Feed her lunch."

He glanced to Cheyenne then back to Amanda. "Yeah, just…don't talk to anyone about what happened. We may need to interview other people about what they may have heard or seen this morning, and we don't want your account to influence others' statements."

She gave him a tight nod of understanding before pivoting on her heel and stalking stiffly toward the door. She gritted her teeth until her jaw ached. Was every man in her life a liar? Was honesty really so hard?

"Amanda."

She stopped but didn't turn. His boots thumped hollowly as he caught up to her, touched her sleeve. Even through her coat, the weight of his hand, the pressure of his fingers holding her arm sent a crackling awareness through her. Damn it, she didn't want to be attracted to him!

"I'm sorry." His tone was quiet, sincere. "My intention was never to deceive you or your family, and certainly not to hurt anyone. Chief Peters and I believed I could accomplish more working undercover."

She said nothing, didn't move.

He sighed. "I still believe working undercover would be best. I need you to not say anything. To anyone. Including your sisters, Cheyenne's guard, the hands…"

"You want me to share in your deception?"

The creases in his forehead and beside his eyes deepened. "If it will get to the bottom of the crimes that have been happening here for months, for *years,* then yes. I want to catch the person who is targeting your daughter. And I want the truth about what happened to Cole when he was kidnapped."

Amanda jerked her chin up. "Cole? What's your interest in Cole's kidnapping?"

Slade's mouth tightened. "I believe Cole's kidnapper is the same person who killed my father."

Chapter 7

Amanda shot him a stunned look. "Your father?"

Slade rubbed the center of his chest when the acid burn kicked up again. He didn't want to get into this conversation here, now, but he owed Amanda at least a cursory explanation. "Do you remember a police officer that was killed by the employees' gate about ten years ago?"

"I..." Her expression brightened with recognition. "Yeah. I was a senior in high school that year. Dad shielded us from most of what happened, unpleasant business that it was." She scrunched her nose as she thought back. "His name was Ronald...no, Roland Kent." The last name had barely passed her lips before her cheeks paled, and she met Slade's gaze, wide-eyed. "Oh, my God."

He nodded tightly, jamming down the cold ball of grief that swelled inside him. "My dad."

Her eyebrows beetled as she glared at him. "So you're here to what? Get revenge?"

"Not revenge. Answers. Justice. The case was never solved."

She grunted. "Turns out Chief Drucker wasn't on the up and up all the time."

"You think?" he asked, his tone heavily sarcastic.

Cheyenne twisted and kicked in her mother's arms, and Amanda shifted her from one hip to her other, murmuring softly to her child. "Just a minute, chickpea."

Cheyenne wasn't the only one growing restless with the conversation. Slade itched to continue his search for the bullet fired at Amanda, head out into the pastures to search for evidence of where the assailant could have gone. Drawing a slow breath, he met Amanda's inquiring gaze. "Now that Drucker's gone I've finally been granted access to the files concerning my father's death. I want his killer caught."

Amanda tipped her head, still rubbing her fussy daughter's back. "And you think the killer is someone here on the ranch?"

Slade shrugged and waved a hand toward the spot where she'd just been attacked. "Considering the events of the past few months, I'd say it's a good possibility. Wouldn't you?"

"Then everything that's been happening, the attacks, the kidnapping attempts…they're connected to your father's death?"

"I don't know that for a fact, but if you blow my cover, we may never know. I don't want whoever's behind the attack on you today and the murders here in recent months to go free for ten years the way my father's murderer has."

She held his stare, her gold eyes wary, intelligent… piercingly beautiful. "All right. I hate lies and deception, but if it will help put an end to the threat against Cheyenne, help bring the mastermind behind the attacks this year to justice…I'll keep your secret. But…" She squared her shoulders and stepped closer to him, poking him in the chest with a finger. "In exchange, I want you to swear to me that from here on out, you'll play it straight with me. I want your complete honesty, no holding back information or softening the truth. I want you to be open with me about everything in your investigation."

Slade tugged out his pack of gum, unwrapped another stick and added it to the one already in his mouth. The gnawing in his chest was growing by the minute, outpacing the effectiveness of the natural remedy.

With a scowl fixed on her, he weighed Amanda's ultimatum. He'd never been able to open himself to people, and more recently, he'd found shutting his emotions down; avoiding certain truths about his life was the only way he got through the day. But she'd qualified her last statement with "everything in your investigation." Facts of a case he could share. Facts were impersonal.

He stuck his hand out. "Deal."

She gave his hand a quick shake, but even that brief contact stirred something in the pit of his stomach. Her hand was small, her skin cold in the raw morning air, and though he knew she'd hate the characterization, *vulnerable* filtered through his brain. Cheyenne wasn't the only one who needed protection. The attacker today could have killed Amanda.

Slade vowed silently to make sure the assailant didn't get a second chance.

Slade escorted Amanda inside, despite her assurances to him that she didn't need his assistance. But when the flood of adrenaline that had fueled her fight wore off and the full impact of what had happened hit her, Amanda's knees turned to cooked pasta, buckling as she climbed the steps to the employee wing back door. Slade caught her with a strong arm around her waist and sent her a concerned look.

"I'm okay," she said, but her tone was unconvincing even to her own ears. She clutched Cheyenne to her chest tighter and stumbled through the door he opened for her.

Slade flagged Hilda down as he helped Amanda to the bench along the trestle table. "Amanda's been hurt. Can someone help?"

"Oh, dear lord! Amanda?" Hilda swooped in to fuss over her and Cheyenne.

"I'll be all right. I just need a minute to rest. Calm my nerves…" She stopped as another shudder rolled through her.

"She needs an ice pack for her jaw," Slade told Hilda. "And something hot to drink to warm her up."

"Miss Amanda? What happened?" Fiona appeared from the back hall and hurried over to check on her.

"I was—" Amanda started but stopped when Slade gave her a stern look and shook his head subtly. "I slipped on the ice. But I'm okay." That much was true, at least.

"I'll get Dr. Colton," Fiona said. "He should check you."

"No, don't bother Levi. I'm—"

But Fiona had hurried up the stairs to the family quarters before Amanda could stop her.

A moment later, Mathilda arrived from the staff wing, carrying an armload of dirty sheets. She took one look at Amanda and Cheyenne, Slade and Hilda huddled around them, and a frown dented her forehead. "Miss Amanda, what's the matter?"

Soon most of the household staff buzzed around her. Amanda did her best to smile and reassure them she and Cheyenne were essentially unharmed. Whenever someone offered to hold Cheyenne for her, she pulled her daughter closer and refused to let go. Someone on the ranch had tried to kill her, had tried to kidnap Cheyenne. That truth was difficult to process. The staff was like her second family. She couldn't comprehend how one of the people she'd grown up trusting, loving, confiding in could be trying to hurt her and Cheyenne.

For several minutes, Slade stayed at her side, and despite the lies he'd told her family about who he was and why he was at their ranch, his strong and stalwart presence gave her comfort, made her feel safe. She watched his keen gaze flick from one face to another as staff members passed through the dining area. When it dawned on her what he was doing, a chill rippled through her. He was looking for scratches on someone's face.

With a sick swirling in her stomach, Amanda sent her own gaze around the room, searching out her attacker.

The whoop of a siren and strobe of colored lights out the dining room window alerted them to the arrival of the police.

Hilda glanced out the window and frowned. "Why are the police here?"

"There was an incident earlier," Slade said cryptically. "The officers will want to talk to each of you in case you heard or saw anything that might be useful."

The gathered staff members glanced at each other then to Amanda with fresh concern and suspicion in their eyes.

"I'll talk to them, take them through the scene of the attack," Slade said quietly as he rose to meet the officers. "They'll want a statement from you."

Amanda nodded. "I know."

He gave her shoulder a firm squeeze before he left, and a chill settled over her as he strode away. What would she have done without him this morning? Not only did he stop the attacker from killing her and stealing her daughter, but his level-headed thinking, his reassuring strength and support had kept her from falling apart.

Slade strode back out into the biting winter air to meet Chief Peters and his officers. The worry that had filled Amanda's eyes as he left her tugged inside him. Although she'd worn a brave face for the household staff as they fussed over her, he'd seen the underlying tension in her face, her protectiveness toward Cheyenne, her uncertainty and doubt in the face of the threat hanging over her. And despite the attack and her rattled nerves, Amanda had treated every member of the staff with warmth and affection and genuine gratitude for their concern.

He shook his head, silently admitting his surprise. He'd imagined a wealthy daughter of Jethro Colton would be aloof and pampered, treating her staff with detached disinterest. But Amanda Colton continued to surprise and impress him.

"Another attack?" Chief Peters asked as he rounded the front bumper of his cruiser.

Slade nodded. "Came after the baby again. Took a shot at Amanda."

Peters gave a low whistle. "The guy's getting brazen, going after the kid when she's with her mother."

"Exactly. *Brazen* is one word for it. *Desperate* is what I'd say. And, therefore, more dangerous." Slade gritted his back teeth at the implication. Amanda and Cheyenne were not safe. But how did he protect them and still have time to conduct his personal investigation into his father's murder?

Peters tugged up his coat collar. "Show me the scene."

Slade led the officers to the holding pen and found Cal Clark squatting beside the squeeze chute.

"Hey!" Slade shouted. "What are you doing?"

Cal looked up, and his expression darkened when he saw the police officers. "Just checking on the cow. Where's Amanda? Why'd she leave the cow in the chute like this?"

"This area is a crime scene." Peters leveled a hard look on Cal. "We're going to need a statement from you."

"From me?" Cal's eyes widened. "What did I do?"

As they walked closer to Cal, Slade noticed a dark smear on the man's chin. He narrowed his gaze, studying the streak as he crossed the holding pen. "Is that blood?"

"What?" Cal frowned.

Chief Peters caught Cal's jaw between his fingers, tipping his face toward the sunlight. "Sure looks like it to me. Harriman, get a swab of this."

Slade caught Cal's wrist when he tried to touch his chin. "How'd you get blood on your face, Clark?"

"I don't know," Cal said, his eyes shifting from Chief Peters to Slade. Then his face brightened. "Wait, I pricked my thumb on the barbed wire when I was fixing the fence. It was bleeding, so I stuck it in my mouth. Must have smeared some of the blood on my chin then."

Slade sent him a hooded glare. "You sure about that?"

"See for yourself." Cal yanked off his glove and held up his thumb. A fresh puncture wound was obvious on the tip. "What happened here? What are you accusing me of?"

"Easy, pal. No one's accusing you of anything." Chief Peters stepped back so his officer could take a sample of the blood on Cal's chin. "Just covering all the bases. Officer Harriman here is going to get your statement."

Cal followed the young policeman to the stable, but

Slade's gut told him the ranch hand was innocent. He'd left the hand in the pasture shortly before the attack, and Cal had been expecting Slade to return, meaning his disappearance at the time of the attack would have been noticed. He hadn't had the sort of outerwear with him that the assailant had worn, and Slade had interviewed enough witnesses to know real shock and honest denial when he saw it.

But he also knew better than to rule out any suspect too soon. Until the assailant was caught, everyone at Dead River Ranch was a suspect in Slade's book.

Chapter 8

Once Chief Peters and his officers had finished collecting evidence and headed back to the station, Slade went upstairs to check on Amanda and Cheyenne. As he made his way through the lavishly appointed family home, he goggled at the expensive decor. One room of the Colton mansion was bigger than his apartment in Jackson, and the furnishings surely cost more than he earned in a year. Somehow the opulent house didn't match the feisty veterinarian he'd gotten to know in the stable. Amanda Colton was an enigma to him. Wealthy beyond his dreams, yet as down-to-earth and unpretentious as any ranch hand he'd ever known.

He climbed the wide staircase, admiring the dark polished-wood hand rail and ornately carved newel posts. At the top of the stairs, he found a sitting area where three hallways to separate wings converged. Hearing soft music down the hall to his left, he headed that direction first. When he found the partially open door where the lullaby music was playing, he knocked softly.

"What are you doing?"

He turned to find the head maid he'd met his first day holding a stack of folded laundry and glaring at him.

"I wanted to check on Amanda. She was—"

"The family quarters are strictly off-limits to ranch hands and kitchen workers." The woman—Mathilda, if he remembered correctly—squared her shoulders. "You shouldn't be up here. There is a proper protocol to be followed if you want to speak to a member of the family."

Slade arched an amused eyebrow. Was she for real? "Protocol?"

Her starched, high-collared uniform dress and pursed mouth added to the air of disapproval she projected. "You heard me."

"Slade?" Amanda called from inside the room. "Is that you?"

He pushed the door farther open, despite Mathilda's sniff of disdain. Amanda was seated in a rocking chair with Cheyenne asleep in her arms. "Hey," he said quietly, "how are you doing?"

Amanda looked past him. "It's okay, Mathilda. I want to talk to him."

The woman looked worried and flattened one hand against her starched bodice. "Are you sure?"

"Positive."

"Can I get you anything? Would you like to have your lunch in your room?" Mathilda asked.

Slade didn't miss the much more ingratiating tone the maid had when addressing Amanda.

"No, thank you. I'll be down in a little while."

Mathilda sent Slade another warning glare before heading down the hall to another room.

With a grunt of disbelief, Slade stepped into the nursery and removed his Stetson. "Didn't know you had a watchdog."

Amanda grinned. "She means well. She's always been protective of our family and her staff, but with all that's been happening in recent months, she's been more on edge." She tipped her head. "What brings you up here?"

A fuzzy orange cat with no tail sauntered over to sniff his boots and rub against his legs. He bent over and gave the cat a cursory scratch behind the ears. "Just making sure you're okay."

"That's sweet of you." She smiled. "I'm a little sore, but I'll live."

Slade cast an uneasy glance around the frilly room, where pastel accents and a mural of flowers and fairies predominated. He forcefully shut out the memory of a yellow nursery and wallpaper with dancing bunnies. When the familiar burn gnawed his gut, he took his gum from his pocket and offered her a stick.

"No, thanks." She glanced down at her sleeping daughter, and the warmth that filled her expression stirred a bittersweet ache in his chest. She drew a fingertip along Cheyenne's cheek. "I've got everything I need right here."

Slade shifted his feet uncomfortably, and after putting the gum in his mouth, he put away the pack. "Chief Peters questioned Cal."

She raised a worried look. "Cal? Why? Wasn't he in the pasture fixing that downed fence?"

"Probably. But he had time to get back to the stable and has no proof he was in the field when the attack happened."

"But Cal's worked for us for years. I can't imagine he'd—"

"Amanda, I know you want to believe the best of all

of your employees and family, but the fact remains that someone on the ranch is behind these attacks. Someone is leading a double life and conspiring behind your back. You need to be careful whom you trust."

He hated the shadows that filled her eyes, but she had to face reality for her own safety. "I know. That's probably the hardest part of this whole mess. It seems crazy to me to think Cal could want to hurt me or Cheyenne, but it's just as ludicrous that it's Jared or George or any of the hands."

Slade fingered the brim of his hat. "Amanda, how sure are you that it was a man that attacked you?"

Her chin jerked up, and surprise filled her face. "You think it was a woman?"

"I didn't say that. We have to consider all the possibilities though. You said the attacker's face was covered with a ski mask."

Closing her eyes, Amanda sighed and leaned her head back against the rocking chair. "I don't know. Maybe. I just assumed…"

"Well, don't assume anything. Did the attacker speak?"

She shook her head. "No." Thinking back to what was reported by her sisters and employees after attacks earlier in the year, Amanda sighed. "I guess it could have been a woman. When my sister Catherine was held hostage earlier this year, she said one of the people who held her was a woman. There's even a good chance the mastermind behind everything that's happened is a woman."

He grunted, digesting that information. Sliding one hand in his jeans pocket, Slade glanced toward the nursery window. "Who lives in the little cabin in the woods on the far edge of the ranch yard?"

She tucked her hair behind her ear and wrinkled her nose in thought. "You mean the Blacks' cabin?"

"Who are the Blacks?"

"Our laundress and handyman. They're an older couple. They've lived on the property for as long as I can remember." Amanda tilted her head. "Why?"

Slade ran a hand through his hair, then jammed his hat back on his head. "That's where the assailant left Midnight when he fled, but when I searched the cabin, it was empty."

She stared at him for several seconds, her expression bleak. Finally she ducked her head and cuddled her daughter closer. "I hate this. Feeling like I have to constantly be looking over my shoulder. Having to hire a guard to protect my baby. Not knowing who to trust."

"You can trust me."

Amanda glanced up at him, her gold eyes wary. "That remains to be seen."

That night at the family dinner table, conversation centered around Jethro's slight improvement that day and Gabriella and Trevor's upcoming wedding. During a lull in conversation, Jethro's ex-wife piped up.

"I hear you had some trouble today, Amanda. Are you okay?"

Amanda glanced up at Darla Colton, ex-wife number three for Jethro. The titillated glint in Darla's eyes, as well as her former stepmother's history, told Amanda that Darla was more interested in juicy gossip than her stepdaughter's well-being.

Across the table, Gabriella shot her a concerned look. "Trouble?"

"I'm okay," Amanda assured her sister. "Someone

tried to snatch Cheyenne again, but our new foreman showed up in time to run the attacker off."

"Oh, no! Why didn't you tell me?" Gabby divided her look between Amanda and Trevor.

"Because I'm all right, and I didn't want to needlessly worry you."

"How can you have such a blasé attitude about being attacked?" Gabby asked, her expression appalled.

"I'm not blasé about anything regarding Cheyenne's safety." Amanda wiped applesauce off her daughter's face. "But the incident is over, and I'd rather use my energy finding the creep responsible than fretting over the could-have-beens."

"We'll get him," Trevor assured her, then gave Gabriella's hand a squeeze. He cut a small bite of potato and put it on his daughter's high chair tray. Baby Avery pinched the bite between her chubby fingers and gave her father a slobbery grin. In the high chair next to Avery's, Cheyenne slapped her tray and reached for Avery's food.

"Hey, chickpea, eat your own dinner." Amanda spooned a few peas and carrots onto Cheyenne's plate, and her daughter took a greedy handful with a squeal of delight. "Good to see your cold hasn't hurt your appetite."

Darla's blond-haired son breezed in and dropped into a chair. Grabbing a serving bowl, he began shoveling food onto his plate. "Hope you saved me some. I'm starved."

Amanda generally tried to avoid her ex-stepbrother, Trip Lowden, who, along with his mother and sister, she considered a leech sucking her family's finances. Given her druthers, she'd kick Darla and her two mooching children off the ranch, but her father allowed them to stay for reasons she and her sisters couldn't fathom. The playboy's face still showed evidence of the black eye Dylan had given him before leaving for Witness Protection with Aurora, and Amanda took secret satisfaction seeing the lingering bruise. How many times had she wanted to slug the smarmy jerk herself when he'd "accidentally" brush up against her or smack her on the butt? Too many to count. She bit the inside of her cheek, holding back a chuckle when she remembered a private joke she and Aurora had shared at Trip's expense, and in the wake of the memory came the familiar ache of missing her dear friend.

"Where have you been?" Darla asked. "You know what time dinner is served."

Trip gave his mother a lecherous grin. "I was…busy."

Trip's sister, Tawny, snorted. "What was her name? Or did you ask?"

Trip shrugged. "Paula or Patty or something. I don't remember."

Amanda angled a look of disgust at her womanizing ex-stepbrother—then did a double take. A long fresh scratch marred his cheek.

Her muscles tensed, and an angry heat began to simmer in her gut. "Trip, where did you get that scratch on your face?"

Around the dinner table, all heads turned toward Amanda and Trip.

"Why do you want to know?" Trip stabbed a bite of roast beef and sent her a blithe look.

Amanda set her silverware down and flattened her hands on the tablecloth. "Where did you get the scratch?" she repeated, enunciating each word slowly.

"Maybe my lady friend liked it rough." He gave Amanda a lewd wink.

Furious with his smug attitude, she slammed her fist on the table so hard the dishes rattled. "Answer me!"

"Amanda?" Gabby murmured. "Why does it matter?"

She sent her sister a brief glance before drilling Trip with an unrelenting glare. "When I was fighting off my attacker this morning, I scratched him somewhere on or near his face."

Trip froze with his fork suspended halfway to his mouth. His blond eyebrows puckered, and he sent a nervous glance around the table to all the eyes focused on him. "Wait...you don't think..." His fork clattered to his plate, and he aimed a finger at Amanda. "I had nothing to do with that! How dare you accuse me!"

"Where'd you get the scratch?" Trevor asked, his tone dark and intimidating.

Trip balled his fists on the table. "Like I said...kinky sex. Paula was a wildcat, okay?"

Tawny made a catty meowing noise and helped herself to another roll.

Narrowing a haughty glower at Amanda, Trip asked, "Jealous?"

Amanda snatched her napkin from her lap and threw it on her plate. "You're disgusting. I'll need this Paula's contact information so the police can verify your story." She shoved her chair back and pulled Cheyenne out of her high chair. "And you better hope she does corroborate your story, because if I find out you had any part of trying to kidnap my daughter, I'll bury you."

Slade sat back in the metal chair in the interrogation room and rubbed his eyes with his palms. He'd come into the Dead River police station three times since arriving in town and had read through the police file regarding his father's murder a dozen times. The only thing clear to him was how shoddy the police work had been. Improper procedure had been followed and incomplete records had been kept, yielding little useful information in finding his father's killer. More likely, the former chief had been covering for someone.

He'd talked to Agnes Barlow, the head cook who'd found his father's body, but she couldn't remember anything more than what was already in the file from her deposition. Mathilda Perkins had also had little to add to her ten-year-old statement, saying she hadn't seen or heard anything the night of the crime. Hilda Zimmerman lived in town with her husband, who'd supported her claim to have been with him at the time his father had been shot. He couldn't question Faye Frick, who'd raised the boy who turned out to be the lost Colton heir, Cole, since she'd been killed that past summer. And that boy, whom everyone knew as Dylan Frick, now lived in Witness Protection with his fiancée. Most of the other employees had joined the ranch after the night his father had died.

He still wanted to follow up with the Blacks, the older couple who lived in the small cabin at the edge of the main ranch yard, former foreman Gray Stark and Amanda's sisters, who'd have been in their teens ten years ago. But when originally questioned by the police, none of them had had any useful information, either.

He slapped the file folder closed with a growl of frustration and shoved the chair back.

Chief Peters was in the hallway when Slade stalked out of the interrogation room, and he sent Slade a commiserative grimace. "Sorry. I told you the file would be of little help."

"Unless you have any other ideas, I've hit a dead end." Slade raked a hand through his hair and huffed a sigh. "Coming here was a mistake."

Peters scratched his chin, his expression contemplative. "No ideas. Unless…"

Slade quirked an eyebrow, his attention drawn fully to Chief Peters. "You have something else? A lead?"

"I don't know what it is. Maybe nothing. Maybe just a crazy person looking for fifteen minutes of fame."

Slade brought his shoulders back and straightened his back. "Go on."

"We took a call here at the station recently from a guy claiming he had dirt on Jethro Colton. He wouldn't give us any details. In fact, he wanted me to fly out to San Diego to talk to him in person. When we traced the call, we found the call had been placed from a hospice."

"A patient wanting to make a deathbed confession or a nurse who'd heard something incriminating from a patient?" Slade suggested.

"Could be. I took the guy's name down but told him our department didn't have the funds to fly me to California without more to go on than the suggestion of something tawdry about Jethro Colton. Especially while we have our hands full investigating all the attacks that have been happening at the Colton ranch." Peters hitched his head toward the front desk. "I think I filed the name out here. I'll get it for you."

Slade followed the chief out to the reception area and rubbed his hands on the seat of his jeans. Could this finally be the tip that would break open the crimes at Dead River Ranch, or was this mysterious call a distraction designed to sidetrack the police's other ongoing investigations regarding the Coltons?

While Chief Peters was thumbing through the files in a cabinet drawer, the front door of the station opened, and Amanda breezed in, her daughter propped on her hip. She exchanged a startled look with Slade, and the officer at the desk said, "Can I help you?"

"Here it is," Chief Peters said, pulling a file and reading, "Scottie Breen was his name. He said he used to work for former President Joe Colton. In fact, he hinted that his information about Jethro had something to do with the former president."

"What does my father have to do with President Colton?" Amanda asked warily.

Chief Peters whirled around. "Miss Colton, I didn't see you come in."

"I just arrived." She furrowed her brow, her cheeks pink from the cold outside. The impulse to wrap Amanda in his arms and warm her kicked Slade like an irate bull. He could almost feel the chill of her skin against his palms, her cold lips brushing his and heating under the persuasion of his kiss. He gave his head a little shake. His instant gut-level reaction to her didn't surprise him. She was a desirable woman by any man's definition. But the extent of his attraction to her worried him. He couldn't afford to be distracted from his mission at Dead River Ranch, especially if that distraction had the last name Colton.

Slade cleared his throat, dragging his attention back to the business at hand.

"Are you aware of any connection Jethro would have to Joe Colton, other than the same last name?" Slade asked. "Does the shared name mean they're related?"

Amanda shook her head. "Not that I've ever heard. And you'd think if we were related to the President of the United States, that might come up."

"Could be nothing, then." Peters showed Slade the note he'd jotted. "Here's the phone number he called from if you want to follow up. Tell him I gave you his name. If you feel he's got anything worth following up on, let me know."

Slade pocketed the note and jerked a nod. "Will do."

Amanda sent Slade a look that clearly said she wanted to grill him further about the chief's tip. Her gold eyes lasered into him, and his body answered with a low thrum. Her determination and confidence were a turn on. He could easily imagine how all that self-assurance and passion translated between the sheets. Her fiery gaze held his a moment longer before she raised her chin and faced Chief Peters. "Trip Lowden showed up at dinner tonight with scratches on his face. I want you to question him and check his alibi."

Slade narrowed a curious gaze on Amanda. "Trip Lowden? I don't know that name."

"Probably because I usually refer to him as my former stepmother's worthless, mooching spawn." Amanda tugged a notepad from her purse. "He claims he got the scratch from a woman during sex. And while that would be completely in character for the reprobate, I find it interesting, incriminating even, that he showed up with a scratch the same day I scratched my attacker."

"So do I." Slade gritted his back teeth, adding Trip Lowden to the list of people he needed to interrogate.

"Here's the woman's name. Supposedly she works nights at the hospital."

Chief Peters stepped to the counter and held his hand out for the paper Amanda ripped from her pad. "We'll follow up." The policeman's serious expression softened as he turned his attention to Cheyenne. "Hey, cutie. How are you?"

Amanda's daughter gurgled, and a beatific baby smile spread across her face. While the officers chuckled and teased their chief about hitting on a younger woman, Slade's gut knotted.

By assuming responsibility for keeping Amanda and her daughter safe, he'd put himself in a position to be near Cheyenne. As cute as the little girl was, all of her sweet smiles and baby babbles were like glass shards on an open wound in his soul. He'd thought he had his grief better in hand when he'd moved onto the ranch, but Cheyenne, and his powerful attraction to Amanda, had brought memories to the surface—along with emotions that had no place in his investigation of the Colton family.

Having followed Amanda back home, Slade parked the ranch truck beside Amanda's small SUV and circled the tailgate to help her unload Cheyenne from her baby seat.

"Thanks, I got her." Amanda took her daughter from him and fell in step beside him as they entered the house. "So…care to share why you were at the police station? Other than digging up weirdo callers who claim to have dirt on my father."

"I told you earlier. I want to know who killed my father. Chief Peters has given me access to the files…for all the good they've done."

Slade placed his hand under Amanda's elbow, steadying her as they climbed the icy steps to the back door to the employee wing, and even through her thick coat, his hand stirred a tingling warmth at her core. Growing up around the ranch hands, Amanda had always been "one of the guys," more likely to get a playful slug in the arm than a gentlemanly gesture. That Slade showed her the courtesy, coupled with the way his gaze lingered on her when they talked, made her feel feminine and attractive in a way she hadn't felt in years.

"Then you haven't learned anything new?" she asked. While she wanted Slade to find the peace and closure he was searching for regarding his father's murder, she was a little scared of what he might find. Bad enough that someone on the ranch was gunning for her and Cheyenne.

What would she do if she discovered someone she loved and trusted had killed Slade's father all those years ago?

"No. Nothing helpful." He held the door open and stood back to let her enter first. "This caller in California may not pan out, either. But I have nothing else at this point, so I'll check it out."

"You'll let me know what this Breen person says?" She started unzipping Cheyenne's coat and her own.

"If I feel it's relevant."

Amanda raised her chin and shot him a hard look. "If it's about my family, then it *is* relevant to me. You promised to be honest with me."

"I did. But he could prove to be a crackpot." Slade hung his coat on the hooks by the door. "Tell me something. Why do you always use the employee door instead of the family entrance?"

She shrugged, Cheyenne propped on her hip. "It's closer to the stable. And I've never paid much heed to the family-versus-employee distinction."

"I bet that drives Mathilda nuts." His hand grazed her shoulder as he helped her remove her coat, and the casual contact shot sizzling sparks through her. In the tight quarters of the entryway, she felt his nearness on a primal level, hyperaware of the scent of hay and wood smoke that clung to him, the low rumble of his voice and the heat behind his bedroom gaze.

Amanda chuckled, working to keep the flutter he caused in her chest out of her voice. "Absolutely."

Slade's cheek twitched in the semblance of a grin, and tiny crinkles framed his eyes. Just that hint of a grin sent a shockwave through Amanda that stole her breath. Damn, he was sexy!

He jerked a nod. "Well, good night."

As he strode through the door to the employee living quarters, the scent of outdoors that surrounded him lingered. She inhaled the sexy aroma and held it in her nose, savoring…and found herself smiling.

Cheyenne patted Amanda's cheek with her cold, chubby hand, and Amanda touched her forehead to her daughter's. "Am I crazy to feel attracted to him, chickpea? We're doing okay without a man in our lives, aren't we?"

But as she climbed the stairs to her suite, Amanda couldn't help thinking what Cheyenne would miss not having a father in her life. Was it time she put David's betrayal behind her and opened her heart to another man? And was Slade that man? Was he a man she could trust not to hurt her, if his reason for being at Dead River Ranch was to unearth her family's buried secrets?

Chapter 9

"What's your interest in Jethro Colton?" Scottie Breen asked, his voice a rasp on Slade's cell phone. After Slade had explained who he was and how he'd gotten Breen's number, the man had started asking questions.

"I'm assisting Chief Peters in investigating a number of crimes that have happened on Jethro Colton's ranch, including the cold case of my father's murder here ten years ago." Slade paced his small bedroom in the employee quarters.

"Your father? Then you have a personal motive for going after the Coltons?"

Slade thought of Amanda and her sister Gabby. Both women had been kind and helpful to him since he'd arrived. His shoulders tensed. "I'm not going after the Coltons. I just want the truth about my father's death. He deserves justice. If I can help catch the culprit behind the recent attacks while I'm at it, all the better. If you have information that can help do either of those things, I'm all ears."

"Oh, yes," the man wheezed. "I've been reading about…the recent trouble at Dead River Ranch. That's largely why…I called Chief Peters." Breen was silent for a moment, then with a grunt he said, "Could be…helpful to you. Maybe not. Either way, I'm dying, Mr. Kent. Lung cancer. I have…information that needs to be…exposed. I've lived with…Jethro Colton's secrets for…years, and I refuse to…die with a guilty conscience."

Slade's grip on his phone tightened. "What secrets?"

"If you…want to know, you come…talk to me in person."

"Is that really necessary? What's wrong with telling me now?"

"I've spent my life in the political world, Mr. Kent. I don't trust phones. I've learned when you have something important to say, you need to look the other man in the eye."

Slade raked his hand through his hair and glanced over at his laptop. "What about a video chat?"

"In person, Mr. Kent. Those are…my terms."

"How can I be sure you're not some prankster? I don't have the time or money to waste flying out there to hear about some old gambling debt or parking ticket."

"Of course not. I wouldn't waste…my time over a parking ticket…either."

Slade rubbed his chin, remembering what the police chief had told him. "Chief Peters mentioned some link to former President Joe Colton."

"Yes. I was President Colton's…campaign manager every election from…his first run for the state senate."

Verifying that information would be easy enough. "What does—?"

"I've said all…I'm going to over the phone," Breen growled, breathlessly. "Are you coming…to see me or not?"

The other ranch hands would return from Nevada by lunch tomorrow, relieving the workload. If he made a quick turnaround and got back to the ranch within thirty-six hours, maybe his absence wouldn't draw too much attention. Solving his father's murder was his priority, and if Breen knew something that could shed light on his investigation or more recent crimes at the ranch, Slade needed to make the trip happen. "I'll be there. Day after tomorrow."

Even as he disconnected with Breen, Slade began pulling up travel websites on his laptop to book his flight and hotel in San Diego. He'd just finished making his airline reservation when a knock sounded at his door.

Amanda waited across his threshold when he opened the door, and she gave him an uneasy grin. "Hi."

"Hi." He checked his watch. Eleven o'clock. He frowned, concerned the late night visit meant trouble. "Is there a problem?"

"Not a new one." She slid her hands in the back pockets of her jeans and tipped her head. "Can we talk?"

He lifted a shoulder. "I suppose." He stood back and let her in. "Where's Cheyenne?"

"Upstairs. Gabby is rocking her to sleep." She flashed a lopsided grin that he felt like a kick in the gut. "Hard to believe all three Colton sisters will be mothers soon."

Slade blinked. "Gabby is pregnant?"

"No, but she's marrying Trevor and will be Avery's mom. And Catherine, whom you'll meet at the wedding, is due in May."

Nodding, Slade made a mental note to be out of town by May. If being around eight-month-old Cheyenne was difficult, being near Catherine Colton's newborn would be torture.

He locked down the pain that reared its head and gave Amanda his attention. "What's up?"

As she strolled into his room, her gaze immediately went to his laptop with his airline reservation glowing from the screen. "Going somewhere?"

He strode past her and pushed the screen of his laptop closed. "Maybe. You wanted to talk?"

She gave him a curious look. "California? Are you going to see that Breen character Chief Peters mentioned?"

Slade saw no point in evading. "I figured it was worth hearing him out."

She squared her shoulders, a gesture that drew his attention to her chest and the fact that she didn't appear to have on a bra under the long-sleeved sleep shirt she wore with her jeans. His imagination conjured an image of her naked breasts and how it would feel to mold them in his hands.

"Take me."

Slade's pulse jumped, and he yanked a startled gaze to her gold eyes as his brain scrambled to process what he'd heard.

When he didn't answer her for several seconds, she said, "Take me with you to talk to Breen."

Oh. Slade drew a deep breath through his nose and slid a hand over his mouth as a cover when he realized how wrong his misinterpretation had been. So…not an invitation to ravish her.

He cleared his throat. "No."

She scowled. "Why not? If this guy thinks he has dirt on my dad, I want to hear it."

Slade folded his arms over his chest. "You came down here to talk about something?"

Amanda opened her mouth as if to argue but seemed to reconsider. She schooled her face, and her shoulders dropped in defeat. "When you were at the police station tonight, did Chief Peters have any new information about my attacker? What did the blood test on Cal show? Did they find the bullet that was fired at me and run ballistics on it?"

"The blood on Cal's chin was his own, and the puncture wound on his thumb backs up his story how it got there. His clothes and hands were negative for gunshot residue."

"So he's not the one behind all the attacks?"

Slade raised a palm. "I can't say that. But it does appear he's not the one who attacked you this morning. We have to wait on the ballistics test. They can take a few days. So far we haven't found a gun to tie to the shooting, either."

"And we still have no progress finding the mastermind behind the attacks. Someone hired Duke, one of the ranch hands, to kidnap Cheyenne and has been manipulating members of the staff to do his—or her—bidding."

She chewed her bottom lip in frustration, drawing his focus to her mouth, and Slade's groin tightened. When she tucked her loose hair behind her ear, exposing the pulse point of her neck, he was blindsided by an awareness of the late hour, the intimacy of having her in his bedroom and a consuming urge to press his lips to the curve of her throat and taste the tender skin there.

"Anything else?"

Again he needed a moment to bring his thoughts back around from his sidetrack. "Not really. Most police work is slow and tedious. A lot of waiting on backed-up labs."

She sighed and plowed her fingers through her hair. "It's hard to be patient when you know someone is trying to kidnap your child. I need to be *doing* something."

He understood her drive to act, not sit back and wait. That ambition was what had brought him to the ranch to search for answers about his father. "You're doing what's most important. Just keep being a good mother and make sure she's guarded."

She shook her head and squared her shoulders again. "It's not enough. I want to go with you to talk to Breen."

He puffed out a breath in exasperation. "No."

She narrowed a disgruntled glare on him then shifted her gaze to his laptop. She made a move toward it, and he stopped her by hooking an arm around her waist, then sidestepping to block her path.

"No," he repeated and noticed that his hand on her hip, his proximity, seemed to rattle her. Fluster her. Her cheeks had flushed, and a tremor rippled through her.

Intriguing. His touch ruffled Amanda's otherwise self-assured and stubborn feathers. He could work with that.

When she'd drawn a calming breath, she glanced up at him and caught him staring. Her nose wrinkled slightly as she tipped her head in query. "What?"

"Honestly?"

Her eyebrows lifted. "Yes. You promised to be completely honest with me. Remember?"

He pursed his lips and nodded. "I do." Stepping close enough to invade her personal space, he caught the silky strands of her hair between his fingers. "I was thinking how much I like your hair down. It's sexy."

Her breath hitched, and her golden eyes widened in surprise.

"But then that messy ponytail you wear in the stable

is kinda hot, too. The mussed and careless thing makes me think about how it might look after sex."

She swallowed hard and gaped at him. "I, uh…"

He tugged his cheek in a grin. "You wanted me to be honest."

"R-right."

Her gaze dropped to his mouth and lingered there as her eyes darkened to the color of well-aged brandy. Slade's pulse hammered. Desire flooded his veins, and his skin flashed hot. He leaned toward her, his focus locked on her lips. Around him the room crackled with a kinetic energy, and his body hummed with anticipation. He lifted his hand to her face to cup her cheek. When he stroked her bottom lip with his thumb, she made a small noise between a gasp and a pleasured sigh.

And he stilled.

Flirting with Amanda, to divert her from her crusade to join him on his fact finding trip to California, was one thing. Kissing Jethro Colton's daughter was quite another matter.

His libido cursed his conscience as he dropped his hand and stepped away. "It's late. I think we should say good-night."

Amanda blinked, and Slade thought he detected a degree of disappointment in the dent of her brow. "Oh." She cleared her throat, and her hand fluttered as she fumbled with the neckline of her shirt. "O-okay."

Color suffused her cheeks as she backed toward the door, and a stab of guilt jabbed Slade. He hadn't intended to hurt or embarrass her. He sobered realizing how willingly she'd responded to his advances.

One more reason to keep his guard up around her. He

had no intention of tangling himself in a relationship of any sort. Not when he still had nightmares from the last time he opened his heart to a woman.

Chapter 10

Thirty-six hours later, as Slade made his way through security at the Laramie airport, his thoughts were still on the almost-kiss with Amanda. He'd spent two restless nights replaying the hurt look in her eyes when he'd backed away from her.

He took a seat at his gate and tugged his hat down over his eyes, hoping to get a few winks before boarding the connecting flight to Denver. He'd just dozed off when a familiar female voice asked, "Is this seat taken, cowboy?"

Jerking his chin up, he confirmed his suspicion. Amanda stood before him, a diaper bag over one shoulder, a carry-on suitcase behind her and—he groaned internally—her baby in a portable baby seat. He sat up from his relaxed sprawl and furrowed his brow. "What are you doing here?"

She grinned saucily. "I'm going to California. I hear

there's a man there with information about my family, and I'd like to talk to him."

"Amanda," he growled in exasperation. "I told you I wanted to go alone."

"And I told you, if there was information about my family to be learned, I have a right to be there." She gave him a sweet smile.

He frowned as she dumped the diaper bag in an empty chair. "How did you know what flight I'd be on? Or where in California I was going?"

"I can be ingenious when I need to be."

"Meaning?"

She set the baby seat on the chair beside him and rolled her suitcase out of the traffic path. "You didn't erase your browser after you bought your plane ticket and made your hotel reservation."

Slade sputtered and sat forward. "You hacked into my laptop?"

"Didn't need to hack. It was sitting out on the desk in your room when I came down to talk to you yesterday afternoon." She pulled out her boarding pass and examined it.

"I was out checking the herd yesterday afternoon."

Another coy smile. "I know."

He gritted his back teeth. "I should arrest you for... something."

"And you should have your laptop password protected." She tsked and shook her head as she settled in the next empty seat.

Slade corralled his emotions, tamping his frustration and irritation. He'd underestimated Amanda, but he'd not make that mistake again. For now, she was here and wouldn't be deterred from accompanying him, so he'd do well to make the best of the situation. Perhaps he could get her to talk about the family, and he'd learn something that would be helpful.

Cheyenne whined, and Amanda turned to tend to her daughter.

"Did you *have* to bring the baby?" he asked and sighed.

Amanda sent him an incredulous look. "She's my daughter. She goes where I go. Besides, with a kidnapper lurking in Wyoming, I think between the two, she's safer in California. In fact, if not for Christmas and Gabby's wedding, I'd consider staying in California for a while."

He crossed his arms over his chest and regarded her skeptically. "So what happens when an animal gets sick tomorrow and you're off following me to San Diego?"

Her gaze casually scanned the other passengers. "There are other vets in Dead River. Cal knows who to call if there's a problem." She flashed another maddeningly calm smile as she patted his leg. "Don't worry, Slade. The ranch will be fine for a couple days without us, and I promise not to interfere with your fact-finding mission. I'm just as eager to hear what this man has to say about my dad as you are."

She let her hand linger for a moment on his knee, and he realized the sense of connection her touch stirred was…nice. In another situation, Amanda was the kind of woman he could see himself asking out. Eventually, he supposed, he'd have to date again if he didn't want to spend his life alone.

"Tell me more about your call with Breen. Just who is this guy we're going to see?" Amanda asked. She unbuckled Cheyenne from the baby seat and held her on her lap.

The little girl gurgled and smiled at her mother and the other passengers. Amanda handed her daughter a cracker to munch while they waited, then faced him with an expression that said he hadn't answered her last questions.

"He used to be Joe Colton's campaign manager. He's bedridden at a hospice with late-stage lung cancer, and apparently he feels compelled to clear his conscience or right past wrongs before he dies." He explained in basic terms how Breen hinted at a scandal and his refusal to explain further over the phone.

"So you don't have any clue what kind of connection he meant?" Amanda wrinkled her nose in consternation, and Slade tried not to think about how adorable she looked when she scrunched her face in deep thought. In the week he'd know her, he'd become well-versed in her quirks, facial tics and unique habits. *Because you've been paying particular attention to her.*

She tipped her head and arched one eyebrow. "Slade?"

"No. No idea. Guess we'll find out together."

One of the airline agents stepped to the intercom and announced early boarding. "First-class passengers, express pass ticket holders and families with small children may now board." The woman sent a smile in the direction of Slade and Amanda when she announced the last category.

Slade's gut tightened. To the observer, he guessed they did look like a family, but the flight attendant's presumption made Slade edgy. He hadn't been part of a family since Krista…

Swiping a hand over his face, he pushed the thought aside before it could fully form.

Amanda returned Cheyenne to her baby carrier and began collecting her possessions…carry-on, purse, diaper bag. Slade had just his backpack with his laptop stowed safely inside. He sighed. So much for easy travel.

Juggling bags, Amanda stooped to lift the baby carrier, and the diaper bag slipped from her shoulder to smack her hip.

Slade tugged her arm. "You take your stuff and board. I'll bring Cheyenne with me."

Amanda sent him an uncertain look. "Are you sure?"

He hitched his head toward the gangway. "Go. Before all the storage bins are taken."

Smiling her thanks, she hurried toward the plane, and he hefted the baby carrier by the handle. The kid was heavier than she looked. How had Amanda dragged all her stuff and the baby through security?

Adjusting his grip on the carrier, Slade joined the flow of passengers onto the plane, noticing Amanda was now several people ahead of him. A guy in front of him stopped in the first-class seating to stuff an oversize bag in the storage bin, holding up the line. Slade craned his neck to see where Amanda had sat down. She was struggling with her carry-on near the bulkhead row in coach…the row of seats he'd selected because it afforded a bit more leg room.

Mr. First Class continued to hold up the line, and Slade waited for the chance to pass, observing Amanda and… the man across the aisle who stood up to help her stow her bag. As he maneuvered out of his seat and into the congested aisle, the guy slyly put his hand on Amanda's butt.

Slade tensed. Mr. Across-the-Aisle smiled at Amanda, brushed against her again as he lifted the small suitcase and they exchanged a private laugh. Slade caught the up-and-down look the guy gave Amanda as she turned to take her seat, and when Mr. Across-the-Aisle leaned on his armrest, continuing to grin and chat Amanda up, Slade's irritation peaked. He reached up and gave First Class's too-big bag a push, jamming it in the bin at last, and once the First Class dude stepped aside, he strode stiffly down the aisle with Cheyenne.

Amanda glanced up from her banter with Across-the-Aisle and gave Slade the same bright smile she'd just been giving the other guy, which made the smile feel less special. Which pissed Slade off for reasons he didn't want to examine.

"I was beginning to think you'd gotten lost," she teased.

Slade didn't smile. Instead, he met Mr. Across-the-Aisle's eyes and nailed him with the glare he used on uncooperative suspects. Hard, menacing, intimidating.

Mr. Across-the-Aisle flicked a startled glance from Slade, to Cheyenne, to Amanda, then back to Slade before shifting back in his seat and losing his come-on grin.

Satisfied that he'd made his point, Slade handed the baby carrier to Amanda and swung his backpack from his shoulder. "Not lost, just detained."

Amanda scooted to the window seat, leaving Slade more leg room on the aisle, and buckled the baby carrier between them.

As Slade settled in, she leaned toward him and whispered, "I saw what you did there."

"Hmm?"

"Next time you could just pee on me to mark your territory."

Slade jerked his gaze toward her. *"What?"*

"That's how most animals do it."

He frowned. "I know that. I mean I didn't—"

Slade snapped his mouth shut, knowing full well he had warned the other guy off with his icy stare. That Amanda recognized the move unsettled him almost as much as his instinctive possessiveness of her. He had no claim to Amanda. Yet the fact that they were traveling together, that they gave the appearance of being a family, that—yes—he was attracted to her, all gave him a sense of possessiveness toward her. A *false* sense of possessiveness, he reminded himself.

Amanda Colton was the most self-confident, independent, headstrong woman he'd ever met. A case in point was that she was on this fact-finding excursion despite his efforts to exclude her.

As the plane pushed back from the gate and taxied to the runway, Amanda talked softly to her cooing daughter, smiling and tickling Cheyenne. And reminding him too painfully of what he'd been denied.

He closed his eyes and tried to relax, tried to sleep, tried to shut out Amanda's obvious love for her baby and Cheyenne's sweet innocence.

Just do the job you came to do and get out.

With a roar of engines, the plane took off, climbing into the gray winter sky. Within minutes of gaining altitude, Cheyenne's gurgling turned cranky. Whines tuned up to cries, then ear-splitting wails.

Slade watched uncomfortably from the corner of his eye as Amanda tried fruitlessly to calm her daughter and gave her drops of some over-the-counter decongestant. Around them, passengers grew restless, and Cheyenne's tears chafed the raw part of his soul where memories of his loss resided. He squeezed the armrests, praying for the flight to end.

"Hey," Mr. Across-the-Aisle called, rousing Slade and drawing Amanda's attention. "Can't you make that kid shut up?"

Slade saw red.

"I'm sorry—" Amanda began.

"You know, you're right." Slade unsnapped his seatbelt and whirled to face the jerk. "Hand me that pillow you're using, and I'll hold it over her face until she stops crying. Okay?"

"Slade!"

"What?" he barked.

Amanda sent him a narrow-eyed look. "You're being an ass."

"And he's not?"

Her warning look was her only reply before she divided an apologetic look among the nearby passengers. "It's the altitude. She's been congested, and the air pressure has to be hurting her. I'm sorry. I'm trying."

Huffing his frustration, Slade shot the jerk another glare as he resettled in his seat. Amanda climbed over his legs with Cheyenne and soothed her baby by walking up and down the aisle, bouncing the baby on her hip, patting her back and distracting her with some success.

Slade turned to look out the window, working to ease the knot of resentment for the guy across the aisle, trying to understand why the guy's callousness toward Cheyenne had pushed his buttons…and dreading the rest of this trip. The plane hadn't even landed, and already Amanda and Cheyenne had him rattled, distracted and as ornery as a rodeo bull. He swiped a hand over his face and heaved a deep sigh. He had to get himself in hand and refocused on the investigation. Scottie Breen could have facts that would blow the lid off any number of cold cases haunting the Colton ranch. Scandalous information. Sinister truths. If so, how would Amanda react to such devastating news?

The taxi ride from the airport to the hotel took thirty minutes thanks to an accident on the freeway. By the time they reached their rooms—adjoining rooms at Amanda's insistence—Slade was chomping at the bit. He'd told Breen he'd be by that afternoon to interview him, and the day was quickly escaping.

Slade sat on the bed with his laptop on his legs and logged on to the hotel's wifi. He'd started a search for directions to Brookdale Hospice when Amanda knocked on the door between their rooms. "Yeah?"

"I feel grimy from the plane and would really like a shower before we go talk to Scottie Breen."

"Go ahead," he said without looking up from his laptop, "We have a little time while I check out a few things."

"Then…you don't mind watching Cheyenne for me for a while?"

Slade's heart kicked, and he jerked his gaze to Amanda. "Excuse me?"

"She shouldn't be any trouble. I just changed her diaper, her decongestant has kicked in and she's had that catnap in the taxi, so she should be in a good mood."

Slade's gut knotted, and when he realized he was gaping at her slack-jawed, he snapped his mouth closed with a click of teeth. Babysit the kid? Traveling with a baby was bad enough without being forced to take charge of her. "I, uh…"

Amanda laughed, a melodious sound that caught Slade off-guard and seeped into his soul. The tension inside him loosened a bit.

She tipped her head, still grinning broadly. "Don't tell me the big bad WBI agent and ranch foreman is scared of a little eight-month-old girl?"

He scoffed. "Of course not. I just…" *haven't held a baby since Emily died.* "I just have a lot of prep work to do before we talk to Breen."

Amanda rolled her eyes. "I'll tell Cheyenne to keep the conversation to a minimum then, so you can work."

"Amanda, I—" But she'd already disappeared back

into her room, only to reappear a moment later with Cheyenne, the diaper bag and Cheyenne's baby seat.

Slade scrubbed a hand over his face. *Buck up, man. You can do this.* Still, an icy shiver slid through him, and his lungs tightened. He set the laptop aside and stood. How long could Amanda's shower take? Five minutes? He could handle five minutes alone with the kid.

Amanda dropped the diaper bag and baby seat on the end of the bed and held Cheyenne out to him. "Don't look at her like that. She doesn't bite."

Slade hadn't been aware his expression gave anything away, but he quickly schooled his face. He placed his hands under Cheyenne's armpits and held her, legs dangling, away from his body.

Amanda tipped her head, studying his I'm-holding-a-bomb grip. "Really?"

"Just…go. And hurry." When she turned to leave, shaking her head, he added, "We need to get to Brookdale before visiting hours are over."

Amanda left him with Cheyenne, giving a little finger wave as she ducked into her room.

Slade turned his attention to the bomb in his hands. Cheyenne kicked her legs and gurgled, her blue eyes flashing. Well, as bombs went, Cheyenne was pretty cute. He sighed and looked around the room. He didn't dare put her down on this floor. God knew what kind of germs were on the floor. And she could roll off the bed and get hurt. But he couldn't keep standing there, holding her bomb-style, either.

He checked his watch. How long had it been? Maybe only four minutes left? Except that he hadn't heard the shower even turn on yet. He muttered a curse, then jerked his gaze to Cheyenne's. "Oh…sorry. You didn't hear that. Don't ever repeat that word. Got it?"

Cheyenne loosed a long, loud squeal. Slade panicked. The squeal sounded happy, but what if it meant the kid was in pain?

He drew her closer to his chest, balancing her on one hip, so he could rub her back with a free hand. "Easy, kid. Quiet down."

Cheyenne reached for his face, and soft hands patted his cheeks.

Startled, he jerked his head back and frowned at her. "Whoa. What the—?"

Cheyenne took one look at his beetled brow and twisted mouth…and released a peal of laughter. If possible, the sound of Cheyenne's innocent laugh was even sweeter and more musical than her mother's.

Slade felt an odd catch in his chest. What would Emily's laugh have sounded like?

Squealing again, Cheyenne grabbed Slade's nose and squeezed. Untrimmed fingernails scratched his face.

"Ow."

More baby chuckles. More strange warmth centered around his heart. More knots in his stomach.

Slade looked around the room, spied the baby seat and hurried to retrieve it. He laid Cheyenne in the seat and buckled her in so she couldn't wiggle free and climb out. "There. You'll be safe there until your mom gets back."

Cheyenne twisted, fighting the restraints. Raising her baby blues to him, Amanda's daughter gave Slade a look of pure betrayal and hurt that slammed into his gut like a fist. Color flushed her face, and her bottom lip poked out.

"No, no, no. Don't start crying again!"

Cheyenne's face crumpled, and a sad little squeak hiccupped from her.

He used both hands to rake his hair as the squeaks

grew to pitiful whimpers. "You're dirt, Slade Kent. Worse. You're horse crap."

In Amanda's room, he heard the shower turn on.

Pinching the bridge of his nose, he mumbled, "Don't think about it. Don't think about it." But an image of Amanda, naked, water streaming down her skin, flashed in his mind's eye. This time he only thought the curse word. Hey, progress.

"All right, here's the deal. I'll hold you, but you can't cry. Got it?" Huffing out a deep breath, he unbuckled Cheyenne, lifted her from the seat and sat down with his back against the bed's headboard. He propped the baby against his bent knees and gave her a stern look. "I have work to do, you know."

The baby sobered and blinked at him, her nose running. He used his thumb to wipe one fat tear off her cheek, and a fast-food napkin to clean her nose. "You are a master manipulator, missy."

He pulled his laptop closer and typed with one hand to finish pulling up the map and directions to Scottie Breen's hospice.

"Ba."

He slanted a wary look at Cheyenne. The infant's face was pure innocence and wide-eyed wonder. Tug went his heart. Knot went his gut.

He glanced back at the computer. Enlarged the map.

"Ba!"

"What?" he said, facing Cheyenne.

The imp grinned, showing off two bottom teeth and at least a quart of slobber. "Ba!"

"I'm trying to work here." He turned back to the laptop, and Cheyenne kicked her feet, thumping his chest.

"Ba!"

He faced her again, growling under his breath.

Cheyenne growled back. Sort of. Then chuckled.

Slade arched an eyebrow, intrigued. He growled again and wrinkled his face in a scowl.

Cheyenne mimicked the growl, then laughed harder.

He snorted and tugged up a cheek in amusement. "I'll be damned."

Cheyenne's eyes twinkled as she gazed up at him with complete trust and childlike mirth.

He stared back at the baby and battled down a kamikaze attack of emotion that grabbed him by the throat. Damn it, this should be his daughter! He should be discovering goofy games and marveling over his own baby's innocent laugh.

His hand fisted in the bedspread, and he swallowed hard, fighting the swell of grief.

Cheyenne growled again, then kicked her feet in joy and giggled.

Releasing the bedcover, Slade raised a shaking hand to the baby's silky hair. He stroked her head, dragged a finger along her soft cheek and exhaled slowly. Emily was gone, and he could do nothing about that.

But he'd be *damned* before he let anyone hurt this precious girl.

Chapter 11

She'd taken longer in the shower than she intended, but she'd really needed to shave her legs, wintertime or not. And the hot water and pounding spray had been so gloriously relaxing after the tense plane trip....

Amanda combed out her wet hair, dried off quickly and wrapped a towel around herself before heading out of the bathroom. She was digging clean clothes out of her suitcase when a curious noise drifted in from the next room. A low rumbling followed by high-pitched squeals and giggles. Cheyenne's laugh.

Amanda smiled and, tucking the towel more snugly around her, tiptoed to the door to peek into the next room.

Slade sat on his bed, his back to the wall, Cheyenne propped on his lap. His Stetson in his hand, he used the hat to cover Cheyenne's face. Cheyenne grew quiet. Then with a bearlike growl, he snatched the hat away and made a comically scowling face. Cheyenne loved it and gave a hearty belly laugh.

Amanda bit her lip and covered her mouth to avoid making a sound that would give her presence away.

Slade returned the hat over Cheyenne's face and repeated the game, this time making a face that was completely cornball as he buzzed his lips. If Cheyenne had been older, Amanda would swear her daughter was laughing hard enough to wet her pants. Slade the comedian. Who knew?

A tender ache burrowed to her core, and bittersweet longing filled her chest. She'd suspected Slade had a soft side, a sweet gooey middle, and that his gruffness was an armor he wore in self-defense. Somewhere along the line, someone had hurt Slade, deeply, and he still bore the scars. But with Cheyenne, when he thought no one was looking, he let that guard down. And Amanda lost a little piece of her heart to him. Was Slade someone she could trust her future to, open her heart to?

As she watched them, she thought about the sultry turn her visit to his room had taken two nights ago. Her heart thumped harder remembering the heated look in his eyes as he'd brushed his body close to hers, touched her face and…hadn't kissed her. She'd been so sure he was about to kiss her, and her body had vibrated with longing and expectation. What had stopped him? Or had his advances been a ploy? Had Slade been manipulating her attraction to him? That possibility hurt.

On the bed, Slade went through the motions of the game again, his expression even sillier this time, and Amanda couldn't cover her own laugh any longer. "What are you doing?"

Slade sobered so fast she was surprised he didn't hurt himself. A red flush spread up his neck and into his cheeks. Clearing his throat, he scooped Cheyenne up and swung his legs off the bed. "I didn't see... I just..."

"I haven't heard her laugh that hard in weeks. You have the magic touch, cowboy."

He held Cheyenne out to her. "You took long enough. Most men can shower in about five minutes."

"Hmmm." She secured the towel again when it slipped. "Most men don't condition their hair or shave their legs."

Slade's gaze traveled to her legs as if on cue, then slid back over her in a sultry perusal. The heat in his eyes when they connected with hers again stirred a heady quiver deep inside her. Maybe the electricity between them the other night had been real after all.

"So here." He took a step toward her, holding Cheyenne under her arms again as if she were a bag of flour. "Take her."

"In a minute. Let me dress. I wouldn't want to interrupt your game of peek-a-boo."

His brow furrowed. "It wasn't peek-a-boo." When she grinned skeptically, he firmed his mouth. "It wasn't. I never said peek-a-boo."

Amanda chuckled as she turned back to her room. "Semantics, tough guy. I'll just be another minute."

Scooting back into her own room, Amanda hurried to the bed where she'd left her selection of clothes and quickly dressed in the khaki slacks and blue blouse. In the adjoining room, more baby giggles spilled through the open crack at the connecting door. Amanda smiled. Plenty of men at the ranch had fawned politely over Cheyenne, but none had touched her as much as Slade's silliness did. Perhaps because most of the time he seemed so serious, so dour...a little sad even. Knowing her daughter had found a way past Slade's gruff exterior filled her with a special sort of maternal pride and joy.

As she buttoned her blouse, a low-pitched rumble joined Cheyenne's baby laugh—a male chuckle, the sound so rich and deep and sexy her skin tingled and warmth spread through her. She stilled, listening to Slade's low voice and remembering the fire in his eyes when he'd studied her moments ago. The raw desire in his gaze had been obvious, and even now her pulse fluttered in a flustered rhythm. She tried to push aside thoughts of his sensual stare, the implicit invitation in his eyes, but her fingers still trembled as she finished buttoning her shirt and putting in her earrings.

She had no business losing her head around Slade Kent, a man who made clear his mission was to uncover her family's buried secrets. While she was all for exposing the truth and finding the mastermind behind all the recent trouble at the ranch, she didn't like the idea that Slade's personal agenda could threaten people she loved.

She needed to stay in control, keep her head in the game and her eyes open when she was around Slade. She had to protect her family's interests. That meant not letting her physical attraction to him cloud her judgment. Problem was, the more time she spent with Slade, the more of his underlying warmth and kindness she saw and the stronger the attraction grew.

Following the directions Slade had downloaded, they drove out to Brookdale Hospice with Amanda navigating and Slade behind the wheel. He parked their rental car outside a Spanish-style ranch house with well-tended landscaping and an inviting water fountain near the front door. Amanda had to admit the hospice was beautiful and had a calming ambiance. After getting Cheyenne from her car seat, she followed Slade inside and waited while he inquired at the front desk for Scottie Breen's room number. He was handed two guest badges, and he clipped one on his jacket as he started down the hall toward the patient rooms.

The interior of the hospice was decorated in warm colors that evoked images of sunshine, summer flowers and sand dunes. Community rooms were tastefully appointed with comfortable furniture, aquariums full of neon fish and lush green plants. Even though this place had all the trappings of home and hearth, Amanda's heart still ached as she caught glimpses of tired families and withering patients in the rooms they passed.

Her own father had lost most of the color in his face, too much weight, and the vitality that she remembered from her childhood. Accepting that Jethro could be near the end of his life was harder than she'd ever imagined. He had always been larger than life to her, maybe because of all his scandals and tragedies. Someone who had lived through so much couldn't possibly be taken out by an illness, even one as vicious as cancer.

She drew a restorative breath as Slade stopped at room 133 and raised his hand to knock. A weak voice bade them to come in, and they entered the dark room slowly, allowing their eyes to adjust to the dim light.

"Mr. Breen?" Slade said. "Sorry to disturb you, but I'm Slade Kent. We talked on the phone earlier?"

"Right, right," the frail man on the bed rasped. "Please come in. You can open the blinds a bit if you wish."

Slade stepped over to the window and angled the blinds enough to ease the gloom in the room. Amanda stood by the door for a moment taking in Scottie Breen's sunken eyes and thin arms. His lips were dry and cracked, but he offered a warm smile when he saw Cheyenne. "Oh, my! Who is this cherub?"

Amanda returned a polite grin. "My daughter, Cheyenne."

Breen looked at Slade and waved a hand toward the two chairs beside his bed. "Please sit. I didn't know you were…bringing your wife and daughter, but I'm…happy for the visitors. I don't see many folks anymore, and… it gets a bit lonely."

Slade waited for her to sit before he lowered himself on the other chair and cleared his throat. "Actually, this isn't my wife. This is Amanda." He paused a beat, his expression hesitant before adding, "Amanda Colton."

Breen's eyes widened, and dismay firmed his mouth. "Colton? You brought a Colton here? I told you what I had to say was…volatile. Is this your…idea of a joke?"

"Mr. Breen, it's not Slade's fault," Amanda cut in. "He tried to dissuade me, but I insisted on coming. If you have information about my family, I have a right to hear it. Even if it's not pretty."

Breen sighed and sank deeper into his pillow. "Ms. Colton, my purpose in contacting Mr. Kent was…not to do harm to your family. I bear you…no ill will. I don't wish to…cause you pain. But I'm afraid what I have to say…will do just that."

"I can handle it." She sat straighter and stroked Cheyenne's back. "I'm strong."

Breen looked away, his eyes rheumy, and began slowly. "Very well. For years, I worked with a single goal in mind—getting the man I worked for elected, then re-elected. In that capacity, I allowed myself…to shut out everything in the periphery, all the…consequences of my actions, in order to focus…straight ahead on my goal." He sighed wearily. "I hurt people through the years… who didn't deserve the backlash I caused. Since being diagnosed with cancer, I've done a lot of soul searching.

I want to come clean. I want to right as many wrongs as I can, and…I want to share the truth where…I was party to hiding facts that…never should have been hidden. Perhaps something I tell you…can shed light on… the events at your ranch."

Slade pulled a small notebook along with a tape recorder from his jacket pocket and flipped the pad open. "May I record you?"

Breen glanced at the small recorder and gave Slade an ironic smile. "I spent my life…avoiding those things. Comments were always…off the record. Now…" He sighed his resignation. "I suppose a recording can't… hurt me if I'm dead. And the truth needs to be said…" He nodded weakly, and Slade pressed the record button.

"Why don't you start with the connection you mentioned on the phone between Jethro Colton and the former president Joe Colton? You claim they have some history?"

Breen coughed and wiped his mouth with a tissue. "History, yes. In fact, they're related."

Amanda blinked. "I'm sorry, did you say my father's *related* to Joe Colton? Former President Colton?"

"They are cousins. Second cousins, I believe. Not a close family tie, but…enough of one that we…on the president's campaign team years ago, when Joe Colton first ran for…state office in California, were concerned about…the media finding the relationship and exploiting it," Breen explained in a labored rasp.

Slade was scribbling in his notebook. "When was this? What year?"

Breen shook his head and furrowed his brow in thought. "Long ago. At least thirty years. No, thirty-four years, I think." He turned his glance toward Amanda. "Well before you were born."

She nodded and pulled a toy out of the diaper bag as

Cheyenne grew restless and started to fuss. "Go on. The campaign discovered a family tie to Jethro and…"

"At the time, Jethro Colton was…" Breen twisted his mouth, and his hands fluttered on his sheets.

"Mr. Breen, you don't need to pull any punches with me." Amanda caught the stuffed monkey Cheyenne had been chewing on when her daughter tired of it and flung it aside. "I'm aware my father has led a less than sterling life. Please, just say what you need to."

Breen gave a tight nod. "Very well. Jethro was… trouble waiting to happen. He was a swindler, a womanizer, a down-on-his-luck drunk…and con artist who approached us, looking to make a profit…off his up-and-coming relative." He paused, gathering his breath. "He was known to have done business with organized crime, even…ran a scam for one crime boss."

Amanda's gut tightened. She grappled to reconcile the father she knew with the picture of an organized crime lackey as Breen described. He couldn't be right…

"We knew we needed to…shut him up and…sever all ties with him quickly and effectively…in order to avoid possible embarrassment or…speculation. Innuendo in the media down the road."

She'd never heard her father talk about his life before she was born. She'd always assumed his reticence had to do with the pain of having lost Cole, his first son, under mysterious circumstances. Hearing now that Jethro had been a drunk womanizer and a con artist with ties to *organized crime* needled her, horrified her. While she knew he hadn't been a saint, she felt the first misgivings about digging up her father's dirty secrets.

"What did Joe Colton do about Jethro? How did he manage to break the ties with his long-lost cousin for all these years?" Slade asked, leaning forward, his expression intrigued.

"Oh, Joe had nothing to do with…what happened next. He'd have frowned upon…what we did, and he…was never told." Breen shook his head. "Joe Colton was a man of honor, and he remained so…until the end."

Amanda's hands grew slick with sweat. Despite her apprehension, she heard herself ask, "What did you do? What didn't Joe Colton know?"

Breen dipped his brow over his eyes and angled a curious look at Amanda. "Did your father ever tell you how…he came to own Dead River Ranch?"

Cheyenne wiggled, and with shaky arms, Amanda repositioned her daughter on her lap. "He bought it before he married his first wife, Cole's mother."

Breen nodded. "Indeed he did. The sale was arranged…through a friend of mine, a broker who got him a steal on…a highly profitable ranch. A ranch previously owned by…a political crony…who stood to profit more in the long run…by selling his ranch at a loss and…helping get Joe Colton in the White House."

When Amanda frowned her confusion, Breen waved a hand in dismissal. "Never mind that part. The sale was legal. Jethro landed the deal of the century. That's not my point."

Amanda and Slade exchanged a look. His asked her to be patient. Hers asked him if he believed what Breen was saying.

"I'm sorry, ma'am," Breen said, turning over a frail hand. "I suppose I'm trying to soften the blow…with all of this setup, but there's just no way…to make the truth less ugly."

"Tell me what happened." She clutched Cheyenne

closer to her, as if to shield her daughter from what was coming. Or protect herself. "What did my father do?"

"Jethro accepted…hush money from the Colton for California Senate…slush fund, in exchange for his… complete silence and…severing all connection with Joe Colton. He was legally required to…stay away from Joe, Joe's family and…the campaign or risk losing his entire fortune."

Amanda stared at Breen, numb and trying to process the staggering information.

Slade shot her a worried look, then asked, "How much hush money?"

Breen's expression was repentant. "One million dollars."

Amanda gasped. "What?"

"Jethro Colton had nothing but debt and…creditors crawling up his—well, you know what. He accepted a cool million in…hush money and used that cash to… buy Dead River Ranch at…a fraction of its value. He's gone on to…turn that million in hush money…into his current fortune."

Amanda opened her mouth to speak, but Breen wasn't finished destroying her illusions about her father.

"But you don't get as rich…as Jethro Colton…simply raising cattle."

A greasy pit settled in her gut.

"Then how—"

"He's laundering money through…his natural gas business for…Vinny Rizono."

Amanda felt cold to the bone. She pressed her cheek to Cheyenne's head and fought a wave of nausea. "Are you saying that everything my family owns, everything we eat and wear and call home, was built with dirty money?

He sold his family connection to Joe Colton and grew that million helping a crime boss hide money?"

"I'm sorry, ma'am. I know that's difficult to—"

"Difficult? We owe our entire family fortune to a cover-up! To ill-gotten gains! To lies and criminals and false appearances—" Her voice cracked, and she blinked back tears. She didn't care about the money, per se, but the deception and secrets that had fed her and put a roof over her head made her ill. "Are…are you sure? Why should I believe you?"

"I'm sure. I've kept tabs on Jethro…through the years. Hired an investigator. Kept a dossier, in case…"

"In case he broke your agreement and tried to cause trouble for President Colton," she finished for him, her voice as strangled sounding as Breen's.

The former campaign manager nodded.

"Amanda?" Slade's voice cut through the fog of disbelief and hurt that engulfed her.

She raised her gaze to his, and the concern that lit his blue eyes burrowed deep inside her. Steadied her. Rooted her when she felt ready to fly apart.

She swallowed hard and gave him a reassuring nod. "I'm okay. I mean, I'm *not* okay with this—" she waved a hand toward Breen "—but I'm not going to fall apart on you. It'll just take time to…sort it out. Cripes. If that's even possible. How do you sort out the fact that your whole life has been built on a lie? On tainted money?"

Slade bent to pick up the stuffed monkey Cheyenne had tossed on the floor again and handed it to her. Cheyenne chuckled at him as she took the toy with her slobbery hand.

What did this revelation mean for Cheyenne's future? How could she continue living at the ranch, raising her daughter on the estate that Jethro had purchased with ill-gotten gains? She needed to tell Gabby and Cath, too. But how could she break the news to them now, with Gabby's wedding in just a few days and Cath expecting a baby? She sighed heavily and looked up to find both Slade and Breen watching her closely.

"If my father still has ties to this Vinny Rizono character, if you have proof he's helping launder money, why not tell the police?"

"And bring the mob...down on me? Stir the media up where...they might draw the connection to Joe Colton that...I'd worked years to keep quiet?" Breen shook his head. "No. It served no purpose...for me or Joe Colton to stir that pot."

"Your silence is a crime in and of itself. Knowledge of a crime..." Slade arched an eyebrow.

"So arrest me. I'll likely be dead...before Christmas."

"And so will my father," Amanda said softly, her heart heavy.

"Do you want to take a break? Go get some coffee or something while I finish the interview?" Slade asked.

She snapped her eyebrows together. "No. I said I'd be all right."

"I think you...should go. In fact, I won't...say anymore with you in the room."

Slade shot Breen a startled look. "There's more?"

He nodded gravely. "Afraid so."

"Something more damning? About my father?" Amanda's face tingled as the blood drained from her cheeks and left her cold with dread. "I'm not leaving. I need to hear what you know about my father."

Breen shook his head. "No. You don't need...to hear

this. I won't be…responsible for hurting you…any more than I have."

"Mr. Breen—" she countered, but he held up a shaky hand.

"I won't." He turned to Slade. "I'll say nothing else… until she's gone. You shouldn't have…brought her."

Slade faced her with an appeal already in his expression, and Amanda tightened her jaw. When he drew a breath to speak, she interjected, "No! I want to hear what he has on Jethro."

Scrubbing both hands over his face, Slade slumped back in his chair. His mouth firmed in a thin line and he furrowed his forehead in the way she'd seen so often that meant he was deliberating.

Amanda squared her shoulders, letting Slade know silently she wouldn't be bullied. When her daughter squawked restlessly, she bounced Cheyenne on her knee.

Finally, Slade stood, a level stare fixed on her, and hitched his head toward the door. "Can I speak to you privately for a moment?"

She glanced to Breen, whose chin was stubbornly set, his fingers gripping his sheets. Clearly they were at a stalemate. She knew before she joined Slade at the door for their private powwow how it would go.

"Amanda, he's not going to talk with you in the room. We flew all this way because he claimed to have important information. It may even help us solve the crimes that have been happening at the ranch, dating back to Cole's disappearance as a baby. If I can figure out what happened back then, I'll be that much closer to finding the truth about my father's murder, too. They're connected. I feel it in my gut."

"Slade, I have a right to know—"

"And you will know. Later." He put his hand on her

shoulder, and the warmth from his palm seeped through the thin fabric of her blouse. "I'll tell you everything he says."

She raised her chin. "You will? You promise?"

He squeezed her shoulder. His hand felt strong, reassuring, steadfast, and her stomach swooped. "I swear I will. But look at him. He's dying. This may be my only chance to get the information he has."

She didn't have to look. Breen's hollow eyes and wan skin were burned in her memory.

Jethro accepted hush money...one million dollars... had connections to organized crime....

A shiver chased through her, and she hoisted Cheyenne higher on her hip. "Fine. Cheyenne's antsy, anyway. I'll take her out to the courtyard to look at the fountain. Meet me there."

His cheek twitched with a hint of an appreciative grin. "Thanks."

She retrieved the diaper bag and faced the frail man in the bed. "Mr. Breen, I wish we'd met under better circumstances. Despite that, I wish you the best. Thank you for your time."

She'd turned to exit the room when Breen stopped her. "Ms. Colton, the past...can only hurt us...if we let it. Be grateful for...the blessings in your life—" he nodded toward Cheyenne "—and put your energy into building... a better future."

Amanda stared at Breen, letting his words wash over her. She recognized the essential truth in his advice, but at the moment, she was still stinging too badly from what she'd learned about her father to do more than acknowledge his admonition. With a jerky nod, she hurried out of his room and headed outside. The California sunshine and fresh December air were a welcome change from the suffocating, dark hospice room.

She sat on the edge of the water fountain and held Cheyenne's hands while her daughter stood on wobbly legs and watched the flowing water with wide eyes.

Jethro had taken a pay-off. Dead River Ranch had been built with dirty mob money. Her family fortune was born from lies, criminal activity and cover-up. The bitterness that had swamped her inside returned, accompanied by a burning shame. After all her preaching to Slade about honesty and integrity, what must he think of her after learning her family's private shame?

And there was more. What was Breen telling Slade even now? How could she face him, knowing the scandals that surrounded her family?

Earlier today, she'd been foolish enough to think that maybe she'd found a man she could open herself to and rely on. But after hearing what Breen had to say about Jethro, would Slade want anything to do with her and her family's lies?

Chapter 12

After Amanda pulled the door to Breen's hospice room closed, Slade turned to the dying man and gave him a no-nonsense look. "All right. She's gone, and I don't need the facts softened with build-up. Just lay it out. What do you know about Jethro that Amanda couldn't hear?"

Breen shifted in the bed, clearly in pain. He already seemed weaker than when they'd arrived, and Slade knew the conversation was taking its toll on the former campaign manager.

"After we struck our…bargain with Jethro," Breen said, then stopped to draw a raspy breath, "I flew to Wyoming…to check up on Jethro. I wanted to be sure he was…holding up his end of the deal. I intended to…drop in at the ranch…unannounced…and repeat the warnings about…never interfering with Joe Colton's political career."

Slade sat forward, rubbing his hands on his jeans impatiently. "And?"

"I arrived at about…2 a.m. one night, and I'd just… checked into my motel room in town. I was almost ready for bed, but…needed a bottle of blood pressure medicine…that was in my car. As I started out, I saw…a truck pull in to the lot. As the truck passed…under a security light, I…recognized the driver. It was Jethro Colton. I ducked back in…the room and watched through a window as a woman came out…from another motel room and…hurried out to the car."

"So Jethro was up to his old tricks," Slade said and shrugged. "It's widely known he was a womanizer. That he had affairs with married women."

Breen shook his head. "No. He opened the passenger door of his truck…and took a baby out. He handed the kid to the woman."

Slade tensed. "A baby?"

Breen nodded weakly. "The woman talked to him… for a few seconds, then…hurried inside her room with the child. Jethro drove away."

Slade gripped the armrests of his chair, a sick certainty that he knew what was coming gnawing his gut. "This was about thirty years ago?"

Breen's eyes lit with a zealous conviction. "The next morning…the town was buzzing that Jethro Colton had… reported his infant son, Cole, missing. He claimed the baby…had disappeared from his crib overnight."

Slade's thoughts spun in a dozen directions. This was explosive, if true. But he had to verify the facts, get some kind of corroboration. "Are you sure it was Jethro you saw?"

"Absolutely."

Slade's heart thundered against his ribs. He found it hard to breathe. "How can you be sure? It was night. Dark—"

"Because I confronted him…later in the day. I went to the ranch. Had a private meeting with him. Told him what I saw. His reaction was…proof enough."

Slade frowned. "Wait…you confirmed with Jethro that you'd seen him hand off a baby—his baby—to some woman, and didn't report what you'd seen to the police?" He dragged a hand over his mouth, aghast. *"Why the hell not?"*

"Because I wasn't…a nice man back then. Everything I did…had one goal. Getting Joe Colton elected. I didn't want to…get dragged into a scandal, a police investigation or…anything that could haunt the campaign. What's more…I had the…best insurance in the world to hold… Jethro to our bargain. I told him I'd disappear, say nothing, keep his secret, so long as…he never came anywhere near Joe Colton…or even hinted to anyone they had…a family tie."

Nausea rolled through Slade's belly. He wasn't sure who he despised more. The man who'd given his own child away and lied for decades about the boy being kidnapped or the political aide who'd helped bury the truth to protect his candidate.

Slade sat back in his chair and stared blankly at the floor, not seeing anything—except his own child, lying in a hospital bassinet, hooked up to tubes and wires that would prove insufficient to save her fragile life. Air balled in his lungs, stagnant and painful. He'd give anything, even his own life, to have Emily back, to give his baby girl a chance at life. But Jethro Colton had had a healthy son and had callously *gotten rid of him.* Then lied about it for thirty years.

Squeezing his eyes shut, he jammed the swell of emotions down, slamming his iron facade in place as he shifted back into investigative mode. He remembered the photographs in his backpack and pulled them out.

"Do you remember the woman he gave the baby to?"

Breen nodded tiredly. "Like it was yesterday."

Slade started with a picture of Agnes Barlow to test the man. "Was this who you saw?"

Breen studied the picture for a few seconds and quickly shook his head. "No."

Slade moved on to a picture of Faye Frick, the woman who'd brought her son, Dylan, to live at the ranch a year after baby Cole disappeared. Dylan had grown up on the ranch in the employee wing and had recently been proven through DNA tests to be Cole Colton. "Is this her?"

Breen knitted his brow as he studied the picture. "No. I don't know her."

Disappointment punched Slade. If it wasn't Faye Frick…

He flipped through the pictures he'd compiled. He pulled out a photo of Mathilda Perkins, the head maid, grasping at straws. "How about her?"

Again Breen shook his head. "Not her. But I remember her being at the ranch that day. She was as distraught over the baby's disappearance as the rest of the household."

Slade grunted. That fit with what he'd observed of the head maid and her relationship with the family she'd worked for the past thirty-odd years.

"Her?" Slade held up a picture of Cole's mother, Britanny Beal Colton, knowing that the woman had been killed in a car accident months before Cole disappeared.

Breen's face creased as he studied the black-and-white photo. He reached for the picture with a shaking hand. "May I see that?"

Slade passed the photo to Breen.

"I…I think this could be her. Something's off, though."

Slade's shoulder's drooped. Since there was no way Britanny could have been the one at the motel that night, he began to seriously doubt the rest of the dying man's wild tale. "I'd say something's off. That woman had been dead for months before Cole, her son, disappeared. That's Britanny Beal."

Breen shot Slade a scathing look. "I know what I saw! Are you calling me a liar?"

"I'm just saying that couldn't be the woman you saw. She was dead." Slade snatched the photo back and jammed the stack of photos into his backpack.

"I said that woman…was close. It wasn't her, but… there were similarities."

Frustration ticked through Slade, but he took a calming breath and gave Breen the benefit of the doubt. They had come all this way to hear Breen's story. He might as well follow this tale through to the end. "Similar how?"

"The face is close, but the hair was too dark."

"Ever heard of dye? Wigs?" Slade said.

Breen glared at him for a moment, then glanced away, his expression full of defeat. "Did Britanny Beal have a sister?"

Slade's pulse tripped. He searched his memory, trying to recall what his research had said about Jethro's first wife. "Maybe." He pulled his laptop out of his backpack. "This place have wifi?"

Breen turned up a palm. "Maybe for the staff's use?"

Slade logged on and checked for a public signal he could use to get on the internet. *Brookdale.* Five bars. Bingo. He accessed the network and quickly typed in his search parameters. *Britanny Beal Colton. Sister.* The first link that came up was Britanny's obituary. He clicked the link and scanned the archived article from the *Dead River Gazette.* "Britanny's survivors include her husband, Jethro," he read aloud, "son, Cole, and—I'll be damned—sister, Desiree."

"Is there a photo of her?" Breen asked, even as Slade clicked the second link, which took him to a photo taken at Britanny's funeral. The picture was of a grim-faced Jethro, standing beside his wife's open grave during the service. To his left, a young Mathilda Perkins held Cole in her arms, and to Jethro's right stood an attractive young woman who bore a striking resemblance to the photo Slade had of Britanny. The caption identified the woman as Desiree Beal.

A tingle of anticipation spun through Slade. He turned the laptop so that Breen could see the image on the screen. "Is that her? Is the woman on the right the one you saw Jethro give his son to that night at the motel?"

Breen squinted at the screen, then tightened his mouth. "Yes. I'm sure of it." He released a weary sigh as if relieved to have his story vindicated.

"So Jethro Colton gave his son to his sister-in-law and told the police Cole had been kidnapped."

Breen nodded, his eyes troubled, sad. "But the question that's…bugged me all these years is *why?*"

"Other than because he's a selfish bastard?" Slade said, grinding his back teeth as he closed the laptop. "That's what I intend to find out."

"What did he say?" Amanda asked when Slade stormed through the front door of the hospice and strode briskly toward the rental car. She had to jog a few steps to catch up to him, which wasn't easy with Cheyenne in her arms and a large diaper bag over her shoulder.

Slade's mouth was set in a grim line and tension rolled off him like heat waves from pavement. "A lot. But nothing I plan to tell you until I can fully verify his story."

Amanda goggled at him. "What? You promised to tell me! That's the only reason I left you alone with him!"

"I didn't say *when* I'd tell you."

Fury surged in her. "Don't you dare jerk me around, Slade Kent!" she fumed, winded from hurrying to keep pace with him. "I am sick to death of lies and cover-ups! You promised me—"

He stopped abruptly, and she had to pull up quickly to avoid running into his back. He reached for the diaper bag and sent her an apologetic look, as if he'd just realized he'd neglected to help her with her load. He nodded to Cheyenne. "Want me to get her?"

"No. She's fine." She hiked Cheyenne higher on her hip. "What I want is answers. Tell me what he said!"

"No." Turning his back, he headed for the car.

"Slade! If you learned something about my father, I have a right to know!"

He used the remote key fob to unlock the car. "You have a right to the truth, which I've yet to determine."

"Meaning?"

He swung the diaper bag onto the backseat and turned back to her for Cheyenne. "Meaning I will look into Breen's allegations against your father, and if I decide what Breen said is the truth…" He paused and clenched his back teeth so that the muscle in his jaw flexed. His eyes were dark with turmoil, and Amanda's gut knotted. When he spoke again, his tone was rough-edged and quiet. "Then I'll tell you."

"Is it that bad?" Her voice, her body, her heart all trembled.

Slade pinched the bridge of his nose and sighed. Which was all the answer she needed. It was that bad.

When he met her eyes, Slade's expression had softened. "Try not to worry, okay. It could all be a big mis-understanding. Maybe—"

Amanda stiffened her back, and her voice hardened. "Do *not* patronize me. Please, Slade. Of all people, you should know I don't like being put off or *managed*."

He held her gaze for several seconds, studying her, then nodded. "All right. Fair enough."

This time when he reached for Cheyenne, she passed her daughter to him and watched him buckle her into the car seat. He seemed to have moved past whatever aversion he'd had to Cheyenne at the start of the trip.

Circling to the passenger side of the rental car, Amanda mulled over what Slade had told her. He had some kind of dirt on her father, something he wanted to verify, something bad enough to have put Slade on edge. Dread coiled inside her.

What had Jethro done? Had she ever really known her father? How many secrets were still buried, and what if the past had the power to destroy her future? To destroy Cheyenne's future?

She had to convince Slade to share what he'd learned with her, especially if it could come back to haunt Cheyenne. She'd do whatever it took to protect her daughter.

Chapter 13

Amanda stood in his hotel room door, wrapped in a towel, her wet hair slicked back from her model-worthy cheekbones. Her skin was dewy from the shower and her smile promised pleasures yet to come. "What are you doing?"

"Waiting for you." He tossed the bed covers back, summoning her.

She crossed to his bed, the towel riding lower on her breasts with each step. He was ready for her, his body humming and taut with anticipation. When she paused, a few steps beyond his reach, he lunged from the bed, capturing her shoulders and tossing her playfully onto the bed. He ripped open the towel, exposing her naked glory, and a growl of satisfaction rumbled in his throat. "I've been waiting a long time for this. For you."

Her body bowed toward him in invitation, and he buried his face in her—

A loud cry yanked Slade from his sensuous dream, and he scrubbed his face, clearing the cobwebs.

In the next room, Cheyenne wailed pitifully, and he heard Amanda's soft murmur, comforting her child.

His heart still thundered, and his body was tense and trembling with sexual energy. Damn but the dream had felt real, had felt…

He huffed in frustration. *Forget it, Kent. You have no business going down that road with a Colton, of all people.*

The Colton family was culpable in covering up the murder of his father. Jethro Colton himself could have even had a hand in killing Slade's father to keep his part in Cole's disappearance a secret. The man had *given his baby away.* The heartlessness galled Slade. How could Jethro have done it? Why had he?

Slade clenched his back teeth. Jethro had no valid excuse in his book. He was a man of means and resources. He'd had staff to help raise Cole after his first wife died, even if he hadn't wanted any part of caring for his child. The man was selfish, arrogant, insufferable…and Amanda's father.

How a woman as strong and upbeat and warm-hearted as Amanda could have Jethro for a parent was a mystery. He sat up, listening for a moment to Cheyenne's crying, before shuffling to the connecting door and knocking. Amanda opened her side of the connecting doors and greeted him with an anxious look.

"She woke you? I'm sorry."

He dismissed her apology with a flick of his hand. "Can I do anything?"

"Cure the common cold. It's her stuffy nose that keeps waking her. This is the eighth night in a row she hasn't slept well." The worry and strain were clearly etched in the creases around Amanda's eyes.

"And therefore the eighth night you haven't slept?"

She lifted a shoulder. "I don't care about my sleep. I'm used to late-night calls. But my heart breaks for her. I wish I could do more."

Slade squeezed the door jamb, knowing intimately the helpless feeling she described. Just one more reason he should stay the hell away from Amanda Colton and her baby. They were a too-painful reminder of what he'd lost. When they got back to the ranch tomorrow, he'd do his best to avoid Amanda.

She shifted her fussy baby from one shoulder to another and narrowed a hard look on him. "Have you reconsidered keeping what Breen told you from me?"

Sighing, Slade plowed his fingers through his hair. "No. I'll tell you if and when I feel the time is right. If and when I prove his allegations. I'm trying to protect y—"

"Then we have nothing else to discuss," she said and closed the door in his face.

He barely got his fingers out of the way before they'd have been smashed. With a grunt of aggravation, Slade turned on his heel and strode back to his bed. As he tugged the sheet back over him, the remnants of his erotic dream flashed in his mind. While her anger with him would make it easier to keep her at arm's length, clearly his desire for her would not be as easy to dodge.

"I'm going to get a bottle of water and something to eat." Slade hitched his head toward the newsstand in the airport the next morning. "Do you want anything?"

Amanda lifted her chin. "Answers about what Breen told you."

He scoffed. "Right. So nothing for you, then."

"Jerk," she grumbled as he walked away.

In the convenience shop, Slade took two chilled bottles of water and two packages of peanut butter crackers to the checkout and waited his turn to pay, scanning the headlines of the tabloids in the nearby rack. "Inside Job!" one headline screamed, with a secondary line that read, "Authorities believe assaults at Dead River Ranch the work of ranch resident."

Slade hated the tabloids' penchant for fixating on the troubles of the rich and famous, sensationalizing a family's pain for the circulation boost a murder meant.

While the tabloid's theory was nothing new to Slade, seeing the claim in print made the reality of the headline resonate differently with him. How must Amanda feel knowing someone she trusted, perhaps someone she loved, was responsible for attacking, even killing people around her. And targeting her daughter for kidnapping. No wonder she found it hard to trust.

"Next?" the cashier called.

Slade laid his purchases on the counter and noticed a small stuffed killer whale on the impulse purchase shelf by the register. Though they hadn't visited Sea World, which the toy was a clear nod to, Slade added one of the stuffed animals to his pile on a whim.

After paying for his loot, he found Amanda and Cheyenne at their gate and handed a water bottle and pack of crackers to Amanda. "Here."

She eyed them suspiciously before taking them. "Thank you."

He sat down beside Amanda and pulled the small killer whale out of the bag. "And this is for the little princess." He handed the toy to Cheyenne, who grinned and immediately stuck the whale's nose in her mouth.

Blinking, Amanda shot him a startled look.

He met her gaze, his gut tightening as he stared into their honey-colored depths. "What?"

"For a jerk, you sure can be sweet."

He harrumphed and looked away. "It was an impulse buy. No big deal."

"Right," she replied, her tone not agreeing at all. She gave his arm a squeeze, and her touch burrowed deep inside him.

The killer whale made it hard to stay mad at Slade. Over the next several days, every time she looked at Cheyenne gnawing on the nose of the toy or waving it in her chubby fist and squealing her delight, Amanda felt her resentment crack. Slade's silence on what he'd learned from Breen didn't seem as unforgivable given a couple days' perspective. In hindsight, what stood out to her was his determination to verify Breen's story before burdening her with bad news. What she remembered most about the trip to California was not Slade's stubbornness, but his gentleness with Cheyenne, the belly laughs he elicited from her daughter and the sweet gesture of buying Cheyenne the whale toy.

But where Slade's kindness toward Cheyenne turned her insides to mush, the memory of Slade's possessiveness toward her on the airplane gave her pause. The heat in his eyes when they'd been alone in the hotel had made her pulse quicken. The image of his muscular chest and taut abs when he'd stood in her door the last night, wakened by Cheyenne's cry, had filled her thoughts in the days since returning to the ranch and kept her awake through several long winter nights.

If he felt the same magnetic pull and crackle of sensuality as she suspected, why hadn't he acted on it? Surely he wasn't hung up on the fact that she was a member of the ranch owner's family and he worked for her. His dismissiveness toward Mathilda's scolding regarding proper family/staff interaction blew that theory out of the water. But she remembered his guardedness and the pain she'd seen in his eyes at times and knew there were layers to Slade she'd yet to uncover, hidden facets of his life. The last thing she needed was to get involved with another man with secrets. And what would happen when he found the answers he was here looking for? Would he walk away from the ranch, leave her behind and return to his life in Jackson without a backward glance? She knew her doubts were David's legacy, but it didn't make his deception and rejection any less painful.

More than once, Amanda had pulled out her cell phone, wanting to call her friend Aurora and get her "Jersey girl" take on Slade. But Aurora—and Dylan— were gone from her life. Permanently. Witness Protection was forever.

With the hands back from the rodeo, Slade spent less time in the pastures and more time shadowing her, even though he pretended the proximity was incidental. If she had her guess, she'd wager his reason for sticking close to her was rooted in the attack from the week before. Not only was he not-so-secretly protective of her, his gaze watched the other hands and the house staff like a wary bird of prey. His vigilance was an unwelcome reminder of the lurking danger on the ranch where she'd grown up, with the people she considered her second family. And while his unrequested bodyguard shtick nettled her innate independence and self-confidence, she had to admit feeling a comforting reassurance having him close by.

On the contrary, the hardest part of returning from California turned out to be telling her sisters what she'd learned about Jethro's dirty dealings. Cath had returned to the ranch to help with the final week of preparation before Gabby's wedding, and Gray would join her here in a few days. Amanda hated spoiling Cath's homecoming but knew she couldn't keep the truth from her sisters. As it was, she needed a couple days to work up the courage to tell them what she'd learned. Finally, one afternoon late that week, she convened her sisters in her solarium while Cheyenne napped.

Reyna rubbed against Catherine's shins, and her sister lifted the fluffy cat onto her lap, scratching Reyna's chin and cheeks. "Hello, little queen. Who's a spoiled girl?"

Reyna purred so loudly Amanda could hear her across the room.

Gabby reached over to stroke Reyna's head, as well. "What's up? You say you learned something in California about Dad?"

"Afraid so." Amanda rubbed her palms on her jeans.

"That doesn't sound good," Cath said, frowning.

"It's not. It's...terrible. Disgusting." Amanda picked up the tiny figure of Mary from the nativity set she'd put out on a table. She turned the figurine over in her hand, fidgeting absentmindedly.

Gabby forgot about the cat and faced Amanda, a furrow in her brow. "Talk. What is it?"

Amanda explained about the hush money Breen had paid Jethro to disassociate himself from Joe Colton. She told them about Breen's allegations Jethro had ties to organized crime, how he'd bought the ranch as part of a deal to assure Jethro's silence and how the family's fortune had grown from that initial payoff and subsequent dirty dealings with Vinny Rizono.

Tears filled Cath's eyes and her hand stilled on Reyna's fur. "I can't believe it. I mean, I knew he had some bad habits and had made some enemies, but…organized crime?"

Gabby shook her head, her expression stricken. "If it's true, then I don't want any part of his money. I don't want any part of this ranch or any inheritance or stock in the natural gas drilling…."

Amanda reached for Gabby's hand. "I know how you feel. But don't do anything rash. Slade is investigating the claims Breen made. There's still a chance Breen was wrong or that there's a good explanation, another side to all this." She squeezed her sister's hand. "At least put it aside until after your wedding." She divided a look between Cath and Gabby. "I hated to say anything, hated to spoil the happiness you've both found."

Cath hugged Reyna closer to her body, like a child clutching a doll. "You were right to tell us, hard as it is to hear." Her sister blinked back her tears and raised her chin. "Do you think this Vinny Rizono could be behind the attacks here? The kidnapping attempts? Could this be revenge of some kind by this crime boss against Dad?"

Amanda had wondered the same but dismissed it. She bit her lip and returned the figure of Mary to the nativity scene, carefully straightening the set. "There's no evidence it is, but I'll mention it to Slade. I'm sure if that's the case, Slade will find it in his investigation."

Gabby tipped her head. "Why is Slade involved? Why would he investigate?"

Oops.

Amanda sat back in the wicker chair and bit down on a fingernail. "Um…" She couldn't lie to her sisters. But she'd promised to keep Slade's position with the WBI a secret. "I'm not supposed to tell you."

Cath and Gabby exchanged a look.

"What if we guess?" Cath said.

"Um…"

"He's not really a foreman. He's really a cop working undercover to solve the murders here," Cath said.

Amanda's eyes widened. "How did you know?"

Cath blinked. "You mean I'm right? That was a guess. I was even joking!"

Amanda raised an eyebrow. "No joke. He's with the WBI." She leveled her shoulders. "But no one is supposed to know. Don't say anything."

Her sisters drew their fingers over their lips, zipping them closed.

"And for what it's worth, he is an experienced foreman. He worked ranches before he joined the WBI."

Gabby sent her a speculative look. "And my guess is that you're sweet on Slade. Anything else about the trip to California you want to tell us?"

Amanda folded her arms over her chest. "Nothing happened."

"But you're interested in him? Something could develop between you two?" Cath asked, a sparkle lighting her eyes.

Though she didn't want to speculate on her relationship with Slade with her sisters, Amanda was grateful for anything that gave her sisters a reason to smile after the damning news she'd given them about Jethro.

Gabby and Cath were resilient and had good men in their lives to support and encourage them. No matter what they all decided about breaking ties with Dead River Ranch and Jethro's tainted fortune, her sisters would be fine, surrounded by love and the companionship of a faithful husband. For an instant, Amanda envied them, but she shoved the jealousy aside, focusing on her own blessings. She had Cheyenne and her career. She'd be fine without Jethro's money.

* * *

On their fourth night back from California, Amanda was finishing her evening chores in the stable and telling Prince William good-night when Jared Hansen burst into the stable.

"Miss Amanda? We need you!" the hand called down the stable alley.

She hurried outside to find Jared and George opening a livestock trailer behind one of the ranch trucks. Inside the trailer, lying on the floor, was an obviously suffering cow. Her gut wrenched for the animal. "What happened to her?"

"She's in premature labor," George answered. "We tried to deliver the calf in the field, but it's hung up somehow."

Amanda's heart sank. The prospects for both the cow and her calf were grim, but she rallied her professionalism and took control of the crisis. "Okay, back the trailer into the livestock barn. Put her in an open stall. I'll get my supplies and meet you there."

Jared rode with the cow as George pulled away, and Amanda jogged into the stable to retrieve her veterinary bag and extra medical supplies.

"Problem?" Slade asked, looking up from a saddle he was rubbing with oil.

"Yeah." She grabbed a box of long gloves, a couple bottles of iodine, and her vet bag from the storage cabinet. "Delivery emergency. Looks bad for the cow and her baby."

Slade's expression sobered, and for a moment he didn't move. Finally he sucked in a deep breath and rose from the bench where he was working. "What can I do?"

"I don't know. They're putting her in the livestock

barn. I'm headed there now." She trotted out of the stable, her arms loaded.

He caught up to her in a few long strides, scooping some of the supplies into his own arms and accompanying her to the barn.

When she reached the stall where the mother cow had been moved, she donned a pair of long gloves and shifted into emergency mode, fully focused on her patient and the two lives that hung in the balance. Her initial exam told her the calf was turned the wrong way and had its umbilical cord wrapped around its neck. She was afraid to sedate the mother, due to her already dropping heart rate, and relied on Slade, George and Jared to hold the mother while she attempted to remove the umbilical from around the calf's throat in utero.

"Miss Amanda?"

Her concentration was so focused on the procedure that she didn't register the female voice until Jared groused, "She's a little busy now, don't you think?"

Amanda glanced up to the stall door. Fiona stared wide-eyed and a bit green around the gills at the blood on the hay and on Amanda's long glove. "I—I'm sorry to bother you, but Mr. Brooks sent me to find you."

Amanda stiffened. "Is everything okay with Cheyenne?"

Fiona nodded hesitantly. "Your baby's okay, but Mr. Brooks is sick. Dr. Colton thinks it could be a stomach virus, and he sent Mr. Brooks out of the nursery."

Amanda surged to her feet, panicking. "Then who's watching Cheyenne?"

Fiona shifted nervously. "Well, Dr. Colton is right now, but he said he needs to get back to Mr. Jethro."

Amanda glanced at the suffering cow and heaved a sigh of distress. She hated to abandon the animal who'd surely die without her help. But given the choice of protecting her daughter or saving the cow, her daughter won hands down every time.

Slade pushed to his feet and gripped her shoulders. "I'll go."

Her eyes darted up to meet his. She remembered how reluctant he'd been to babysit Cheyenne earlier in the week at the hotel. "Are you sure?"

He jerked a nod. "You're needed here."

"I…" She held his gaze, knowing instinctively he was the best option, knowing on a gut level that her daughter would be safe with him, and appreciating more than she could express his understanding of her need and voluntary help. "Thank you."

He gave her shoulders a firm squeeze, then followed Fiona back to the house.

With a cleansing breath, Amanda shoved aside the distraction and set back to work saving the cow and her calf.

Hours later, well after midnight, the calf was delivered stillborn, but Amanda managed to spare the mother. Though heartbroken over the calf, she considered the cow's survival a victory. Things had been touch-and-go many times, and they could easily have lost the cow, as well.

Jared volunteered to sit up with the cow, promising to send for Amanda if the mother took a turn for the worse. After thanking George and Jared for their help and washing up thoroughly at the sink in the stable, she trudged wearily back to the house and upstairs to her suite. Slipping off her boots, Amanda tiptoed into the nursery, her sock feet silent on the plush carpet. She was already yawning and anticipating overdue slumber. If Cheyenne was asleep. She sighed wearily. *Please let Cheyenne be asleep.*

The room was dark. A good sign. She hurried to the crib and peeked in.

Empty. Cheyenne's pink blanket hung askew over the railing.

Panic swelled in her chest. "Slade?"

Turning on the nearest lamp, Amanda cast a glance around the room. Slade's Stetson was on the floor beside the rocking chair, but he was nowhere in sight. "Slade!"

Amanda rushed into her bedroom, flipping on the overhead light as she entered. Nothing. No one.

"Slade!" she heard the desperation that filled her voice, the dread. Where were Slade and Cheyenne?

Chapter 14

Without hesitation she snatched her phone from her back pocket, ready to call the police, ready to sound the alarm that her daughter had been taken, that Slade could be hurt…when a noise in the bathroom caught her attention. Water running.

Heart in her throat and phone still in her hand, Amanda crept toward the closed bathroom door. Twisted the knob. Prayed. *Please don't let Slade or my baby be dead!*

When Amanda cracked open the door, a cloud of scented steam billowed out. The humid, pungent air wrapped around her like a suffocating quilt.

But it was the sight that greeted her that stole her breath. Slade, dripping sweat, sitting on the floor, propped against the side of the bathtub with Cheyenne lying facedown against his chest. His *bare* chest. His long muscled *bare* legs stretched out in front of him.

Amanda blinked, her pulse jumping. Slade wore only

his boxer briefs, damp now and clinging to his… Oh, my! She released a stuttering breath.

Hot water poured from the bathtub spigot, renewing the supply of steam. The closed toilet seat beside him was littered with a vial of menthol rub— so *that* was what she smelled— a nasal aspirator and a box of facial tissues. Her daughter had been stripped to her diaper and, rosy cheeked, snoozed soundly beneath Slade's splayed hand.

Amanda tried to process the scene, her brain slow to shift from panic over a potential kidnapping to…*this*. A full-scale respiratory intervention…with a heavy dose of drool-worthy, oh-my-god-what-a-bod man sprawled on her floor.

Hearing her enter, Slade raised bleary eyes to her and swiped perspiration from his face. When she opened her mouth to speak, he pressed a finger to his lips and whispered over the whoosh of rushing bath water, "I just got her to sleep. If you wake her, I will douse you in honey and stake you to an ant hill."

She choked on a throttled laugh, shaking her head in wonder.

"What happened here?" she asked, even though the evidence was clear.

He sighed. "It's been a rough night. She does *not* like having her nose suctioned."

"Can you blame her?" Amanda smiled, even as tears of gratitude and awe puddled in her eyes. The rough, tough ranch-hand-slash-WBI agent had spent the evening sweating and dealing with her cranky, snotty baby. He'd stuck with the task, putting Cheyenne's needs first, and hadn't abandoned her when it got hard and dirty and uncomfortable. Her chest throbbed with a tender ache. Slade had definitely won major "prince" points tonight.

And it didn't hurt that he looked so damn sexy for his

efforts…even if his hair was frizzing a little in the humidity. Especially because his hair was frizzing in the humidity. She had the same problem with her hair, and somehow it humanized him and endeared him to her all the more that he suffered from the same annoyance.

She shook her head, a grin tugging her cheek. "I can't believe you voluntarily suctioned my baby's stuffy nose. Most guys I know would be grossed out and run the other way. Fast."

He matched her lopsided grin. "I'm a ranch foreman. Gross is in the job description. I don't scare easily."

"Well…thank you. This was…" She stepped farther into the steamy room and squatted to turn off the tub facet. "Above and beyond the call of duty."

He shrugged a muscular shoulder. "I did what I had to. She was miserable, and I couldn't let her suffer." He nodded toward Cheyenne. "Wanna take her so I can get up? My butt is numb."

"Sure." Amanda reached for her daughter, and quickly realized there was no way to lift her sleeping child off Slade's chest without touching him. A lot. Her breath hung in her lungs as she wedged her hand between Cheyenne's cheek and Slade's sweat-slickened skin. When she scooped up her baby's legs and wiggled her hand carefully under Cheyenne's belly, the back of her arm grazed his taut stomach and came dangerously close to his, er… clingy briefs.

Cheyenne squawked once as Amanda started lifting her. Slade tensed, and Amanda froze, waiting for her daughter to resettle. Her gaze latched on to his, and Slade's azure eyes wordlessly repeated his threat of torture if she woke the baby. The bright blue intensity of his stare, the feel of his damp skin against hers and the heavy, humid air in the bathroom were a potent mix.

Amanda's pulse scrambled. Her limbs were flooded with a throbbing heat that left her flesh tingling and her belly feeling hot and tight.

A bead of perspiration tickled her temple as it ran down her face, and she inhaled slowly to steady herself before trying again to stand with Cheyenne in her arms. As she turned to carry Cheyenne out to her crib, Slade stopped her with a short, soft whistle.

"You need to dry her off before you put her in bed, or she'll get chilled."

Amanda jerked a nod. Dry Cheyenne off. Of course. She knew that. She did. And she would have remembered…before too late. She gritted her teeth. She would have remembered *now* if she hadn't been so distracted by six feet two inches of kind-hearted, broad-shouldered, nearly naked eye candy.

He shoved to his feet, took a hand towel from the bar above the toilet and draped it over her shoulder. "Here."

"Thanks," she replied, her voice far too breathy. The twitch of his sexy lips and amusement in his eyes told her he'd heard it too. Damn it.

Amanda chastised herself for her schoolgirl reaction to Slade as she carefully dried Cheyenne and dressed her in fresh pajamas. She lingered by the crib for a moment after settling her daughter in, buying a few moments to regain her composure before facing Slade again.

By the time she returned to the bathroom, he'd put the bathroom back in order, had helped himself to a towel and was rubbing down his arms and face. He was still in his damp boxer briefs.

Her mouth dried. *Steady girl.*

She found his discarded jeans behind the door and retrieved them, shoving them toward his chest. "Okay, cowboy, you can put your pants back on now."

He flashed a wicked grin as he took them from her. "It bothers you, me being in my skivvies?"

Amanda hiked up her chin as she gathered the aspirator and menthol rub he'd set beside the sink. "Well… no." *It turns me on.*

She put the items in the medicine cabinet over the sink, and when she closed the cabinet door, she caught Slade's smug expression in the mirror. She scowled back. "What?"

"I turn you on, do I?" His lopsided smile was pure seduction.

Amanda gasped, horrified. "I said that out loud?"

A rich, low chuckle rumbled from his throat. "You did."

Snapping her mouth closed, she shot him a warning glare. "Don't gloat. It will tarnish the shine on the knight's armor you earned tonight taking care of my daughter."

He took a step toward her. "I want you, too, Amanda."

Her breath snagged. "What?"

"You asked me to be honest with you." Dropping his jeans on the floor again, he took another step, backing her against the door frame. With his fingers, he traced her chin, then cradled the side of her head in his palm. "I'd think that truth was rather obvious."

"Slade…" She pressed a hand to her swirling stomach and searched for her usual control. Damn it! Why did he fluster her so much? She'd been around plenty of handsome men before. She'd even been around her share of naked men without turning into a blushing, babbling schoolgirl. But somehow Slade's sensual good looks and sexy build unnerved her, *aroused* her like no one else.

She swallowed hard. "You should go."

"What's the rush?"

"It's late, and…I need to get to bed."

He arched a black eyebrow, his thumb lazily skimming her cheekbone. "I agree."

The smoky look in his eyes and low pitch of his voice made it clear he wasn't talking about sleep. He twisted his hand in her hair and tugged so that her head angled up. His gaze zeroed in on her mouth, and anticipation fluttered through her. He touched his lips to hers softly at first, but even the gentle brush of his mouth sent shock waves through her. Then, with a rough growl from his throat, he angled his head and deepened the kiss.

Amanda curled her fingers into his muscular arms, steadying herself as the earth shifted and her head spun. Slade's lips commanded hers, moving with tantalizing persuasion and earning her fervid response. He tasted like peppermint gum, like sweet temptation, and for the life of her she couldn't remember any of the reasons she'd told herself to stay away from him. Not while his kiss was muddling her brain and setting her body on fire.

He released her hair, moving his hands to her waist. He worked his fingers inside the hem of her shirt, and the heat of his touch against her bare skin sent fresh tremors of heady sensation rolling through her. When he skimmed his hands up, she was so enthralled by the sensation of his calloused palms scraping lightly over her ribs that she didn't recognize his goal until he'd pushed her bra out of the way.

Her pulse kicked hard, even as desire puddled, warm and heavy at her core. He broke their kiss only long enough to divest her of the shirt and bra, leaving her exposed to him. Her mouth dried as he dropped the clothes on the floor and his gaze dipped to take in her naked breasts. Cupping her with his palms, he shaped her flesh and tweaked her nipples between his thumbs and index fingers. A powerful current of sensation shot through her, leaving her trembling with need, clamoring for him.

Slade pressed another hard, soulful kiss to her lips… then stepped back. He gave her a long, piercing look that reached deep inside her, and without a word, he turned and walked away.

Amanda blinked, stunned, breathless and more than a little disappointed. But as she stood there, cold in the wake of his absent body heat, mute from confusion, she heard the creak of bed springs.

She rallied her senses and made her way on shaky legs to her bedroom. In the golden glow of lights from her miniature Christmas tree, Slade lay on one side of her bed, the sheet draped over his hip. His boxer briefs were discarded on the carpet.

"Wh-what are you doing?" she asked, though the answer was obvious.

His cheek twitched in amusement. "Waiting for you."

She should kick him out, send him on his way. She should put any crazy notion of tangling in the sheets with him far from her mind. But her feet shuffled forward, drawn by the lure of his dark blue eyes, his beguiling grin, and the memory of the sweet fatherly care he'd taken with Cheyenne.

She could resist a sexy man. But a sexy man who'd shown such tenderness and consideration for her daughter's needs shattered her defenses. In that moment, all she wanted was to curl against him, pull the covers over their heads and not come up for air for a very long time.

She moved to the side of the bed, holding his hot gaze, and unbuttoned her jeans. Hooking her thumbs in her panties, she shoved them and her jeans down her hips and past her knees in one swift motion. After stepping out of the jeans, she stripped off her socks and tossed them aside. The room was cool, but Slade's gaze, as he studied her from hooded eyes, made her skin flush with heat and anticipation.

He lifted the covers, and as soon as she'd taken a condom packet from her bedside stand, she crawled in beside him. Slade slid an arm around her waist and tugged her closer. Amanda's breath hitched as he stroked his hand along her spine, over her hip, and down her thigh before reversing the path with his fingertips. They lay on their sides, facing each other, so close his body heat enveloped her and she could see every one of the thick eyelashes that framed his deep blue eyes.

"What are you doing here?" she asked.

"Again…I'd think that was obvious."

"I mean…that face, those eyes, you could have any woman you wanted. Why are you here with someone who smells like horses most of the time, only wears makeup and high heels when she has to, and hasn't seen the inside of a beauty parlor in too many years? You could do better. Or is it just that I'm convenient and willing?"

Slade locked gazes with her and remained silent for so long she thought he might not answer. His fingers combed idly through her hair, and he pressed a kiss to her nose. "All I ever smell on you is alfalfa hay, which I like, and your peach shampoo, which I find a turn-on." He traced the shell of her ear with his thumb and shivers raced through her. "And why wear makeup and heels when you look so hot in boots and jeans?" He tweaked her chin. "This face doesn't need makeup to be beautiful."

She smiled, ridiculously touched by his sweet words. "I really wasn't digging for compliments."

He put a finger over her lips to silence her. "As far as the inside of a beauty parlor, I much prefer what the outdoors does for you. The pink the cold air puts in your cheeks, the sexy mussing the wind gives your hair, the shine of the sun in your hair."

Warmth spread through her chest. "What do you know? You're a poet."

He scoffed. "If you think that's poetry, you're clearly not well read."

"What I think is that beneath your tough guy, cowboy, lawman mask beats the heart of a gentle soul. A sweet man."

He scowled again. "For the record, most men I know don't like to be called sweet."

She flashed him a lopsided grin. "Well, to me, you are. Sweet and gentle and ki—"

With a growl, he pushed her back on the mattress and pinned her with his body. His eyes narrowed, and some dark emotion flickered in their depths. A muscle in his jaw twitched as he clenched his teeth. "Don't."

"Wha—?"

His mouth captured hers, silencing her. His kiss was hot and thorough, his tongue probing and exploring her mouth with a firm authority. A guttural sound rumbled in his throat as he raised her arms above her head, pinning them with one hand on her wrists. With his other hand, he covered a breast, shaping and kneading it, rolling her nipple between his fingers. Fiery sensations flowed through her, quickly heating her body and spiking her arousal.

She settled into his demanding kiss, returning his fervor, even if the change of pace and mood was rather abrupt. Clearly he was bent on banishing ideas of soft and gentle from her mind. Their teeth clicked as he deepened the kiss, and when he wedged his knee between her thighs, she wrapped her legs around him.

He stroked his hand down her body, squeezing her

bottom and angling her hips so that her most sensitive area was pressed against his hard flesh. He rocked his hips, and the friction of his body against hers shot sparks through her blood. He moved his mouth to the curve between her neck and shoulder, and he raked her skin with his teeth and tongue.

"Slade," she gasped, her need quickly spiraling tighter, ready to spring, and he answered with a low moan of pleasure.

He took the condom from the bedside stand and ripped it open with is teeth. He sheathed himself with amazing one-handed dexterity while his hot gaze bore into hers. Hooking an arm behind one of her knees, he bent her leg, lifting it toward her belly. Then with one long thrust, he sank into her. She was ready for him, but the sudden pressure as he stretched and filled her made her gasp. As soon as her body accommodated him, he withdrew and entered her again with jolting force. Then again. And again.

This forceful, rough-and-tumble version of Slade kickstarted her pulse, but she wasn't afraid. Her instinctive trust in him, her certainty that she was safe, allowed her to free her inhibitions and follow where he led. She wiggled her arms, longing to free her hands from his restraining grasp and sink her fingers into his back, to cling to his shoulders as she bucked and matched the fierce clash of his body pumping into hers.

The sweet tension inside her torqued higher and hotter until she shattered. Waves of bliss, more powerful than she'd ever experienced, ever known possible, shook her to the core. A cry rose in her throat, and he quickly muffled it with a mind-numbing kiss.

His grip on her hands tightened to the point of pain as he climaxed. His body shuddered, and he buried his face against her neck, his breath hot on her skin. As the ripples of pleasure faded and her pulse slowed, she whispered, "Wow."

Slade collapsed on her, and the tension in his body eased. He lay on top of her, unmoving, his weight and size immobilizing her. In the stillness and the soft glow of the Christmas tree lights, she listened to the ragged sough of his breath and hers, listened for Cheyenne's whine and prayed they hadn't wakened her.

They hadn't been terribly loud, and he'd caught her spontaneous cry of ecstasy with a kiss. Had that been intentional? Was he, even in the throes of passion, thinking about her daughter's welfare? It seemed unlikely, and yet…

"I'm sorry," he murmured finally after several minutes of silence.

She wrinkled her nose. "For what?"

"I was…rough. More than I intended." He angled his head and met her eyes with a deep furrow in his brow. "Did I hurt you?"

Amanda lifted her cheek in a half grin. "No. I can handle a little rough now and then. I used to ride broncs, don't forget."

He grunted and gave a little nod, though his eyes were still dark and chagrined.

"I am starting to lose feeling in my hands, though." She tugged her arms, wiggling them in the grip he still had on her wrists.

"Oh," he whispered, releasing her, "right. Sorry."

She opened and closed her hand in a fist, then wrapped her arms around him. Plowing her fingers into his hair, she massaged his scalp and neck. "Ah, much better."

He flashed a contrite grin and kissed her cheek.

She rested a hand on his chest, felt the steady thump of his heart beneath her palm, and met his eyes. Even before the vigorous sex she'd been bone-tired, but she felt compelled to get a handle on where things stood between her and Slade. Where did they go from here?

"So…now what?"

He tensed a bit. Sighed. Turned to pull her body back against his, spoon-style. "Now you sleep."

"But what does—"

"Sleep, Amanda. We're both beat. We'll talk tomorrow."

She started to protest, but the minute she opened her mouth, a jaw-cracking yawn overtook her. Maybe Slade was right. Maybe…

But curled against his body heat, sated from their lovemaking and worn out by the long day, she succumbed to the slumber weighting her eyelids.

As sleep claimed her, one last thought filtered through her brain. Did the warmth in her heart mean she was falling in love?

Chapter 15

Tom reported for duty the next morning, claiming to feel much better and blaming his illness on his wife's cooking. "I knew that chicken didn't taste right, but she swore it had baked long enough."

Amanda, who'd had food poisoning once in college, cringed in sympathy. "Well, I'm glad you're better. And the good news is, chickpea seems to feel much better, too."

Standing in her crib, holding the side railing, Cheyenne cooed at Tom and flashed two bottom teeth as she grinned.

"That's the best news I've had all morning." Tom winked at Cheyenne and handed her the killer whale toy she'd tossed out on the floor.

Cheyenne squealed her delight at having her new favorite toy back and stuck the whale's tail in her mouth to gnaw.

"I'd like to check a few things in the stable, and then I thought I'd take Cheyenne to visit the animals in the petting barn. You feel up to joining us?"

"Absolutely. Lead the way."

Tom followed Amanda out to the stable, where the morning buzz of activity was in full swing—feeding, grooming, stall mucking and ribald teasing among the hands.

"Watch your language, men," Tom said, his tone and manner fully reminiscent of the military and police officer he used to be. "There's a lady on deck."

"That's no lady, that's Amanda," George said with a grin, and the other men laughed.

Amanda gave the hand a playful punch in the arm. "That's right. You're the lady around here. Aren't ya, George?"

The other hands hooted and guffawed even louder, and George shook his head, his face red.

Slade emerged from the storage room at the back of the stable and cast a curious look around the hands. When his gaze found Amanda's, his cheek twitched in a private grin. "Morning, Amanda, Tom."

"Don't mind us," Amanda said. "I just wanted to visit PW and have a quick look at the sore on Ranger's hoof."

"It looked better to me when I checked it a while ago," Jared said.

Slade's attention shifted to Cheyenne, and Cheyenne gave Slade a shy grin before hiding her face in Amanda's shoulder. In her hand, Cheyenne clutched the killer whale he'd bought her.

Slade stepped closer to tickle Cheyenne's belly. "What's new, little girl?"

"Her cold is almost gone. She's been all grins this

morning." Warmth swelled in Amanda's chest watching Slade interact with her daughter.

Cheyenne held out the killer whale and said, "Gee!"

"Translation?" Slade asked her.

Amanda shrugged. "Beats me. But she loves that thing. It's her new favorite toy."

He glanced up, his face sobering as if he just remembered they had company, and he cleared his throat. "Tom, would you mind watching Cheyenne for a while? I'd like to discuss some important matters with Amanda, and I thought we could take a ride out and check fences while we talk."

Stewie made a taunting, "Ooo," while George chuckled, "Uh-oh. You're in trouble. Boss wants to talk to you."

Amanda flipped her hair over her shoulder and gave George a playfully haughty look. "He's not my boss. But I am yours, and I don't currently see a lot of work happening out here."

George gave her a wink and a thumbs-up.

Jared poked at George with another hoot of laughter, and the hands scattered to finish their chores.

Tom took Cheyenne from Amanda, tweaking the baby's chin. "Princess and I will head over to the petting barn, then, and meet you inside later."

"Thanks, Tom." Amanda gave Cheyenne a quick kiss on the cheek then headed into Prince William's stall to saddle him for her ride with Slade. When she finished, she took an old straw-colored cowboy hat from a hook where she kept it for sun protection when she rode the pastures. Slade had his horse, which he'd had delivered the weekend before, ready to go by the time she led PW out to the corral.

She thought about putting her hair up in a ponytail, but when she remembered Slade saying he thought her hair looked sexy down, a tingle of pleasure raced through her, and she left it loose to blow in the chilly breeze.

As she approached, Slade sent a circumspect glance around the ranch yard, then cupped her cheek and gave her a warm kiss. "Morning, beautiful."

She smiled up at him, feeling every bit as cheerful as the bright yellow sun streaming down on the rolling Wyoming landscape. "Morning, stud. What did you want to talk about?"

He hitched his head toward the pasture. "Let's ride."

They swung up onto their horses and headed out into the north pasture. As they rode, Amanda tipped her head back and savored the warmth of the sunshine on the cold morning. "It's such a beautiful day. I'm glad you suggested we take a ride."

"This is about business, not pleasure."

She turned to face him and chuckled. "That doesn't mean I can't enjoy the sunshine. Lighten up, sourpuss."

"I—" He snapped his mouth closed and shook his head as he gave her a half grin. "Sourpuss?"

She shrugged and lifted her chin matter-of-factly. "Well, you don't smile nearly enough. I know things around the ranch are tense. But even with someone gunning for me, I know to be thankful for my blessings."

He arched an eyebrow inviting her to continue.

"My daughter is feeling better and is safe with Tom, I have the best horse on the ranch and the sun is out." She watched Slade's ease in the saddle, enjoying the way he looked in his faded jeans, black Stetson and sexy confidence. She added him to her list of blessings. She didn't know where their relationship was headed, but she had no doubt he was a man of integrity and kindness—despite the often-gruff face he showed the world.

He glowered at her now. "Best horse on the ranch?"

She smiled smugly and patted Prince William's neck. "Absolutely. Right, PW?"

"Maybe before Zeus arrived. But this fella is champion stock. Top-notch." Beneath the brim of his Stetson, a teasing light flickered in Slade's blue eyes, and a grin ghosted over his lips.

"Is that a challenge?"

His lips tugged sideways, his eyes bright. "Maybe. What are you thinking?"

"A race. To the fence at the top of that rise." She pointed to a far hill.

He glanced the direction she pointed, then back to her. "All ri—"

"Go!" She kicked Prince William to a run, laughing as she left Slade behind.

"Hey!" His shout rang over the rolling fields.

As she raced across the frozen ground, she looked back over her shoulder and found him gaining on her. She goaded PW to run faster, and he ate up the ground, enjoying the speed as much as she did.

The thunder of galloping hooves caught up to her, and Slade gave her a cocky look as he pulled even with her. Her competitive drive flared. She leaned low over Prince William's neck, urging him to go faster. As they neared the agreed finish line, she pulled ahead and flew past the fence line, ahead of Slade by a half a length.

She gave a victory whoop as she reined PW and rode up to Slade, glowing from adrenaline, her win and the temporary release from the tension on the ranch. "Good race."

He narrowed his eyes, but a genuine grin spread his mouth. "You cheated."

She feigned affront. "Did not!"

He half grunted, half laughed.

"So…where's my prize?" She pushed her hat back and tilted her head.

"Prize?" He guided his horse alongside hers. "What prize?"

"How about a kiss?" She reached for the front of his ranch coat and tugged him closer.

He slid a hand into her hair and cradled the base of her skull as he leaned toward her. "Kissing you would make me the winner."

"Oh, smooth, cowboy," she teased as he caught her lips with his. His mouth was warm, and his kiss made her forget races, sunny pastures and the troubles waiting back at the ranch.

After thoroughly muddling her mind with his skillful lips and gentle caress, he leaned back and looked deep into her eyes. For a change, his blue eyes were clear and happy and reflected the sunlight like a sparkling lake. He tugged lightly on a wisp of her hair and flashed a crooked smile. "You still cheated."

A laugh burst from her, and she nodded. "Okay, a little."

His eyes widened, along with his grin. When he smiled, Slade Kent was hands down the sexiest man alive. "A little? How do you cheat a little? Is that like being a little pregnant or a little dead?"

Amanda brushed a hand along the stubble on his chin, remembering the sensual scrape of his day-old beard when they'd made love last night. She sighed contentedly. "No, it's like being a lot happy."

His dark eyebrows shot up. "Happy?"

She swatted playfully at him. "Don't look so surprised."

His horse shifted his hooves, moving Slade a few

inches farther away from her, but it was the fading light in his expression that made her feel he was pulling back.

Amanda leaned farther toward him, grabbing the lapel of his coat and smacking another kiss on his mouth. "You make me happy, Slade Kent. I like being with you."

He moved her hand from his coat and gave her fingers a brief kiss before dropping her hand and flashing a smile that didn't reach his eyes. "I like you, too." He straightened and cast an awkward glance around the pasture before returning his gaze to her. "But what do you say we talk about what I brought you out here to discuss?"

Amanda felt sucker-punched. *I like you, too?* What kind of halfhearted, lukewarm sentiment was that? His kiss certainly said his feelings were deeper than *I like you.* Why had he withdrawn like that?

She straightened in her saddle and tried not to let her disappointment show. "And what did you bring me out here to discuss?"

"Motives."

"Pardon?"

He motioned toward the long barbed-wire fence marking the end of the grazing pasture. "Let's check fence while we talk."

He flicked his reins and headed down the fence line, leaving her to follow. When she caught up to him, he said, "The police aren't getting anywhere tracking down the person who shot at you, and I've hit a dead end on my father's case, so I thought we could brainstorm, look at things from a different angle."

The joy that had filled her earlier evaporated, leaving a hollowness inside her. "As in who has a motive to attack me?"

"More specifically, who has motive to kidnap Cheyenne? You were attacked because the suspect was trying to take Cheyenne. All the attacks this summer and fall have centered around people who were protecting Cheyenne or investigating some aspect of Cole's kidnapping or the crimes this summer."

"We already know Cole's aunt, Desiree Beal, kidnapped him. That was confirmed months ago. And we know Faye Frick brought Dylan, who it turns out is Cole, here when he was one year old."

He gave her a long skeptical look. "Maybe. But what if there's more to the story you don't know."

She studied the stern set of his jaw, and an uneasy prickle chased up her spine. What did he know? "Does this have to do with what Scottie Breen told you?"

He sent her an unreadable look. "I didn't say that. I just want to consider every angle."

"But you think all of it, from Cole's kidnapping and your father's murder, right through the attempts to kidnap Cheyenne, are all connected?"

"Certainly seems possible. But we're brainstorming, okay. Let's not dismiss any theories, no matter how unlikely it sounds."

She gnawed her bottom lip and huffed her frustration. "Believe me, I've done nothing for months now but brainstorm wild theories about who could be responsible. I just can't wrap my brain around the idea that a member of my family or someone on the ranch staff could be trying to kidnap Cheyenne."

"That's the first theory I want to challenge."

She jerked a startled gaze toward him. "What?"

"We've assumed, with good reason, that the mastermind behind the attacks is living on the ranch, connected to the ranch in some way. What if they aren't?"

Amanda blinked and opened her mouth mutely.

"Can you think of anyone, anyone who could have a

grudge against you or want to kidnap Cheyenne for monetary or other personal gain?"

The obvious answer stuck in her chest like a knife blade. "David," she rasped.

Slade sent her a dark frown. "Who?"

"David Gill. Cheyenne's father."

His brow creased. "Tell me about him."

"I met him at a veterinary conference a couple years ago, and we kept up a long-distance relationship for several months. We'd meet up in different cities, wherever he was traveling for business or on the weekend several times a month."

"What business?"

"Veterinary equipment sales."

Slade nodded. "Okay. Go on."

"When I learned I was pregnant, I told him, and… he freaked. He wanted nothing to do with a baby. Turns out he was married." She glanced at Slade, and he returned a frown.

"Married?"

"To a prominent Boston socialite. He was terrified she'd find out and his reputation, his marriage, his gravy train would be ruined." She scoffed. "He signed away his rights to Cheyenne and Cheyenne's inheritance as fast as he could, in exchange for me staying out of his life."

A muscle in Slade's tense jaw worked as he stared down the fence line. "He disowned his kid. Just like that." He muttered an unflattering epithet under his breath.

Slade's disgust with David made her feel a little better, and she flashed him an appreciative smile. "I honestly think he's the last person who'd want to kidnap Cheyenne. He has too much to lose."

Slade tipped his head to the side in assent. "What about Hilda Zimmerman?"

Amanda almost choked as she goggled at him. "Hilda? Hilda is the kindest, sweetest, most motherly woman I know!"

"And yet by talking to her, I learn she has no children of her own, a fact she mourns deeply."

"She always called me and my sisters the children she never had. She doted on us as we grew up. She'd never hurt us."

"Are you sure? What if she decided she wanted to take Cheyenne and disappear to raise her as her own, much like Faye Frick did with Cole?"

"I... She wouldn't—" Amanda fumbled, aghast.

Slade raised a hand. "Brainstorming, remember? We can't dismiss anything if we're going to catch this person."

She chuckled without mirth. "Fine. While we're at it, let's accuse Mathilda or my sisters or Tom."

"*Could* your sisters have a reason to want Cheyenne gone?"

She nailed him with an angry glare. "My sisters love Cheyenne. Besides, Cath is about to have her own baby and Gabby is going to adopt Avery. Why would they want to kidnap Cheyenne?"

"To get rid of a second-generation heir that would cut into their own inheritance?"

She glared at him. "Don't even go there. My sisters aren't mercenary like that."

"Okay, then what about Mathilda or Fiona?"

She rolled her eyes and groaned. "Fiona has only worked for us a few years, so that rules out your theory about the attacks this summer being connected to your dad or Desiree Beal kidnapping Cole."

"And Mathilda?"

"Is the most loyal employee we have. You've seen how protective she is of us and her fellow staff members."

"She seems kinda stiff and high-strung to me."

Amanda shrugged. "Her views on employee-family interaction may be a bit outdated, but she's got a good heart. She's been with us longer than anyone other than maybe the Blacks, and she has true affection for our family. Just because she's type A and likes to keep the house running smoothly doesn't mean she doesn't have a softer side." She shook her head. "It's not Mathilda."

"I found the horse your attacker escaped on near the Blacks' cabin. What about them?"

Amanda took a slow breath, battling down the frustration that made her edgy. This whole conversation felt like an exercise in futility to her. But Slade was trying to help, trying to protect Cheyenne, trying to connect the dots to his own father's killer. And he was a WBI agent. He wouldn't be pursuing this line of questioning if he didn't think it would be helpful.

"The Blacks keep to themselves for the most part. They are old, hard of hearing and getting frail. If they kidnapped Cheyenne, where would they hide her? They've never lived anywhere but that small cabin for as long as I've been alive." Amanda pulled the lapels of her coat together at the throat when a cold breeze buffeted her. "It's completely illogical that they have anything to do with what's been happening. Why would they want to kidnap Cheyenne?"

"Same reason any of the others would. Money. Face it, Amanda. Your family is loaded. Greed is a powerful motivation."

"Well, if greed is behind all this, then put my dad's ex-wife and her kids at the top of the list. Trip is as smarmy as they come, and although I can't prove it, I think he sells drugs. He could be in debt to a dealer."

Slade lifted an eyebrow in interest. "Go on."

"Darla is a master manipulator. She was while she was married to my dad, and she's still got some unexplained hold over him. She has to. That's the only reason my sisters and I can come up with to explain why he lets her live in the guest wing. And Catherine has confirmed that there is a woman connected to everything, possibly as the mastermind. Did I tell you Chief Drucker confessed to covering up crimes to protect someone he was in love with? Darla definitely fits that bill. She's a user, and I wouldn't put it past her to have been stringing Drucker along."

"And the daughter? Tawny?"

Amanda rolled her eyes. "Spoiled, lazy, self-centered…frankly, I might rule her out simply because masterminding everything that's happened and getting away with it takes more intelligence and initiative than Tawny has. Darla is cunning and heartless enough to have people helping her. But Tawny is…" She let her grunt of disgust finish her sentence.

Slade nodded and steered his horse around a rough patch of ground. "I'll keep them on my radar, then. What about the hands?"

"Certainly any of them would be physically capable of the attacks. Duke Johnson, a former hand, was working for the mastermind this summer. But whether any of the current hands could be involved…" She shrugged. "You've worked with them. What do you think?"

"I think they're all too smart to show their hand if they are behind this or helping someone."

Amanda shifted in her saddle to face Slade more fully. "The thing that bothers me…if this is about greed, then why now? My family has always had money. Why would someone try to extort money from us now?"

"Plenty of reasons. A baby is easy to kidnap. They don't scream for help or resist. The first attempt to take Cheyenne was not long after Cheyenne was born."

Amanda chewed her bottom lip and digested that fact.

"Second, Jethro is dying. Maybe whoever is doing this thinks their best chance to get at his money is while he's on his deathbed. Maybe the point is to torture Jethro by attacking his family and his wealth when he's vulnerable."

"Some kind of revenge?" She frowned as she mulled the idea.

"It's happened before. Worth considering. And don't forget—all of this could date back as far as when Cole disappeared."

Amanda dropped her shoulders and growled. "Jeez! This is giving me a headache." She pinched the bridge of her nose, fighting the throb growing behind her eyes, when a thought came back to her. "Do you think the organized crime faction Breen mentioned could be behind all this? Could Vinny Rizono and his crime buddies be making it look like an inside job to throw the cops off their trail?"

Slade twisted his mouth skeptically. "Unlikely, but I won't rule them out. From what I've learned, the attacks earlier and the attack on you aren't the work of a pro. I'd say a lot of luck and a minimum of skill, perhaps an inside knowledge of the ranch operations and layout, arc the only reasons the person behind this has not been caught."

"Luck?"

He lifted a palm. "But this character is going to mess up eventually. His—or her—luck will run out, and I'll nail him." Slade's gaze echoed his promise with an intensity that sent a sensual heat curling through her.

She gave him a confident smile. "I believe you. And I believe *in* you."

He seemed startled by her trust in him and covered by shifting his attention to the pasture fence. "Everything looks good out here and…that's all I had to talk to you about if you're ready to head back in."

So in addition to compliments about his kindness, Slade was uncomfortable with expressions of faith. Why would a man with so much good in him eschew any recognition of his integrity and gentleness? Why would he hide it behind such a stern face most of the time?

As they rode back toward the stable, Amanda moved the conversation to a safer topic. "So other than finding your father's killer and the person behind the recent attacks—" she shot him a side glance "—what do you want for Christmas?"

His dark eyebrows drew together. "Christmas?"

"You know…December twenty-fifth. Lighted trees and exchanging gifts with friends and family? It's just over a week away."

His shoulders drooped. "Crap."

She snorted a laugh. "Well, aren't you full of the holiday spirit?"

He flashed a chagrined smile. "I didn't mean… It's just I haven't even thought about Christmas."

"Then you don't have any ideas what you want?"

He gave her a hooded look that smoldered with meaning. "Oh, I know what I want."

An image of Slade in her bed flashed in her memory, and a sensual heat flowed through her. "Hmm, I think the same thing is on my list."

His cheek hitched up in a sexy crooked grin. "Good."

When he sobered and gave her a worried look, Amanda's gut clenched. "What's that look for?"

"About last night…"

Chapter 16

She swallowed hard, not liking the dark turn in his mood. They'd put off talking about where their relationship would go. If they even had a relationship…

Amanda took a deep breath of winter air. "What about last night?"

He hesitated, then met her gaze with a penetrating stare. "I just want to be sure we're on the same page about what happened. Next time, I'll—"

"Next time?" she asked with a grin. "Are you saying you think there'll be a next time?"

He cocked an eyebrow. "Amanda, we have good chemistry, and we're consenting adults. I'll go back to Jackson when the case here is closed, but until then…"

Her heart dropped to her toes. When he went back to Jackson…

She'd known Slade's presence on the ranch was temporary, warned herself not to develop feelings for him.

"Until then I'm convenient and willing?" she asked, repeating the words she'd used in jest last night and not bothering to hide her hurt.

"I didn't say that."

"But it's what you meant. Right?"

He sighed and looked away. His silence spoke for him. It seemed she was more right about Slade's unavailability than she'd known. Pain lanced her heart. He was leaving soon, and clearly only wanted a fling while he was at the ranch.

After a moment, he nudged Zeus and rode closer to her. Touching her face, he narrowed a sorrowful gaze on her. "Amanda, the last thing I want is to hurt you. I'm just not in a place in my life where—"

"No, no…I get it." She forced a smile, determined not to let him see her disappointment. "We made no promises to each other, and there are no hard feelings. But I'm not the type to indulge in a meaningless fling. I need more, so…" She took a breath for courage, gave him a brave smile, and pulled away from his touch. "There'll be no next time."

She gave Prince William a little kick and headed back toward the ranch. Clearly she'd picked the wrong man. *Again.* But that was her fault, not Slade's. She wouldn't punish him for her own mistake.

Was she so eager to have what her sisters had found, so desperate to build a family for Cheyenne that she'd imagined feelings that didn't exist?

When they returned to the stable, she swung down from Prince William and started unbuckling his saddle.

"Here," Slade said, nudging her out of the way, "I'll get that for you."

Amanda opened her mouth to tell him she'd been handling her own tack since she was nine. Jethro had insisted his daughters be self-sufficient in such things and not be a nuisance to the ranch hands. Instead, she stepped back, giving Slade room to work, and knowing he was simply acting from his code of honor and respect.

"Thank you," she said, forcing a smile. "It's good to know chivalry isn't dead."

And it was this side of Slade that she'd found so easy to fall in love with.

Slade cut an irritated side glance at her as he pulled the saddle off Prince William. "Chivalry?" He grunted and twisted his mouth in disgust. "It's called doing my job. Every cowboy knows taking care of his horse is his first priority."

She sighed. "True, but when you take care of my horse, too, I call it thoughtful and sweet."

Another withering look. "Whatever."

He turned his back and draped the saddle over the storage rack, and she recalled his reaction to being called "sweet" last night. Amanda frowned. "Why do you do that?"

"Do what?" he asked, pulling off the saddle blanket next and folding it in halves.

"Whenever I thank you for doing something nice or being especially tender with Cheyenne, you get all bristly and dismiss it as if I'm imagining things."

His brow furrowed. "I do not."

She barked a humorless laugh. "You just did!" Shifting her weight and angling her head, she folded her arms over her chest. "Why does it bother you for me to see your softer side? For me to point out to you that you *have* a softer side?"

He gave her a hooded look. "I told you before, no real man wants to be called soft."

"I'm not calling you soft. I said *softer side*. I'm talking about when you're considerate or polite to the maids. Or when you do nice things for me without being asked and take it upon yourself to protect me. Or when you look at Cheyenne with that tender look on your face."

He jerked his head up, his expression dark. "I do *what?*"

Amanda blinked. What had she said that upset him? "You're good with Cheyenne. Most men handle babies like they were footballs, but you're careful with her. Gentle. And, yes, you're swe—"

"Damn it, Amanda." He swung the folded blanket onto the shelf harder than he needed, his body tense. "Would you drop it?"

"Why are you mad?" She stared at him, baffled by his attitude. "This is what I'm talking about! If I even hint that you have a good heart under your tough-guy exterior, you go all squirrely and hostile on me. Is this because I cut you off, because I won't have a sex-for-sex's-sake fling with you?"

His expression darkened. "Is that really what you think?"

She grunted her frustration. "Then why does it bother you so much that I see good qualities in you?"

He snatched a bridle up from the ground and slung it onto the shelf. His jaw was tight, and a muscle flexed in his cheek.

She crossed the floor to him and laid a hand on his shoulder. "Slade—"

"Don't," he growled, swinging around to face her and aiming a finger at her face. His nostrils flared as he dragged in a ragged breath. "Don't fall in love with me."

She gave a startled laugh. "Who said anything about *love?*"

His eyes widened as if he feared he'd just made a colossal mistake, and he yanked his finger back, balling his hand in a fist. "Forget it."

"I mean, we just decided there was no relationship to pursue, right? That you'll be leaving when you're done here." Amanda stared at his back as he continued to toss tack equipment about with more force than necessary. What had just happened? She hated that the conviviality of the afternoon had disintegrated into this…this whatever it was. Not a fight. She wasn't mad at him. Disappointed, yes. But she was more puzzled by his unexplained attitude and brusque behavior.

"Slade?"

He faced her with an impatient huff. "Just because I'm nice to your daughter or I help you with your saddle doesn't mean I'm all hearts and flowers and romance. Okay?"

She raised her palms. "Okaaay. I got that. You don't love me. Last night was just sex. But why are you so mad?"

Did he think she was angling for a commitment, pushing him for a marriage proposal because they'd slept together once? Did he think she was withholding sex to manipulate him? She'd learned her lesson with Cheyenne's father about expecting too much and getting her heart broken. She would not make the same mistake with Slade. Somehow she'd rein her heart in and move on.

Amanda set her mouth in a firm line. She was quite content to build her life around raising Cheyenne—alone, thank you—and concentrate on her career.

After another moment of her confused silence and his slamming things around, he heaved a disgruntled sigh and marched back over to her. "Look, last night the sex was good…hell, it was great, all right? And I know

I shouldn't have misled you by staying last night and making love to you."

"Making love?" She scoffed, her hurt seeping to the surface. "I thought we decided it was just sex."

He slapped a hand down on her saddle. "Damn it, Amanda, I never said that! It *was* more than just sex. We both know that, but…"

Her breath stilled. What was he saying?

"I'm just…I'm not looking for anything permanent. I don't need another wife to—" Again he cut himself off, a stricken expression crossing his face as he clamped his mouth shut and staggered back a step. He bit out a curse and pinched the bridge of his nose.

Then his words permeated her fog of confusion over his drastic reaction. *Another wife…*

Ice slithered down her spine. A bone-deep cold filled her. "You're…m-married?"

Not again. Please God, not again. A stabbing ache slashed to her heart, and she admitted that, yeah, maybe she did have feelings for Slade. Otherwise why would the idea of his betrayal hurt so much?

Slade raised his head, his eyes troubled, pained. "Was. I *was* married."

The weight in her chest eased a fraction, but before she'd relax completely she had to be certain. "And the divorce is final?"

If possible, the misery in his face deepened. He looked ready to cry, though the rigid set of his jaw and black expression he wore said he'd never yield to the tears. "No divorce," he rasped. "She died."

Amanda raised a trembling hand to her mouth, the tears he wouldn't let himself cry spilling from her eyes. "Oh, Slade, I'm so sor—"

"Save your pity." He jerked his shoulders back and

stormed past her. When he reached the stable door, he paused long enough to add, "If all you want is sex, I'm your man. But I'm not husband material. Spare yourself the trouble of learning that the hard way, and start looking for good qualities in another man."

Amanda returned to the house, her chest heavy with grief and confusion. Slade had been married. His wife had died. It explained so much about his dark mood, his resistance to a relationship.

And he'd called what happened between them last night making love. *It was more than just sex. We both know that...*

Damn it, why had he given her that seed of hope? She'd have been better off believing he didn't care. She could more easily move on and curb her own feelings if she thought there was no chance for them. But the torture in his eyes just now in the stable said he did care, that he was torn, that he was hurting. And his pain sat heavily in her chest, gnawing at her.

The sound of a car door slamming brought her head up as she approached the house.

"Amanda!" her sister Catherine called, giving a wave and a smile. "Wait until you see what I just bought for the baby's nursery. They had the cutest accessories at the shop next door to the seamstress in town."

Amanda's mood lifted a little, seeing her sister's broad grin.

"Why were you at the seamstress?"

Catherine laughed. "Gabby is worried my growing belly means my bridesmaid dress won't fit. She sent me to get alterations." Cath moved to the trunk of her car, and Amanda bumped her aside when she reached for her packages.

"Nope. I'll get that. You don't need to be lifting anything heavy."

As she lugged the bag out of the car, Amanda flashed back to Slade's similar gesture with her saddle moments earlier.

Catherine rested a hand on Amanda's shoulder. "Hey, why the sad face? What's happened?"

Amanda slammed the trunk lid closed and shook her head. "Long story. If you're truly interested, I'll bore you with it later. For now, let's go see what treasures you found in town."

"First I want lunch. The baby is demanding food. Now!" Catherine hooked her arm in Amanda's and walked inside with her. "By the way, was that Slade I saw crossing the yard toward the barn when I first pulled in?"

Amanda flashed an ironic grin. "Yep. He's the protagonist of the long and tragic tale of my bad mood."

Cath arched a shapely eyebrow. "Uh-oh."

"Exactly."

Later in the week, after Amanda finished her morning rounds, checking on all the animals she was currently treating for various ailments and feeding the animals in the petting zoo, she headed upstairs and stuck her head into Cheyenne's nursery. Tom was flipping through a magazine while Cheyenne gummed her killer whale toy in her baby swing. "Tom, are you busy?"

He glanced up and chuckled. "Do I look busy?" He set the magazine aside. "What do you need?"

"Distraction. I've been preoccupied with all the horrible things happening on the ranch and my dad's failing health and…" She heaved a weighty sigh.

"You want to talk?" The older man shifted forward on his seat but looked uneasy about a heart-to-heart.

"No…thanks. I thought the house could use a little Christmas cheer. Would you help me bring the decorations in from the storage building out by the barn?"

"Sure. What do you want to do about princess? I saw Mathilda in the hall earlier."

Amanda shook her head. She'd grown increasingly worried about having anyone other than Tom babysit Cheyenne. Except Slade. And what did it say about their relationship that he was one of the few people she trusted with her daughter's life?

An image of Slade, nearly naked and sitting in the steamy bathroom, flickered through her mind's eye, stirring her pulse, and she quickly pushed the sultry image aside.

"No, we can, um…take her with us." Amanda retrieved the baby backpack and slipped it on. Tom helped dress Cheyenne warmly in her pink winter snowsuit and load her in the carrier, and they headed out.

Mathilda was vacuuming in the hall as they left, and she cut the machine off as they passed. "Heading out, Miss Amanda? I can have Fiona clean your suite while you're gone, if you'd like."

"Oh, not necessary. We'll only be gone a few minutes. We're heading down to the storage building to get Christmas decorations." She flashed a smile as she started down the stairs. "Thanks, anyway."

Mathilda nodded. "Let me know if you'd like help putting the decorations up."

Tom followed Amanda out the back door of the ranch house, and they crunched through the thin layer of snow that had fallen that morning. The dusting of white made the trees and outbuildings sparkle in the winter sunlight.

"Beautiful, isn't it?" she asked, inhaling a deep breath of fresh air, so cold it bit her lungs.

Tom smiled as he cast his gaze around. "No prettier place on earth than Wyoming, I say. Lived here my whole life and wouldn't want to live anywhere else."

When they reached the outlying storage building, Amanda keyed open the lock and flipped on the lights in the cavernous room. "The tree ornaments are up there." She pointed to a middle shelf. "And the garlands and nativity set are up there." She aimed her finger to a top shelf.

Tom groaned. "Clearly someone on your staff doesn't believe in making Christmas easy for the decorator."

"Fortunately the boxes aren't heavy." Amanda retrieved a step ladder and set it up. Glancing over her shoulder, she said, "Chickpea, this will be easier without you on my back."

"Agreed." Tom helped lift Cheyenne from the pack and spread his coat on the floor.

"Tom, you'll freeze!"

"It's only for a few minutes while we climb the ladder, and I won't have the princess sitting on the cold, dirty floor." He set Cheyenne in the middle of his coat and handed her the killer whale toy to chew.

Amanda headed up the ladder, chuckling. "You softie."

"Guilty as charged." He took the first box from her and set it on the floor, then moved back in place to take the next one from her. "Just don't let my old police squad hear—"

The storage room door crashed open, and someone in a ski mask darted inside.

A ski mask...Amanda's blood ran cold.

"No! Tom, get Cheyenne!"

But the bodyguard had already headed toward her daughter. Amanda let the box of decorations crash to the floor. She started down the ladder, desperate to protect

Cheyenne. Time seemed to move in slow motion, as the ski-masked figure raised a gun. Fired. The ear-shattering blast echoed through the storage building.

Tom clutched his chest. Staggered…and fell, face-down, mere feet from her daughter.

"Tom!" Amanda screamed, stumbling as she hurried down the ladder. She missed a rung in her haste and fell, landing with a bone-jarring thump.

Cheyenne let out a terrified wail. The gunman charged forward. Amanda scrambled, head throbbing, to reach her daughter.

To no avail. Horrified, she watched the assailant scoop Cheyenne in his arms and race out of the storage building.

"Noooo!" Her cry was a ragged sob, a howl of agony and numb disbelief. She staggered to her feet, ran through the door in pursuit. But the assailant had climbed on one of the ranch's ATVs. Driving with one hand and holding Cheyenne in his other arm, the kidnapper drove away.

Her feet slipping on the icy snow, Amanda raced after them, screaming for help. The ATV quickly outpaced her and disappeared over a hill into the north pasture.

Legs quivering, Amanda dropped to her knees, racked by sobs and gasping for breath. "Nooo!"

Seconds later, or minutes—time had no meaning anymore—Amanda rose on shaky legs and stumbled back to the storage building. She dropped beside Tom and rolled him to his back. His face was slack and blood stained his shirt. "Tom? Tom, can you hear me?"

She felt for a pulse in his neck, even though his fixed gaze gave little doubt he was dead. Tipping her head back, Amanda let a loud keening moan pour from her shattered soul. Tom had died trying to save Cheyenne, and her daughter was in the hands of killers.

Chapter 17

A knock on his room door roused Slade as he changed out of a machine-grease-covered shirt. He'd spent the morning repairing a hay baler in the barn, and it felt good to shower and clean up. His pulse spiked, simultaneously hoping Amanda had forgiven him his outburst and also praying it wasn't her. He needed to keep his distance from her, for her own good. He needed to put his investigation in high gear, solve his father's murder and get the hell out of Dodge without hurting Amanda any more than he had.

He pulled the door open and blinked his surprise. Jethro's ex-wife Darla and her daughter, Tawny, who was a younger version of her mother, smiled at him with cattish grins. Both women were bottle-blonde, made up with a thick coat of makeup and about as warm-looking as a snowman. Though surprised to see the women who tended to keep to their suite and eschewed mingling with the hired help, according to Amanda, he had been meaning to interview Darla and her children. He'd been in a hurry to get out in the pasture to check on the hands, who were working in the south field, but figured he ought to seize this opportunity while he had it.

"Afternoon, ladies. Can I help you?"

"Hello, Mr. Kent. We need a few minutes of your time."

He noted it wasn't a question, but rather a subtle demand. "All right. Shall we talk in the dining—" He stepped out of his room, but Darla stopped him with a hand planted firmly on his chest.

"No." She gave a none-too-gentle shove. "We'll talk in here. It's more private."

Tawny swept into his room behind her mother and closed the door.

Darla let her hand linger a moment longer than necessary on his chest, and when she finally withdrew it, her fingers slid along his ribs.

Slade's skin crawled. Not only was the woman twice his age, the glint in her eyes told him she and Tawny were up to no good.

"Well, well," Tawny said, eyeing him like a tasty snack. "No one told me the new foreman was so… handsome. Had I known, I wouldn't have taken so long to come down and meet you."

Darla strolled across his floor examining the things on his dresser and touching his personal items—his comb, his razor, his cell phone. Her uninvited familiarity rankled.

"You wanted to talk?" he said coolly when she continued snooping without saying anything.

"I do." She faced him and tipped her head. "Rumor has it you've been asking a lot of questions since you arrived."

Slade said nothing, only stared at her blankly.

"There have been a lot of snoops around here over the past few months. Employees who fancied themselves as spies, long-lost sons of Jethro's coming out of the woodwork, even an investigative reporter pretending to be Cole."

When she picked up his picture of his father and studied it, Slade bristled and snatched the framed photo from her. "What's your point?"

Her back stiffened, and she lifted her obviously surgeon-sculpted nose. "My point is we don't welcome outside interference and prying in our home."

"Now, Mother," Tawny said with a false smile. She stepped closer to him and took her turn manhandling him. She put a hand on his arm and sidled close to him. "Let's not be hasty. Perhaps Slade is just friendly and wanting to get to know all of the employees." She sent him a wink. "I'm free tonight if you want to get to know me better, cutie."

Slade stepped away from Tawny, his back teeth grinding. "Sorry. I have plans."

Tawny flashed a comically disappointed pout. "Aw…"

He sent a flat look to Darla. "I'm here to do a job. Nothing more. A job I need to get back to, if there's nothing else." He put a hand on the doorknob.

"I know who you are, Mr. *Kent,*" Darla said with a smug grin. "The picture confirms it." She nodded to the photo in Slade's hand. "I recognized the name. Your father was the policeman killed here ten years ago."

Slade gritted his back teeth and placed the photo back on his dresser. "So?"

She lifted overplucked eyebrows. "So I'm not stupid enough to think it is coincidence that you were hired as foreman. What sort of game are you playing, Mr. Kent?"

"I don't play games."

"Does Jethro know who you are?" Darla asked, her eyes narrowed.

"You'd have to ask him."

"The man is dying, Mr. Kent. I'm sensitive enough to his illness not to upset him with troubling events from the past. I hope you'll show him the same kindness."

"Why would—" He started when a popping noise filtered in through his window. "Did you hear that?"

"Jethro can't be bothered with—"

"Quiet!" he ordered sharply, lifting a hand to echo his command.

"Don't tell me what to—"

"Quiet!" he repeated, shouting down Darla's complaint. "I hear something."

Everyone in the room stilled, straining their ears. A scream rang from outside, and Slade's gut pitched, recognizing the voice. "That's Amanda."

He turned and ripped open his door, even as Darla's voice chased him.

"Wait! We're not finished!"

He ignored Darla, his only thoughts of reaching Amanda. *Fast.* The first sound he'd heard, the noise that caught his attention, sounded far too much like a gunshot. If Amanda was hurt…

Acid pooled in Slade's gut as he sprinted down the stairs and out the back door. He swept his gaze around the ranch yard. The stable and pens were eerily empty and quiet. Because he'd sent the hands to the south field to do maintenance on the irrigation system. Damn!

"Amanda!" He jogged toward the stable, still casting an encompassing glance around the yard. His heart tapped an anxious tattoo against his ribs. Where was she? "Amanda!"

Bingo and Betsy trotted out of the stable wagging their tails, and he started that direction.

"Slade!"

He spun around, searching the area from which Amanda's cry had come. The fear that vibrated in her cry sent a chill to his bones. "Amanda?"

Finally he saw her stagger from the storage building, her steps unsteady as she stumbled drunkenly toward him. Heart in his throat, he bolted across the ranch yard toward her, his feet slipping in the snow.

Before he reached her, she dropped to her knees.

He skidded to a stop beside her, seizing her arms and quickly scanning her for injuries. "Amanda, what happened?" he panted, winded from his sprint.

The eyes she lifted to his were so full of pain and distress that icy dread shot straight to his core. She shook from head to toe and was clearly suffering from shock.

He gave her a shake. "Tell me what happened!"

"Ch-Cheyenne..." she moaned and shuddered, staring blankly at the snow.

Knowing she was in no shape to explain, he eased her down to the ground and stroked her hair. "Wait here."

Drawing his service weapon from his shoulder holster, Slade crept toward the storage building. He found ATV tracks in the snow by the door, and inhaling deeply, he could still smell exhaust, telling him the vehicle had been there recently. He pushed the storage building door open with one hand and led with his gun as he sidled inside. Between the long walls of shelves, he found a body sprawled on the ground.

Tom Brooks. Cheyenne's bodyguard.

Rushing in, he checked Tom for signs of life. But found none. Slade bit out a scorching curse then ground his back teeth in frustration. Another pointless death at Jethro Colton's ranch. If it was the last thing he did, he'd—

Slade cut the thought off without finishing it as Amanda's stuttered response replayed in his head. *Ch-Cheyenne.*

He lurched to his feet. Swept another glance around the storage room. And froze.

Beside a man's coat, which had been spread on the floor, lay the small stuffed killer whale he'd bought Cheyenne in the San Diego airport.

She loves that thing. It's her new favorite toy.

Grief slammed Slade with the force of a wrecking ball. His breath whooshed from his lungs, and he had to brace a hand on the nearest shelf to stay on his wobbly legs. Closing his eyes, he fought for control, battled to keep his emotions locked down. Cheyenne had been taken, a good man had been murdered and Amanda was, understandably, in shock. He had to hold it together for her sake. He had to keep his head and do his job.

He reholstered his weapon, then pulled out his cell phone to call Trevor Garth. While he waited for the head of ranch security to answer, Slade took a step toward the stuffed killer whale, then stopped. The toy was part of the crime scene, and he couldn't touch it. Fisting his hand, he turned and headed back out to Amanda.

"Tom Brooks has been murdered, and the killer took Cheyenne," he said without preamble when Trevor answered. Hearing the strain in his voice, he paused only long enough to pull in a deep breath. "Get Chief Peters up here, then radio to the hands to organize a search of the property. They're in the south field, so they can fan out from there. The killer has about a five-minute lead. We need to hurry."

Trevor's only response was a mumbled curse that echoed Slade's feelings.

Amanda was still huddled in the snow, shivering violently. As he approached her, she raised a hollow, stricken gaze to him that caused a wrenching in his chest. "M-my baby…"

He nodded somberly. "I've called Trevor. The cops are on their way."

With a hiccup and jerk of her shoulders, Amanda dissolved in plaintive sobs. Sobs so deep and pained she could barely catch her breath. "She's…my world.…"

Slade dropped to his knees and scooped her into his arms. "I know, honey."

Amanda clutched at his back, holding him as if her life depended on it. At that moment, Slade was sure her sanity did. He knew how dark and hopeless the well of grief could be when fearing for your child's life.

He held her tightly, pressing her head to his chest and fighting the sting of tears that burned his sinuses. He absorbed the guttural sobs and spasms of anguish that racked her body, sharing her heartbreak.

Moments later, when he heard footsteps crunching through the snow, he glanced up to find Gabriella and Trevor leading a small crowd hurrying toward them.

"Amanda!" Gabriella rushed to her sister's side. "I heard…I—I'm so sorry!"

Slade levered Amanda back and framed her wet face with his hands. He swiped at the tears on her cheeks with his thumbs as he drilled her with a penetrating stare. "I have to go now, but your sister is here. Trevor and I are going start searching for her."

Amanda's face crumpled, and her hands gripped his sleeves. "Find her. You h-have to f-find her."

Slade pressed a lingering kiss to her forehead, then

met her eyes again. "I will bring her back to you. I promise." As he pulled away from Amanda, he faced Gabriella. "Get her inside. Have Levi check her. She's in shock." Then jerking his chin toward Trevor, he rose to his feet and headed to the stable. "The assailant's on an ATV. We can follow the tracks in the snow. Tell the hands we're headed to the north pasture."

Trevor lifted a two-way radio to his mouth and conveyed the message to Cal.

Slade pulled out his gun, double-checked that it was fully loaded then clicked the magazine back in place. "Let's catch the sonofabitch."

"I should be out there looking for her," Amanda said as she paced the nursery, biting fingernails that were already down to a nub.

Catherine sent her a worried look. "No, you shouldn't. I know it's hard to wait for news, but the whole police department and every available person on the ranch is out searching. Gabby, Levi, the hands…even some of the cooks and maids."

"But she's *my* daughter."

Cath wrapped an arm around her sister's shoulders and guided her back to the rocking chair for the umpteenth time that evening. "And you were understandably in no condition to ride out with the search party when they left."

Amanda perched on the edge of the chair, nausea swirling in her gut every time her thoughts replayed the kidnapping, Tom's murder, her helpless scramble to reach her daughter as the attacker fled. Levi had wanted to give her a sedative and she'd refused. She wanted her mind sharp and fully able to help Slade and the police identify and locate the person who'd stolen her baby.

Only Cath had stayed behind, partly to take care of Amanda when she'd been in shock, and partly because a cold, bumpy ride into the pastures was not advisable for a pregnant mother.

"Besides," her sister said, rubbing Amanda's icy fingers between her warm palms, "if the kidnapper holds to form from this summer when Avery was taken, you should be getting a ransom call soon. You need to stay by the phone."

A ransom. Amanda launched herself from the rocking chair again, unable to sit still. She'd gladly empty her account and sell all her possessions for the safe return of her daughter. After what she'd learned from Breen about how the Colton fortune had been created, she wanted no part of the tainted money, anyway. Knowing that the same ill-gotten riches were the reason Cheyenne had been targeted made her all the more furious and disgusted.

"Do you think Jethro will help with the ransom if I can't pay it all?"

Cath blinked, her expression stricken. "Cheyenne's his granddaughter. He has to!"

"He wouldn't help Trevor get Avery back." A fact Amanda found unforgivable, and judging from Cath's expression, her sister shared the opinion.

"This is different. Cheyenne's family."

"But Avery will be family in another few days." Amanda stalked across the floor and back, her hands fisted and pent-up adrenaline coursing through her. "He knew how Gabby felt about Avery…"

Cath stepped in front of her and chafed Amanda's arms. "Hon, you're dwelling. Take a deep breath and come sit down. Everything's going to be fine. I know it will."

"I can't sit. I should be out there looking for her."

Cath gave her a sad smile as the conversation came full circle…again.

Amanda stepped over to the window where Reyna sat looking out, watching stray snowflakes drift down from a darkening gray sky. She stroked her cat's fur, trying to find solace in the simple act, but her nerves were frayed. "It'll be dark soon. What if they don't find her by then?"

"Then they'll shift gears and do other things to find her, like making fliers to put up in town, or going house to house knocking on doors, talking to the FBI and Center for Missing Children."

For several moments after that, Amanda simply stared out the window at the deepening dusk and repeating silent prayers for Cheyenne's safe return.

When a knock sounded on the nursery door, she spun around, holding her breath. Slade pushed open the door and walked in, his weary gaze finding hers. Amanda's heart rose to her throat.

But he removed his Stetson and slowly shook his head. "Nothing yet. I'm sorry."

Amanda covered her mouth with one hand as fresh tears stung her eyes and disappointment crushed her chest, making it difficult to breathe.

Slade crossed the room to her and folded her into his embrace. As he held her, the chill of outdoors still on his clothes, he spoke to Cath. "Gray just arrived. He's looking for you."

Amanda lifted her head and sent Cath a startled look. "Gray came back from the police academy?"

Her sister smiled. "Of course he did. He loves Cheyenne, too. He wanted to help."

Amanda sniffed, touched by the outpouring of love from her family and friends. "Thank him for me."

Cath nodded, then disappeared into the hall, clearly eager to see her fiancé.

Slade pulled her close again, pressing her head against his chest and holding her tightly. "Have you gotten a ransom call yet?"

"No." She clutched the back of Slade's shirt as if it were a lifeline. His arms soothed her when she thought nothing could, keeping her from falling apart. "What did you find? Anything?"

He heaved a burdened sigh. "No. We followed the ATV tracks in the snow out into the pasture, but they got mixed with a dozen other tracks farther out, where the hands had been working earlier today. We lost the trail. There was no sign of her or the kidnapper anywhere on the property."

Amanda heard his frustration in the dark rumble underlying his tone. She tipped her head back and met his gaze. Slade's eyes were framed by creases and shot with red as if he'd been crying. Her pulse stumbled at the notion of the tough, stoic WBI agent and ranch foreman ceding to his emotions. And that Cheyenne's kidnapping would be the catalyst.

Slade's thumbs stroked Amanda's cheeks, and he drilled her with a penetrating stare. "She's going to be all right. We'll find her. Okay?"

She blinked as tears filled her eyes. "We don't know that. The animal that took her has killed before. He killed Tom. He shot at me, he's attacked and murdered other members of the house staff."

Slade's hands tensed, his fingers digging lightly into her skull. "We can't think that way. Cheyenne's just a baby. We have to believe that whoever did this is just after the money. If it's an inside job, as we believe, surely they care about Cheyenne, and they'll be careful with her."

A fire of conviction blazed in his eyes, a hope she wanted to share.

"How can you be so sure?"

"Because—" he started, but his voice cracked, and she saw the shadows of doubt and fear that appeared in his gaze. Moisture crept into his eyes, and her heart stilled. "Because…" he tried again, his voice rough and heavy with emotion, "I can't believe God would be cruel enough to let *two* babies I loved die."

Two babies? Amanda was still processing that startling revelation when another truth hit her. He loved Cheyenne. He was hurting as deeply as she was over Cheyenne's kidnapping. With her head and heart full of grief and worry over Cheyenne, she hadn't thought she could feel anything else. But a tender ache swelled in her chest and stole her breath seeing the emotions filling Slade's eyes.

The same moment she recognized his pain, however, he closed his eyes, clenched his teeth and drew a deep breath. Shoving the pain and tears down. Pulling out the mask of stoicism. Putting the walls back up.

When he stepped back from her, turning his face away, hiding his tortured expression, frustration and desperation surged through her.

Amanda lunged forward, slamming her fists against his chest. "No!" He raised a startled look as she pounded her fists against his chest again. "Don't you dare do that!"

He seized her shoulders, his brow furrowed, confused. "Do what?"

"Retreat into yourself again! Withdraw from me!" She poked his chest hard with a shaking finger. "That emotion from you, your tears, is the most honest you've been with me, ever! It's what I want from you. What I *need* from you. Don't hide it. Not now. Especially not now!"

He stared back at her, clearly stunned by her outburst. "Amanda, I...I don't—"

Curling her fingers into the front of his shirt, she pleaded with her eyes, her tone. "You said *two* babies you loved. Tell me about the other baby. What other baby?"

Beneath her hands, his heartbeat raced, and his breathing grew rapid and shallow. A haunted expression filled his face. "This isn't the time to—"

Her grip tightened on his shirt. "This is the perfect time. Talk to me, Slade. Please. Tell me what happened."

His hands raked through his hair, leaving it disheveled as he tried again to take a step back from her. But she clung to him, knowing somehow he needed her as much as she needed him.

"Slade?"

He dragged in a tremulous breath. "Her name was... Emily." He paused. Swallowed hard. "She was my daughter."

Air froze in Amanda's lungs. Slade had lost a child? She could only imagine the pain she'd feel, the agony if she lost Cheyenne....

He turned bleak eyes to her, clearly struggling to speak. "She was born with a heart defect and...died when she was three weeks old."

Her throat clogged with grief for him, but she rasped, "Oh, Slade...I'm so sorry...."

Tears dampened his eyelashes. "She never left the hospital."

Moisture blurred her vision as she framed his face with her hands and kissed his cheeks. Wrapping him in a hug, she held him close as his shoulders shook, and he released his grief.

"My wife...took it especially hard."

Amanda leaned back to meet his gaze, remembering

he'd said his wife had died, as well. A deep-seated chill settled in her gut. "Slade…no," she whispered, fearing the truth.

"She refused to go to Emily's funeral." His tears dripped down his cheeks, and his face crumpled in torment. The raw pain in his eyes shredded her heart. "When I got home…I found her on our bed."

She shook her head mutely, pain stealing her breath. But he continued, confirming her fears.

"She'd taken a bottle of sleeping pills." His voice broke with grief, but he finished, despite his choked tone. "I was too late to save her."

Amanda murmured an unladylike curse and dragged him into a fierce embrace. She held him, squeezed him hard, both of them shaking. "Slade, I—"

Her cell phone jangled, a perky Christmas tune completely incongruous to the dark moment. Amanda stiffened, then spun to the window sill where she'd left her phone. The screen read Unknown Caller.

Slade was on her heels as she darted over to pick it up. She put the phone on speaker. "Hello?"

"Cheyenne is alive," a mechanically distorted voice said. Amanda's gaze darted to meet Slade's damp eyes. "If you want her to stay that way, her ransom is five million dollars. You have twenty-four hours to get it. I want a hundred thousand in cash, the rest in a cashier's check. You'll get delivery directions later."

"Don't hurt her—" Amanda started, but the screen flashed Call Disconnected.

The cell slipped from her fingers to the carpet and Amanda slumped where she stood, her knees buckling under her. Slade's arm circled her waist before she could drop. As fresh sobs racked her body, he scooped her in his arms to carry her to her bed. For long minutes he stroked her head and back, his body rocking as he comforted her.

Finally, he levered away and thumbed a tear from her cheek. "I'll take your phone to Chief Peters and get them started tracing the call."

With a hiccup, she nodded. "I'll c-call the bank. I don't have that much money, but maybe my d-dad—"

Five million dollars. She prayed Cath was right about Jethro paying the ransom for his own granddaughter. If not…

"Will you be okay if I go?" Slade caressed her cheek, his eyes dark with worry.

When I got home…I found her on our bed.

Her chest gave another squeeze of grief for Slade's losses.

She nodded and touched his face. "I'm hurting, but I'm not a quitter. I'll be here when you get back."

He pressed a kiss to her forehead and pushed off the bed.

"Slade." She caught his hand before he could leave.

He faced her, already shifting into battle mode, his expression grim and determined.

"Thank you…for telling me about your family. About Emily."

A muscle in his jaw twitched as he gritted his teeth, his only outward reaction. For a strained moment he said nothing, then with a jerked nod, he strode toward the hall. Pausing in the door, he glanced back at her. "I will get your daughter back safely, Amanda. I promise. Whatever it takes…I won't let you suffer what I did."

Slade retrieved Amanda's phone on the nursery floor where it had fallen from her hand and headed out to the police station. He'd made it as far as the top of the stairs when an overwhelming fatigue swamped him. He was physically and emotionally drained.

He gripped the newel post at the top of the stairs and bent at the waist, digging deep for his second wind, the energy to face the long hours ahead. Telling Amanda about Emily's too-short life and Krista's suicide had been one of the hardest things he'd ever done. Yet he also felt relieved to have shared it with her, to have someone else sharing his deepest grief and darkest moment. At the same time, knowing Cheyenne was in the hands of kidnappers chilled him to the bone. He couldn't bear the thought of going through the loss of another baby or seeing the fathomless anguish of a dead child in another mother's eyes.

"Slade, are you all right?"

He glanced up to find Catherine and Gray coming up the stairs. Catherine hurried to him as he straightened and gathered his composure. "Yeah. I— The ransom call came in. I'm headed to the police department with Amanda's phone now. She's in her room, if you don't mind staying with her."

Cath nodded. "That's where I'm headed."

"What can I do?" Gray asked.

"Ride with me. We'll talk, plan our next move." Slade started down the stairs, and after giving Cath a kiss goodbye, Gray followed.

Chapter 18

Late that night, Slade returned to the ranch, having met with Chief Peters for hours, discussing their options. The FBI was called in to help, and two agents were slated to arrive tomorrow morning. He headed upstairs to Amanda's suite to report to her, though he hated arriving without good news.

Mathilda Perkins spotted him as he started up the wide stairway to the family quarters and called to him. "Mr. Kent, where are you going?"

"Amanda's suite," he said without stopping.

"Mr. Kent, wait!" Mathilda's tone sharpened. "You're not permitted in the— I said stop!"

"She's expecting me," he said, his jaw tight. He was in no mood for this woman's antiquated policies.

"Mr. Colton has been very clear about the rules for employees," Mathilda protested, dogging his steps as he reached the family quarters, "and he doesn't want—"

"Mathilda, give it a rest. Will you?" a woman said.

Slade glanced up to find Amanda standing in the door of the nursery, glaring at Mathilda. In her arms, Amanda held her long-haired orange cat. She clutched Reyna to her chest like a child might cling to a teddy bear.

Behind him Mathilda gave a hurt-sounding grunt. "Miss Amanda, I'm only trying to look out for you and your family. Your father has always insisted the line between family and employees be strictly enforced."

Amanda sagged visibly. "I know your intentions are good. I'm sorry I snapped. I'm just so worried about Chey—" Her voice cracked, and she squeezed her eyes shut.

Mathilda brushed past Slade and stroked Amanda's back. "I know you are, dear. Can I get you anything? You never ate any dinner. How about a sandwich? A glass of warm milk?"

Amanda shook her head. "No. Thank you." Her gaze found Slade's. "Please tell me you have good news."

His gut clenched. "I wish I could." He glanced at Mathilda, then stepped forward, guiding Amanda into the nursery. "We'll talk in here."

Once the door was closed, he led Amanda to the rocking chair to sit. He gave Reyna a quick scratch on the head before the Manx jumped from her arms and strolled away.

"Tell me everything. Don't try to protect me." Her gold eyes searched his, and the desperation clouding her gaze tugged at him.

"We have no leads yet. No one saw anything, and the ATV tracks led to a mishmash of tracks out in the pasture. No help there. We've called in the Feds to help, though. We will find her."

"I tried to talk to my dad while you were gone about

arranging the ransom, but Levi had just given him a shot of painkiller, and Jethro was asleep." Amanda scowled and growled in frustration and agony. "How could this have happened? I hired a bodyguard for her! I kept her with me as much as possible. And you…" She narrowed an accusing look on him. "You promised to protect her! You said you wouldn't let anything happen to her!"

She thumped a balled fist against his chest, but her recriminations were what cut him. Because she was right. He had failed her, and he'd failed Cheyenne. Pain fisted in his chest. "Amanda, I—"

"Where were you? If you'd been with us, you could have stopped him. You could have saved her!" She was growing hysterical again, and he pulled her close, smoothing his hand down her hair and back.

"God knows, I wish I'd been there. I was in my room, talking to Darla and Tawny."

Amanda jerked back. "Darla and Tawny? Why on earth did you have them in your room?"

"Not my idea. They found me. Insisted we talk in my room for privacy."

Amanda scrunched her nose. "Talk about what?"

"I think Tawny was just there to hit on me."

Amanda scoffed in disgust. "Typical."

"But Darla…" He pulled her close again, tucking Amanda's head under his chin as he held her. "Your stepmother is suspicious of me because I've been asking questions. She recognized my name, saw the photo I have of my dad and began connecting dots. She wasn't happy."

Amanda wiggled free of his hold and glared up at him. "Why would she care what you—" She paused abruptly, her face blanching. "Wait, she sought you out? Insisted on talking to you *then,* in *your room?*"

"Yeah. Why?" But a tickle of suspicion crawled down his spine.

"Doesn't the timing bug you?"

"You think she was purposely distracting me, occupying me while you were attacked and Cheyenne was taken?"

"Makes sense to me!" Her eyes brightened as the theory clearly jelled for her. "She could have sent Trip to take Cheyenne!"

"But why? Why would she risk her position here, the cushy arrangement she has? Where's her motive?"

"Money, of course! Maybe she thinks that with my dad dying her gravy train is about to derail." She stiffened. "And she'd be right about that!"

Slade squeezed her shoulders and shook his head. "Amanda, calm down. You have no evidence—"

"Then I'll get some!" She wrenched free of his hands and stormed toward the door.

"Where are you going?"

"To Darla's suite. I have questions for her."

Slade sighed, following her down the hall. "Amanda, wait. If you charge in there making accusations before the police can interrogate her, you give her a chance to cover her tracks or arrange an alibi or—"

She didn't stop. Amanda marched militantly down the corridor, yanking her arm free when Slade tried again to stop her. "I want her to look me in the eye and tell me the truth. That freeloader is not going to get away with this!"

"Amanda, it's after midnight—"

She banged on Darla's door. "Darla! Tawny! Open up!"

Slade raked his hand through his hair, considered throwing Amanda over his shoulder and carrying her back to her suite. "Amanda, let Chief Peters question her in the morning. I know you're desperate for answers, but this—"

"Ya think?" she snapped at him. "My baby has been kidnapped at gunpoint, and you think I might be desperate for answers?"

Tears had puddled in her eyes again, softening the edge to her voice.

Darla's door opened, and a bleary-eyed Trip glared at her. "What the hell is your problem?"

"Where's Cheyenne?" Amanda demanded, grabbing the front of Trip's pajamas.

"How the hell should I know?" He pried her hands off him and sneered at her.

"You took her!"

"No way! I didn't touch your snot-nosed brat!" Trip growled.

Amanda lunged again, her fingernails bared like cat claws, and Slade caught her around the waist, hauling her back.

Trip tried to slam the door, but Slade stiff-armed the door before it closed. "Where's your mother?"

"Out."

"Out where? When did she leave?"

Trip shrugged. "I don't know."

Slade shot him a hard look. "Think about it."

"I don't know. She and Tawny took off hours ago. An overnight shopping trip or something."

"Shopping?" Amanda shrieked. "My daughter has been kidnapped, and they think it's a good time to go *shopping!"*

Slade pressed a finger to Amanda's lips, then faced Trip. "If you hear from either Darla or Tawny, tell them to get back here immediately. The police need to talk to them. And in the meantime, don't *you* leave town. Everyone on the ranch is to stay put until Cheyenne is returned."

With that, Slade pulled Amanda with him as he headed back toward her suite.

"They're not shopping, Slade." As she stumbled along with him, her fingers gripped his arm, digging deep into his flesh. "They have Cheyenne, and they took her out of town."

"You don't know that."

"Don't I?" She raised wide eyes. Lack of sleep and worry etched lines in her ivory skin. "Darla has always been a greedy, selfish witch. I don't doubt for a minute that she'd stoop to stealing my baby if she thought she'd profit!"

"Look, I'll call Chief Peters and tell him to post a BOLO for her and Tawny, but we have no proof that either of them have anything to do with Cheyenne's kidnapping."

"They could have taken her out of the country! What if they sold her to some black market adoption ring or child pornography ri   "

Slade did the only thing he could think of at that moment to silence her. He kissed her. Deeply. Thoroughly. And in addition to quieting her panicked tirade, he found it help center himself, as well.

When he pulled back from the kiss, she blinked up at him. "Why did you do that?"

"Because I like kissing you." He stroked a hand along her cheek. "And because you were spinning out of control and needed to be reeled back in."

A crease dented the bridge of her nose. "I'm not—"

"You were." Slade rubbed her arms, then pulled her into a hug. "We have absolutely no reason to think Cheyenne's kidnappers are connected to child porn or the black market. Your imagination is running wild, and it serves no purpose but to make you crazy."

She wilted in his arms. "Oh, Slade…this is so hard."

"I know, honey. I know."

She tipped her chin up, and her expression said she understood where his thoughts were. His daughter, his wife.

"Come on." He escorted her to her bedroom and helped her undress and tumble into bed. When he'd stripped off his own jeans, he climbed in next to her and cuddled her against his body. "Now sleep. You'll be better prepared to help us find Cheyenne tomorrow if you get some rest tonight."

She tucked her head under his chin and sighed. "I'll try."

After shifting restlessly for more than an hour, Amanda finally stilled, and her breathing grew deep and slow. Slade tried to sleep, as well, but whenever he closed his eyes, he saw Cheyenne's whale toy lying next to a puddle of Tom Brooks's blood.

He clenched his teeth and held Amanda closer. Despite what he'd told Amanda, he knew if the kidnapper was desperate enough to kill the people around Cheyenne, they had no guarantee the baby was safe. The longer it took to find Cheyenne, the more danger Amanda's daughter would be in.

Chapter 19

The trill of Slade's phone woke them the next morning at dawn. Amanda bolted upright in bed, a suffocating grief and worry swamping her the minute she blinked the world into focus. The previous day's events crashed down on her, and nausea swirled in her belly.

"What d'you have?" he said without preamble as he answered his cell phone.

Amanda pressed her ear close to Slade's, listening to Chief Peters's report.

"Found Darla Colton and Tawny Lowden at a hotel in Jackson. They claim they were planning a day of Christmas shopping. We've brought them back for questioning, but the baby's not with them."

Amanda's heart sank. Cheyenne might not be with her stepmother, but she wasn't ready to write Darla and Tawny off as suspects.

"We'll reassemble the search team and head out again,

but at this point, my bet is the kidnapper has Cheyenne stashed at a motel or safe house somewhere," Chief Peters said. "Our time would probably be better used arranging to get the ransom and setting up a sting to catch the kidnapper at the drop-off."

Slade nodded. "I agree."

Adrenaline flowed through Amanda, wiping away the last wisps of sleep from her brain. She tossed back the covers and dressed hurriedly, energized by purpose.

Slade finished his call with Chief Peters and slid out of bed. "Where are you off to in such a rush?"

"You heard the chief. We need to arrange Cheyenne's ransom. I have part of it in my account, but I need Jethro to cover the rest. I'm going to see if he's awake."

Slade yanked on his jeans and boots and followed her down the hall to Jethro's suite. Amanda knocked but didn't wait for a summons before entering her father's sitting room. Levi was already awake and cradling a mug of coffee as he chatted intimately with Kate. The fragrant plate of fresh croissants on the side table was, no doubt, Kate's excuse to come up to visit her fiancé. Amanda's stomach rumbled, but she shoved aside thoughts of food. How could she think of eating until Cheyenne was safely home?

"Is Dad awake?" she asked Levi.

"He was a few minutes ago."

Kate sent Amanda an anxious frown. "I'm so sorry about Cheyenne. If I can do anything to help, please let me."

Amanda nodded. "Thanks."

She bustled into her father's bedroom, and as it always did in recent weeks, her father's frail form and hollow eyes shocked her anew. Pain shot to her heart. Despite the horrid things she'd learned in California about her father's past, he was still her father, the only parent she had. Despite his flaws, she loved and needed him. Watching her once robust and handsome father fade away was difficult on a good day. Today, with Cheyenne missing, she longed for the security she once knew, having her father in charge and reigning over his ranch like a medieval lord.

A sob caught in her throat as Jethro turned his head to face her. "Amanda. About time you came…to see me again." He drew a slow shallow breath.

"I'm sorry. I've…"

"Been busy." He wheezed as he drew a breath. "I know. I…invented that excuse." Her father's eyes shifted to Slade as he stepped up close behind her, a wall of strength and support.

"Dad…" Amanda sucked in a shaky breath. "The kidnapper struck again. He…he killed Tom Brooks and took Cheyenne."

Jethro's graying eyebrows dipped low in a scowl. "Took Cheyenne?"

Amanda felt panic climbing her throat, and she swallowed hard, determined to keep her composure today in order to help her daughter. "Yes. She was kidnapped yesterday, and they're demanding five million dollars for her return."

Jethro's eyes widened, and he struggled to sit up, not making it before collapsing against his pillows again. "Five million!"

A knot lodged in Amanda's chest, remembering Jethro's cruel refusal to pay the ransom for Trevor Garth's daughter this summer. Though baby Avery had been safely rescued, Amanda still held her father's selfishness against him. Surely he wouldn't refuse to help his own granddaughter, too!

"I have about half of it, but I need your help with the balance. Please, Daddy!" she cried. "For Cheyenne…"

Jethro stared at her, his expression stunned. "Of course I'll pay her ransom. She's my granddaughter!"

Relief poured through Amanda so sweet and strong that her knees buckled. Slade caught her and wrapped her in a firm hug. He gently kissed her hair and murmured, "See, I told you not to worry. We're going to get her back, honey."

Jethro raised a gnarled finger. "What's this? You and the Kent boy…are involved?"

Amanda angled her head toward her father. "The Kent boy? Daddy, he's hardly a *boy*."

"I only mean…" Jethro paused. "I remember his father."

Slade stiffened.

Amanda glanced up at Slade, then back to Jethro. "Yes. His father was the policeman killed on our property ten years ago." She squared her shoulders. "And, yes, I have feelings for Slade. Is that a problem for you?"

Jethro eyed them for long silent seconds. "Doesn't seem as though I have a choice."

Amanda twitched a grin and squeezed Slade's hand. "No. You don't." She drew a deep breath. "The sooner you can arrange for the money to be withdrawn, the better. The kidnappers will be calling soon with directions for a drop."

Jethro nodded, his eyes blazing and more alive than she'd seen them in months. "Consider it done."

Amanda turned and headed out of her father's room, and when Slade tried to follow her, Jethro said, "Mr. Kent, wait. I need…a word with you."

When Amanda hesitated, Slade said, "Go on. I'll catch

up." He turned back to Jethro, stepping closer to the side of the man's bed, meeting his eyes. "Yes?"

Jethro waited for the bedroom door to click shut, then narrowed a keen gaze on Slade. "Well, you heard my daughter," Jethro said slowly, his breath weak. "She has… feelings for you. Deep feelings…judging by the look in her eyes."

Slade rubbed his chest. The familiar gnawing still bit at him but was softened by a gentle warmth when he thought of Amanda. "Yes, sir. I heard her."

"So what are your…feelings toward her? Because if you…hurt my daughter…I'll—"

"I have no intention of hurting Amanda."

"Then you love her?"

Yes. The answer came to him immediately, with no need for debate, but somehow he wasn't ready to admit the truth.

"Amanda is beautiful, intelligent, warm and vibrant and—"

"Hell, boy! I know all that!" Jethro sniped. "She's my…daughter! Answer…the question."

Slade felt a bit like a schoolboy called out for tugging a girl's pigtail. He squared his shoulders. "I care very much for Amanda. And Cheyenne."

Jethro made a face. "Care very much…I have feelings for him," he grumbled under his breath. "Damn youngsters. Don't equivocate. If you…love her, say it!"

"Fine. I love—"

"Not to me!" Jethro scoffed. "Tell her. My daughter… deserves to be happy."

"I agree."

"Good." Jethro jerked a nod and closed his eyes wearily.

Taking Jethro's silence as a dismissal, Slade turned to leave.

"It was an accident," Jethro said darkly.

Slade hesitated, faced Jethro again. "What was an accident?"

Jethro opened his eyes, and the anguish and guilt in his expression made Slade's pulse ramp into high gear.

"If you're going to…have a future with my daughter—" Jethro drew a slow ragged breath "—you should know the truth."

Slade's hands balled at his sides, struggling for patience. "What truth?"

"It was me," Jethro whispered, then coughed and said louder, "It was me. I shot your father."

Slade's gut pitched, and fury flooded him like a tide of hot lava. *"What?"*

"I thought he was…an intruder. I've made a lot of enemies in my life, some who…settle their business with a bullet in the brain. I never meant…to kill anyone."

"You murdered my father?"

"Not murder. It was an accident…."

"That you failed to report. You even covered it up by taking evidence from the scene." His volume rose as all the implications sharpened in his mind. "You pried the bullet out of the fencepost, then left my father's body lying there—"

"I panicked. I had too much at stake," Jethro said, his voice stronger than it had been moments earlier.

In his peripheral vision, Slade saw Levi step into the room, clearly concerned by the shouting.

"Like being discovered as a fraud? Having the world learn your firstborn child was never kidnapped. That, instead, you *gave him away!*"

"What?" Levi asked, his voice heavy with disgust.

"How…where did you hear that?" Jethro asked. "Did Darla tell you?"

Slade took a second to absorb that question. "Darla *knew* you gave Cole away?" Slade asked, stunned.

"I…yes. And…she knew I killed your father."

Beside him, Slade heard Levi mumble a curse.

Jethro looked away, grumbling, "She's been holding it over me for…years now. Blackmailing me. That's why she…and her brats still live…on my ranch. The *only* reason." He scoffed. "But not anymore. Now that…you know the truth, she has nothing…that can hurt me or my family."

"As if you ever cared how any of this would hurt your family," Levi scoffed, then turned to Slade. "You said he gave Cole away. How did you find out?"

Slade explained briefly about visiting Breen and learning about the hush money, Jethro's association with organized crime and his distant relationship to the former president.

"Breen had no right…to tell you any of that. We had a deal!" Jethro grumbled.

"After Amanda left with Cheyenne," Slade continued, undeterred by Jethro's glare, "Breen said he came to Dead River to check up on Jethro and saw him hand over a baby to a woman in the parking lot of the motel late one night. The next morning the news was full of reports Cole had been kidnapped."

A gasp drew everyone's attention to the bedroom door. Amanda stared back at Slade, her face pale.

Slade's heart sunk. He hadn't wanted her to find out this way. Hadn't wanted her to find out at all if he could have protected her from the truth…. "Amanda, I—"

"Is it true?" she rasped. But her gaze was no longer on

Slade. She held the door frame and stared at her father, shaking. "Did you give Cole away? Kill Slade's father? Lie to all of us all these years?"

Jethro held his daughter's gaze, his breathing more labored and wheezy than before. "Amanda, I can... explain."

"No! You can't explain away thirty years of lies! You can't explain away the fact that you got rid of your own son like so much garbage. That you murdered a man and covered it up. No deathbed confession or last-minute feigned affection for your family can make up for the years of hurt you've caused! It's...unforgivable!" Her voice broke and tears rolled down her cheeks. Slade took a step toward her, and she threw up a hand. "No. You knew about this and didn't tell me."

"I wanted to verify—"

"Save it." She jerked a harsh glare back to her father. "You are dead to me, old man. I want nothing to do with you, your lies or your dirty money ever again!"

With that, she whirled around and nearly knocked Darla and Chief Peters over as they arrived at Jethro's door.

Slade started to follow Amanda, but Chief Peters grabbed his arm. "Hey, Kent, I need you to take charge of Ms. Colton here. Question her, take her statement. The department is slammed following up on the tips coming in about Cheyenne's kidnapping."

"I—" Slade glanced past the chief, down the hall where Amanda had disappeared. She was probably in no mood to talk to him, and he had a job to do. "Sure. I'll do it."

With a tip of his hat, Chief Peters left Darla with him.

"What's all this about?" she asked. "I had nothing to do with Amanda's kid disappearing!"

"But you have, for the past several years, concealed your knowledge that Jethro Colton shot and killed my father, a police officer, and that he hid evidence of that crime." Slade narrowed a menacing glare on Darla. "Am I right?"

Her father had given Cole away, had lied about it for years. Numb and cold to the core, Amanda sat in her solarium and stared blankly ahead. How could he be so unloving, so despicably deceitful? The man who'd taught her to ride a horse, had encouraged her to pursue veterinary school and had given her a diamond solitaire necklace when Cheyenne was born couldn't have thrown away his own son. Could he?

Of course he could. Because the same man had been a distant, demanding father. Those horseback lessons had been grueling, with Jethro expecting perfection. Veterinary school had satisfied Jethro's wish to have a full-time vet on the ranch. The diamond necklace had been his attempt to assuage his conscience over not visiting her in the hospital. Not meeting his first grandchild—in fact—for almost a week. Because he didn't care, Amanda admitted to herself after months, years, of making excuses for her father.

Amanda, I can explain...

Reyna brushed against her shins and, absently, Amanda reached down to pat her. After a few more minutes of stewing, the scene across from her came into focus. The nativity. Seeing the baby Jesus in the manger sent a fresh stab of pain through her.

She missed Cheyenne. Was worried sick about her. Ached for her.

Plucking the figure of the Christ baby from the manger, she squeezed the figure in her hand, a sob rising in her throat. *Please, God, keep my baby safe! Bring her back to me!*

Suddenly the room seemed to close in on her. She couldn't breathe. Needed air.

Still clutching the baby figurine in her hand, she bolted from the room and raced down the back stairs, nearly knocking Mathilda over in the process. She burst through the door and staggered out into the icy morning, gulping in the cold air. Without any conscious intent, she wandered toward the storage building where Cheyenne had been kidnapped. When she reached the outbuilding, she stood in the open door, staring into the dark storage room.

"Miss Amanda?"

She spun around to find Mathilda watching her.

"Are you all right, dear?"

"No." Amanda dissolved into tears. Though Mathilda had always been pleasant and kind to her, Amanda had never considered her especially maternal. Faye Frick, her nanny growing up, or Hilda had always filled the mother role when Amanda or her sisters needed a woman's comfort or advice. But Faye had been murdered in July, and Hilda was somewhere in the ranch house busy with her duties. The sympathetic look on Mathilda's face reached out to Amanda. And she needed a motherly hug and guidance more than ever.

Throwing herself into Mathilda's arms, she clung to the head housekeeper and sobbed. "Everything is falling apart. My whole world..." She drew a ragged breath. "Cheyenne's been kidnapped, everyone around me keeps getting killed, and...and my father..."

Mathilda patted her back awkwardly. "I know, Miss Amanda. It's hard to see your father die."

Amanda levered back, shaking her head. "No, it's worse than that. He— He's a murderer!"

Mathilda blinked, her body stiffening. "What?"

"Ten years ago…Dad's the one who killed Slade's father! I overheard him admit it to Slade and Levi. And… there's more."

The housekeeper gripped Amanda's arms, clearly stunned by these revelations. "What else did he say?"

"Cole was never kidnapped," she said, then swallowed hard as grief tightened her throat. "My father gave his own son away and lied about it to the police. It was all a big cover-up! Darla knew and used the truth to blackmail him. That's why he lets her and her horrible kids live here!"

"He what?" Mathilda frowned, shock making her complexion pale.

"What will Slade think of me now?"

Mathilda furrowed her brow. "Slade?"

"I think I…I love him. But my father murdered his dad!" she sobbed, stepping close to embrace Mathilda again and bury her face in the housekeeper's coat. "How can he get past that?"

"That is…big. I, uh—" Mathilda patted her back.

"I had enough to deal with today arranging the ransom money to save Cheyenne from the kidnappers. But now my father has apparently decided that he needs to confess all his sins on his deathbed." She leaned back again and swiped moisture from her eyes. "Did you know my dad had connections to organized crime? That he took hush money from a political slush fund and used it to buy this ranch? His entire fortune was built with tainted money!"

"Miss Amanda, I—"

"I know." She sighed and backed a step away from the housekeeper. "You think I should keep family business to myself and not be dumping all this on you. I'm sorry... I just...needed to vent. Needed someone to listen." Another rush of tears spilled from her eyes and she shivered in the icy air. She wished Aurora were here. Never had she felt so alone, so out of sorts....

"No, Miss Amanda, it's fine. Clearly you needed to get things off your chest." Mathilda opened her arms again, and with a sad smile, Amanda hugged her back.

"Thanks for understanding. I don't really know what else he said. I'd gone back to my suite long enough to arrange for the ransom money to be withdrawn from my father's and my accounts and brought here to the ranch."

She felt Mathilda flinch. "The money is being brought here? Today?"

Amanda nodded, sobering a bit. "I guess I need to stop blubbering over all the ways my father has betrayed my family and arrange for Chief Peters to escort the bank employee with the cash."

As Amanda pulled away from the housekeeper's comforting embrace, her watch clasp snagged on the high collar of Mathilda's uniform. "Uh-oh. I'm snagged. I'm sorry." She used her free hand to try to unhook the catch without tearing the fabric of Mathilda's collar. "Hold on. I can—"

She stopped, spying three long scratches low on Mathilda's neck. Amanda froze, flashing back to her struggle with the masked person in the holding pen ten days earlier. "I— Mathilda, where...where did you get these scratches?"

The housekeeper tensed and snapped a sharp look at her. "What?"

"You have scratches on your neck. How—?"

But the flash of guilt that crossed the housekeeper's

face, followed quickly by a cold, hateful glare, answered for her.

Amanda shuddered, stunned. "Mathilda?"

The woman who'd taken care of her family since before she was born grabbed Amanda's wrist and yanked it free of the snag at her collar. "You gave me those scratches when you fought me in the cow pen!"

Chapter 20

"That…that was *you?*" Amanda sputtered, too startled by the revelation to think clearly. "How… Why… You shot at me!" She straightened her back as rage filled her. "You tried to take Cheyenne!"

"Correction, I *took* Cheyenne! Maybe not then, but I have her now, don't I?" Mathilda gave a smug grin that sent shivers down Amanda's back. "Well, Jared is the one who actually snatched her, but he did it on my orders." She sent Amanda a self-satisfied grin.

Amanda shook from the inside out. "Where? Where is she?" She grabbed at Mathilda's coat. "Give her back!"

Mathilda wrenched Amanda's hand from her coat and flung it away. "Don't worry. She's safe. For now…"

Betrayal, horror and anger coalesced in a hot pool in her gut. "*Why?* For God's sake, Mathilda! Why would you want to take my daughter?"

Mathilda snorted. "For the money, of course. Five million dollars in ransom, remember? Although now I'm thinking I should ask for more. How about ten million?"

"But you've worked at the ranch for years! We trusted you. You were like family to us!"

"Bull!" she snapped. "You high and mighty Coltons always thought you were better than anyone else. Jethro thought he breathed rarified air, and he lorded his money over the staff. But as you've discovered, your sainted father was nothing but a fraud. A low-life liar. A cheating, dishonest criminal who took advantage of people and didn't care whom he hurt to make his millions."

A sharp ache sliced Amanda to the bone. She wanted desperately to defend her father and deny the harsh claims Mathilda made, but she couldn't. She had learned on her own that her father was everything Mathilda accused him of being.

The housekeeper's eyes narrowed to slits. "I stood by him when even his slutty wives didn't. And how did he thank me? Brushing me aside like common trash. Treating me like a second-class citizen only good enough for the occasional tumble in his sheets, then sent away to wait on him hand and foot."

Amanda shook her head as if to clear it. Mathilda and her father had had an affair? She could believe it of her womanizing father, but Mathilda was so straight-laced and starchy and... Amanda braced a hand against the wall of the storage building for support.

"I could have made him happy, you know. But for my loyalty, he gave me nothing but a cold shoulder. He treated me like trash!" Bitterness filled Mathilda's voice, and her lips pursed.

"But I never treated you that way! I loved you like family. I never took you or any of the staff for granted..."

She swallowed hard. "And Cheyenne...my daughter is an innocent! How could you do this to her?"

Mathilda grunted and straightened her back. "Given time, she'll grow up just as spoiled and pampered as the rest of your lot."

The woman's posture was hard and unyielding. Amanda knew she wasn't going to change Mathilda's mind here and now. Clearly the housekeeper's resentment—including her plan to extort money from Jethro as some type of revenge—had festered for a long time.

Amanda's mind reeled, and her emotions were so convoluted and suffocating, she didn't know where to begin sorting out the horrible truths she was learning today.

Her father had coldly given Cole, her *brother,* away. Lied to everyone for years. Allowed Darla to blackmail him. Mathilda had been her father's lover. Had nurtured a hatred toward her family. Had conspired to kidnap Cheyenne for the ransom....

Cheyenne! Everything else fell away in an instant. Mathilda had Cheyenne!

An iron will and blazing purpose swept through Amanda. She locked a steely stare on Mathilda and seized the lapels of the woman's coat again. "Give me back my daughter! *Now!*"

"Not until you pay the ransom." Mathilda leaned close, sticking her nose right in Amanda's face. "Not until Jethro pays for all the pain he's caused me for thirty years!"

Gritting her teeth, Amanda tightened her grip. She shook with rage and horror. "I want Cheyenne back now! Take me to her!"

"No," Mathilda snarled back.

With her heartbeat thundering in her ears, Amanda tried to sort out her thoughts, to tamp her roiling emotions long enough to think logically.

Slade. She didn't want to analyze why his name came to her above all other options, but having him at her side now, relying on him to help her in this moment of crisis, felt right. Fated.

Stepping back from Mathilda, she dropped her hands from the housekeeper's coat and fumbled in her pocket for her cell phone. Her hands shook from the cold, from the rush of adrenaline pumping through her veins.

"What are you doing?"

"Calling Slade, then the police. I won't let you get away with—"

With a swift slap, Mathilda knocked the phone from Amanda's frozen, trembling hand. As soon as it clattered on the storage building floor, the older woman stomped it into a useless heap.

Amanda saw red. She was about to launch herself onto Mathilda, ripping into her like a wildcat, with fingernails and teeth and anything else she could find. But as she tensed her muscles to strike, Mathilda startled her again.

"Fine. You want to see your daughter? I'll take you to her."

Amanda stilled. "You will?"

Joy and relief coursed through her, an instinctive reaction to Mathilda's offer....

Until she noticed the scheming look in Mathilda's eyes. Amanda hesitated, her brain scrambling. Why would Mathilda have such an abrupt change of heart? What was Amanda missing? Could it really be so easy, that Mathilda would give up and take her to Cheyenne?

Her heart galloped, thrashing against her ribs with almost painful urgency. She had to find Cheyenne. If there was any chance...

"Sure. I'll take you to her now." Mathilda grabbed

Amanda's wrist in a viselike grip, and the first wings of panic fluttered in her chest.

"Wait! I want Slade to come with us." Amanda struggled, trying to pull her arm free.

"Fat chance of that," Mathilda cackled and headed out of the storage building with Amanda in tow.

Mixed emotions battled for dominance as Amanda stumbled behind Mathilda. The icy wind blasted her when they stepped outside, as if to warn her against venturing farther with the older woman. Shivering, Amanda dug her heels into the snow, fighting the woman's grip. "No, wait!"

"Don't you want to see your baby?" Mathilda's grin bordered on a sneer and boded ill.

"Of course. But I—" Amanda cast a frantic glance around the ranch yard.

Empty. Still. Even the animals were safely ensconced in warm shelter. Her breath clouded as she gasped shallow, panicked breaths. Despite all her doubts about Mathilda's intent, how could she pass up even the tiniest chance that Mathilda might truly take her to Cheyenne? Her mental battle continued as the older woman yanked hard on her arm, her grip like a shackle. In her indecision and confusion, Amanda allowed herself to be dragged several steps through the snow. Away from the main house. Away from help. Away from Slade.

"Help!" she shouted, praying someone, anyone, would hear. "Someone help me!"

A palm cracked against her cheek, stinging all the more because of the icy cold. "Shut up! Keep your mouth shut and come with me." Mathilda's glare was glacial, cruel. And soberingly serious.

Warning bells screamed in Amanda's head. *You can't help Cheyenne if you're dead....*

"No! Bring her here. To me." Again she fought to free herself.

Mathilda's face crumpled with malice. "I'm in charge now, missy. You do what I say if you want your brat to live!"

Ice raced through Amanda's blood. "Don't you dare hurt her!"

"Then come with me," Mathilda grated. "Quietly!"

Amanda stumbled behind the woman she'd considered family, the friendly face she'd never suspected could harbor such hatred for her family. A strange elixir of hope that she would really be taken to Cheyenne and fear that she was walking into a deadly trap swirled inside her. Mathilda squeezed Amanda's wrist so hard, her hand grew numb. The farther they walked away from the main house, the ranch yard and the people who could help her, the more worried Amanda became. Finally she recognized where Mathilda was leading her, and a fresh wave of betrayal swept through her.

The Blacks' cabin. Was the old couple in on the kidnapping? Were they part of a conspiracy to extort money from the family?

Mathilda paused on the front step of the small shack and peered in a front window. Then without knocking, she opened the door and poked her head inside. "Horace? Bernice?"

When no reply came, Mathilda shoved her way inside and pushed Amanda into the cabin's main room. The cabin was still and silent except for the loud ticking of a clock over the small fireplace. Amanda had the passing thought that such a loud ticking would drive her nuts…and remembered that both of the elderly Blacks were hard of hearing and probably didn't even hear the annoying ticking.

She faced Mathilda, her hands balled at her sides. "All right. Where is she? Where's Cheyenne?"

Mathilda crossed to the kitchen table, pulled out a chair, rolled back a small throw rug under the table and lifted a section of the wood plank floor. Amanda goggled at what she was seeing. A trapdoor? She'd had no idea...

Mathilda pointed down into the dark hole below. "You first."

Holding her breath, Amanda sidled over to peer into the inky darkness. And heard a muffled whimper. Her heart jumped. "Cheyenne?"

"Maaa!" a tiny voice wailed.

"Cheyenne!" Amanda scrambled under the table and into the hole, finding a ladder against one wall.

Mathilda followed her down the ladder, closing the trapdoor behind them. As she descended, the house-keeper flipped a switch which lit a bare light bulb that dangled from the ceiling of the cellar pit.

At the bottom of the ladder, Amanda turned and searched the small room frantically. She took in the two wooden chairs and shelves of canned foods, blankets, batteries that lined the walls, but her interest was only in finding Cheyenne. Had she been tricked?

"Where is she?"

Mathilda stepped over to one of the shelving units and pulled on it. It swung open like a door, revealing a dark tunnel.

In the dim glow from the bare light bulb, Amanda spotted an old, shabby playpen. Cheyenne stood in the playpen, clinging to the side rail. When Cheyenne spotted her mother, she loosed a loud cry and reached for Amanda. "Maaa!"

"Oh, baby girl!" Amanda started toward the tunnel, only to have Mathilda step in her path. With a gun.

Mathilda aimed the weapon at Amanda's heart. "I took you to her. I didn't say you got to hold her."

Amanda stared at the gun, her anxiety climbing. "Wh-where did you get that?" She was certain Mathilda hadn't had the gun in the storage building or she'd have used it to threaten her.

"The Blacks aren't the only ones who store things down here. Didn't you ever wonder why the cops could never find the gun that shot Jenny Burke or that fired at you in the holding pen?"

Amanda swallowed hard as a lot of things from the past months began to make sense. "It was your gun the whole time. You hid it here."

"Exactly. Along with the .45 I took from Chief Drucker during one of our—" she gave a smug grin "—late-night interludes."

Amanda quickly processed this new tidbit. "You and Chief Drucker had an affair?"

Her grin spread. "Poor shmuck was in love with me. He'd do anything I asked. Sleeping with him was a small price to wield that kind of influence over the chief of police."

Amanda's gut rolled. How could she and her family have been so blind to Mathilda's manipulation and cold ambition? The woman had hidden her secret life well, given Oscar-worthy performances, pretending to care about the family, the ranch.

Now Mathilda took another gun, a bigger one, from a shelf and showed it to Amanda before she stuck it in her coat pocket. "Jared preferred using the .45, and it has the bonus of matching the weapon the police use, since it was Drucker's." She chuckled. "Which confused the poor fools plenty when that snooping reporter, Jagger what's-his-face, was here this summer. When I needed

Jared to handle a job, he came and collected one of the guns, then hid it again here."

Cheyenne continued crying, her distress breaking Amanda's heart. "Please, let me pick her up. Comfort her."

"No. Crying never hurt a kid."

"But—"

"No!" Mathilda stretched the gun toward Amanda.

Raising her palms, Amanda tried to pacify the housekeeper. "Okay. Okay…" *Get her to talk. Fill in more of the blanks.* "So the Blacks are in on this with you?"

Mathilda scoffed. "Hardly. Those old geezers have no use for money. They wouldn't live like this if they weren't perfectly content with this lifestyle. Old Horace has a small fortune sitting in the bank he never touches."

She blinked. "He does?"

"Most of it was his father's money. His old pop got rich selling moonshine during prohibition. This tunnel goes all the way to the basement of the main house. It was built as a secret escape route in case the police came after Pop Black during prohibition. The Reverend Horace and holier-than-thou Bernice are ashamed of that legacy and never speak of it. While they still use the root cellar as a doomsday shelter—yes, the idiots believe all that end-of-times nonsense and these are their supplies." She waved the nongun hand at the shelves of food and dry goods. "But they never use the tunnel…on principle. Because of its immoral original use." She gave a gloating grin. "Which served my purposes. I found the tunnel quite by accident several years ago and never told anyone."

"My father doesn't know about the tunnel?"

The housekeeper scoffed. "Of course not. No one does besides me, the Blacks…and now Jared, since he had to have a way to disappear, a way to hide the gun from the cops." She gave a quick glance behind her at Cheyenne. "And a place to stash your kid while we waited for the ransom."

"How could all of this have happened under the Blacks' noses…under their *table*…without them finding out?" Amanda shook her head, baffled.

"As deaf as those two old birds are? Ha! Easy." Mathilda shrugged. "And we always planned our attacks to coincide with the Blacks' work hours. They keep a routine, entirely predictable schedule. They never knew anything about what was happening right below their feet." Mathilda's expression was pure self-satisfaction, and her gloating fueled the disgust and anger that writhed in Amanda's gut.

Cheyenne's wails continued, and Amanda couldn't take it any longer. Daring Mathilda to defy her, she strode boldly toward the playpen.

"Stop!" Mathilda shrieked.

"My daughter needs me!"

An earsplitting gunshot echoed through the dark cellar, and a jar of preserved green beans shattered near Amanda's head. Cheyenne's plaintive whines became a frightened cry. Amanda's heart raced, and she raised a wary look to Mathilda.

"The next bullet goes in the baby's head, if you don't do exactly as I tell you."

Amanda shook all over. "You're insane."

"Not insane. Just sick to death of bowing and scraping for you Coltons. Now it is my turn to be rich, to have people do my bidding." She waved the gun in Amanda's face. "Starting with you. Go sit in that chair and put your hands behind you."

Amanda didn't move. Her thoughts spun wildly as

she tried to think of a way to get the gun from Mathilda and rescue Cheyenne.

"Now!" Mathilda roared, stepping closer to the play-pen and waving the gun toward the chair again.

Much as she despised the idea of capitulating, Amanda couldn't risk anything that would rile Mathilda or give her cause to shoot Cheyenne. Numb with fear for her child, Amanda eased back to the wooden chair and sat down. With one hand still holding the gun, Mathilda took a rope from one of the shelves and slid the pre-made lasso loop around Amanda's wrists. She tightened the loop, pinning Amanda's hands together, then wrapping the rope around Amanda and the chair several times before securing her feet. When Amanda was tied, Mathilda walked over to the playpen.

Icy terror flashed through Amanda. A cold sweat beaded on her lip. "Stay away from her! I did what you asked! Don't hurt her. *Please!*" she sobbed.

Mathilda scoffed and stashed the gun in her pocket. "A dead baby won't bring a ransom, now will it?"

Relief made Amanda wilt against the chair.

"You, on the other hand, are a different matter," Mathilda said as she lifted Cheyenne in her arms and headed deeper into the dark tunnel. "I can't let you live now that I've shared my secrets with you. No, my dear, once I have that ransom money, you are expendable."

Chapter 21

"You *told* them?" Darla screeched, stomping closer to Jethro's bed. "Are you crazy? You'll be charged with murder!"

"Not crazy...dying." Jethro's eyes narrowed on his ex-wife. "Only crazy to let you stay...on my ranch...all these years. Holding this over me..." He drew a wheezing breath, his glare fiery. "No more. Get out! You and your lazy kids. I want you...off my ranch!"

"You can't do that!" Darla drew herself up, lifting her chin to a haughty angle. "I'll tell everyone what you did! Even if it's too late to charge you with the murder, your reputation will be ruined!"

Slade gritted his teeth as the woman's high-pitched whine scraped through him. What had Jethro ever seen in this harpy? "Perhaps you should be more worried about being charged as an accessory for withholding knowledge of a murder and false kidnapping allegations," Slade said, narrowing a glare on Darla.

"What? But I didn't do—"

"Exactly. You had a legal and moral obligation to report what you knew about my father's murder. And you chose to stay silent for personal gain." Slade balled a fist. If Darla weren't a woman... "You disgust me."

She raised her chin and sniffed haughtily. "How dare you talk to me like that! You're nothing but a ranch hand. It'll be my word against yours. No one will believe—"

"Actually, I'm a Wyoming Bureau of Investigation agent, working here undercover to find my father's murderer and solve the open investigations from the past months."

Darla gasped. Jethro sighed and closed his eyes in resignation.

"You're what?" Levi asked.

Slade glanced quickly to Levi. "I'm sorry to have deceived you. I needed to protect my cover to root out the truth."

"Does...Amanda know?" Jethro asked hoarsely.

Slade jerked a nod. "She's been working with me to find answers to a lot of questions. Things are finally beginning to make sense. The pieces are lining up." From the corner of his eye, he saw Darla edging toward the door. "Hold it, Ms. Colton. I'm not through with you." He stepped over to Darla and pinned her with a hard stare. "What do you know about Cheyenne's kidnapping?"

"Nothing!" Darla's face flushed red, and her hand fluttered at her throat. "I was shopping with Tawny. Ask the police chief! Didn't he just bring me back from there?"

"A convenient alibi. You could have had Trip take her with plans to share the ransom money."

"Trip will have to answer for himself. I don't know

what he may or may not be involved with. But I did not touch that baby!"

Darla's shrill voice grated Slade's already frayed nerves. Amanda's hurt expression as she'd stormed out moments ago knifed through him. He needed to catch up with Amanda. Darla would keep.

"I swear, I had nothing to do with—"

Slade aimed a finger at Darla as he stalked for the door. "Don't leave the house. You're under arrest as an accessory to murder. Levi, watch her."

"No! You can't—" she yelped, but Slade didn't stick around to argue.

He hurried to Amanda's suite and knocked. Got no answer.

"Amanda?" He opened the door, searched the solarium, bedroom, bathroom. Empty.

The stable? Maybe she'd gone out to be with the animals she loved.

He raced down the back staircase, taking the steps three at a time and snagging his coat as he trotted past the employee coatrack. As he stepped outside into the frigid air, he sent a searching glance around the empty ranch yard. Would she have ridden out in the pastures to think?

He hurried across the yard to the stable and burst through the alley doors. "Amanda!" He headed first to Prince William's stall. Amanda's horse tossed his mane and snuffled at Slade. He patted the gelding's nose while he sent a glance around the other stalls. "Amanda?"

George strolled out of the tack room and gave a nod. "Howdy, Slade. What's up?"

"Have you seen Amanda?"

The hand knitted his brow. "Naw. She hasn't been in here. But I did hear someone hollering earlier, sounded a little like her. I thought it was just someone playing around, though. Sounded like it came from down by the petting barn or the storage building."

The storage building. Where Cheyenne was snatched. Slade's chest tightened. "Thanks," he called as he dashed out of the stable and ran toward the far end of the ranch grounds.

"Amanda!" He skidded to a stop, slipping on the icy ground, when he reached the door of the storage building. "Amanda!" No one was around, but tracks in the snow cleared indicated someone *had* been there.

Spotting something dark in the snow, he crouched to pick up the small object, bringing it up close to study it. His heart thumped when he recognized it—the baby Jesus from the nativity set in Amanda's room. What was it doing out here? Was someone trying to send a message about Cheyenne? He tried to remember if the figure had been missing this morning when they woke.

Shoving the Jesus figure into his pocket, he followed the tracks in the snow with his gaze. Some of the footprints were messier than others, more elongated, as if the person who made them had dragged her feet. Or resisted being led away.

Adrenaline spiking, Slade traced the path made by the two sets of footprints, jogging through the snow. The trail ended at the small cabin where he'd found Jethro's stallion, Midnight, wandering after Amanda's attacker had used the horse to escape. Slade had searched the cabin then and not found anyone there. Had he missed something?

Now, he stepped onto the small weather-beaten porch and knocked. Amanda had said the cabin belonged to the old couple who worked as the laundry lady and handyman. When no one answered the door, he tried the knob and found the cabin unlocked. Letting himself in, he called, "Hello? Mr. Black? Mrs. Black?"

Nothing.

"Amanda?" Then louder, "Amanda!"

"Help!"

The muffled cry seemed to come from below him. He glanced around the small cabin again, confused, searching for a stairway or door he'd missed. "Amanda? Where are you?"

"In the cellar!" Amanda's distant voice cried. She said something else, but muffled as her voice was, he only made out "trap."

He stiffened, his senses on full alert. Had he been duped into coming here for Amanda? He scoped the cabin again, paying particular attention to places a person could hide, waiting to jump him. He cursed himself for bolting from the house without stopping in his room for his gun. If someone had set a trap for him, he was unarmed and at a disadvantage.

"Slade!"

Following the sound of Amanda's voice, he moved across the room—wary, tensed, ready. "Where are you?" he repeated.

"Under the table!"

He frowned at the simple wooden table in the center of the floor, dropping to his knees to examine the wood planked floor. On closer examination, he noticed light shining through a knothole in one of the planks. Squinting through the hole in the floor, he could make out shelves and jars of vegetables. *Trap...*

Trap*door!* He poked his finger in the hole and lifted. The flooring opened to a pit, complete with a homemade ladder. "Amanda?"

"Down here! Hurry, Slade. She took Cheyenne!" The panic in Amanda's voice was unmistakable.

Slade scrambled down the ladder, and his pulse jumped when he found Amanda tied up on a rickety chair in the corner of the cellar.

"Good God! Are you hurt?" he asked, hurrying to her.

"No. I—I'm okay."

He framed her face between his hands and pressed a desperate kiss to her mouth. "When I saw the signs of a scuffle in the snow, I was so scared I'd be too late. I couldn't stand losing you."

She hiccuped a sob, nodding her understanding of his fear. "You found me in time, but…Mathilda has Cheyenne! She took her that way—" she jerked her chin, motioning across the cellar "—down that tunnel."

"Tunnel?" Slade paused to look over his shoulder. "I'll be damned. Where does it go?" He turned back to Amanda. "And what does Mathilda have to do with all of this?"

He started working the knots that bound her.

"Everything! She's the mastermind behind all the terrible things that have happened!" As Slade finished untying the ropes binding her hands, Amanda recapped everything she'd learned from the head housekeeper.

"And you never had a hint of her duplicity?" But even as he asked, Slade admitted the housekeeper had fooled him, too.

Amanda bit her bottom lip and shook her head. "No. Apparently, she's a grand actress. She's played her part well for years. If anyone caught on to her act or got in her way, she killed them…or had her minion kill for her."

"Her minion?"

"First Duke, then when he screwed up and got caught,

she went after Jared. Chief Drucker was also under her spell apparently. She said they'd had an affair."

"The former police chief? The one they found was crooked and who hanged himself?" Slade finished freeing her hands and rubbed her chafed wrists between his hands.

"The same." She furrowed her brow in consternation. "But his suicide should be investigated. I bet she had a hand in it. To keep him from talking."

Slade bent to untie her feet, considering these revelations. "If she was willing to reveal so much to you, she clearly feels she's won. That this whole thing she has planned is coming to an end."

Amanda leaned forward to help him with the knots at her ankles. "She said she'd be back to kill me once she had the ransom money."

Her fingers were shaking, and Slade wrapped her cold hands in his. "That's not going to happen on my watch. We're going to find her and Jared and finish this, once and for all."

Amanda raised damp eyes. "She has Cheyenne. What if she gets the money and still kills my baby?"

Slade kissed her hard, again. "I *will not* let that happen. I swear." Clenching his back teeth, he finished pulling the rope away from Amanda's legs and helped her to her feet. "Let's go get your daughter back."

Chapter 22

"Where is Jared Hansen?" Slade demanded as he stormed into the stable where several of the hands were returning from the pastures and finishing the morning chores.

He'd taken Amanda back to the main house and left her in Kate McCord's and her sisters' care. Kate was practically forcing hot tea down Amanda's throat to warm her up. After Slade had called Chief Peters and explained the turn of events to Trevor and Gray, the two men joined him in mounting a search for the missing head house-keeper, her lackey and their tiny hostage.

Cal Clark gave Slade a considering look, then shrugged. "Jared got a text message a few minutes ago and lit out of here like his tail was on fire."

"He didn't say what the text was about or where he was headed?" Trevor asked.

"Nope," George replied, "but he took an ATV and headed toward the north pasture. Why?"

"We now know that he's the one behind many of the kidnappings and violent attacks over the last several months," Trevor said. "He's been working with Mathilda since he got here, and they're on the run."

"Wait. Mathilda? The housekeeper?" Stewie said and laughed. "Is this some kind of joke?"

"No joke." Slade sent the hand a hard, silencing glare. "The details are too long to get into now, but Mathilda attacked Amanda this morning and tied her up. She confessed to having plotted everything before she disappeared again with Cheyenne."

"God help me," Cal snarled and made a fist, "if those two hurt little Cheyenne, I'll break every bone in their bodies!"

"Get in line," Slade growled, then addressed the group. "Chief Peters and his officers are on the way, along with agents from the FBI who have been working the kidnapping case with the police."

"Seriously? *Ms. Perkins* is behind everything?" Stewie said, his expression baffled.

Slade narrowed his gaze on the stunned hand. "Let's focus here. This thing's coming to a head, and I need all of you to help."

Stewie sobered and gave a stiff nod.

Slade aimed a finger at him. "Stewie, I want you to wait here for Peters and his men. When they get here, have them follow you out to the north pasture on ATVs, unless we radio with new orders."

Stewie nodded. "All right."

Slade pointed to George. "Saddle my horse and yours." He moved his aim to Cal. "You take the last ATV out. Gray, saddle up. You can ride with me. Trevor, I want you to drive a Jeep around via the county road and cut off that escape route. If you have weapons, take them, but don't—"

Slade stopped short when his cell phone rang. He glanced at the number and froze. "It's Jared." He motioned for quiet before answering the call. "Jared, it's not too late for you to give yourself up."

"It's not Jared, Mr. Kent," a woman at the other end of the connection said. "It's Mathilda Perkins. Listen carefully, and do exactly as I say."

Slade tensed. "Ms. Perkins, what have you—"

"I said *listen!*" she snapped. "I'll do the talking, and you'll do what I tell you, if you want Cheyenne Colton back alive."

"If you hurt that baby girl, I'll—"

"Yes, yes. I know that you've fallen for Amanda and her daughter, and they're important to you. That's why I called you. I knew Amanda was a little…tied up right now." She chuckled at her own joke. "So it falls to you to bring me the ransom money that I know is being delivered to the house."

"How—"

She cut him off with a scolding, "Ahn, ahn, ahn!"

Slade gritted his teeth and let the woman continue, holding the phone out so that Trevor and Gray, who were nearest him, could hear, as well.

"I know you are more than just a ranch foreman, and even now you are probably calculating and working on a plan to trap me when you deliver the ransom. But hear me well, Mr. Kent. I'm not with Cheyenne anymore. Jared has her, and he has instructions to kill her if even one thing goes wrong."

Slade tried to mask the gut-wrenching fear that spiraled through him at the thought of Jared hurting Cheyenne. He raised his gaze to Trevor, baby Avery's father, and he saw in the other man's eyes an understanding of that level of terror.

"If I see even one policeman or ranch hand with you at the drop-off, I'll give Jared orders to shoot Amanda's kid. If the money doesn't arrive at the drop by noon, she's dead. If the money is rigged with exploding ink, or is padded with blank paper, or is hiding a tracking device, Cheyenne dies. And Amanda, too." She paused and gave a satisfied hum. "That's right. I've got Amanda stashed away as insurance that you comply. So don't even think of pulling anything stupid. Got it?"

You had *Amanda, you witch, but I found her.* Slade's jaw was so tight his back teeth throbbed. He wouldn't tip his hand on that score. He couldn't risk riling Mathilda until Cheyenne was safe. "Where do you want the money dropped?"

"There's a fallen, hollow tree along the fence line in the north pasture. Do you know the spot?"

"Yes." He didn't, but he was sure the other hands would.

"Leave the money there in a satchel or bag of some kind. No locks. Then walk away. I'll be watching. When I verify the money is all there, I'll tell you where to meet Jared to get the baby. Do you understand?"

Slade scanned the grim faces of the other men. "I do."

The screen flashed Call Ended and Slade lowered the phone, his chest tight.

"Jared would never kill a baby," George said. "I know I haven't known him as long as you all, but that…killing a kid is just…evil."

"I wish I thought you were right about Jared," Trevor said. "But all the attacks and murders the last few months say otherwise."

"How do you want to play this?" Gray asked, his gaze hard and troubled.

Outside, the rumble of car engines and crunch of snow signaled the arrival of Chief Peters and the FBI agents. Slade walked to the stable door at the end of the center alley and waved the police officers in.

Having seen the police cruisers arrive, Amanda burst through the back door from the house with Gabby on her heels. She jogged across the ranch yard and joined the circle of men. "Do you have the ransom money?"

Chief Peters handed her a leather satchel. "It's all there. Checked it myself."

Slade related to the new arrivals the context of Mathilda's call, including her directions and warnings.

"So we do what she says," Amanda said, a note of panic in her voice. "I don't care about Jethro's tainted money! All I care about is getting my daughter back unhurt."

"We won't let your daughter be hurt," Chief Peters said. "But we can't let her or Jared Hansen escape again."

"And we can't give them a *reason* to hurt her by defying her warnings!" Amanda replied, her voice rising in pitch.

Slade pulled Amanda into his arms and stroked her back. "Let me go. Alone. Like Mathilda said." A murmur of disagreement rumbled through assembled men, and Slade raised his voice to be heard over the din. "I've worked cases like this before for the state Bureau. I'll be armed, I'll stay in contact via radio and *I'll* be watching *her* when she comes to collect the money."

Chief Peters exchanged a look with one of the FBI agents, who'd introduced himself as Agent Colby and who was clearly the senior agent in charge. Colby gave a terse nod.

"She just contacted me using Jared Hansen's cell phone." Slade looked to the FBI agents. "Can you get people working a GPS trace on the phone? If she keeps it with her for further communication, we can track her using the GPS signal from the phone."

"Good thinking. I'll set it up," Agent Colby said.

"All right," Peters said, facing Slade. "We have a helicopter on standby to help locate Ms. Perkins after she leaves the drop-off, and we'll be ready to move out as soon as you have word where Hansen has the baby."

"Meanwhile, take your positions surrounding the north pasture from every direction," Slade said. He gave Amanda a kiss on the forehead and gently moved her aside as he sprang into action. "But stay back, stay quiet, stay hidden."

Two-way radios were distributed, horses saddled and a map of the ranch property and surrounding terrain spread on a worktable for the FBI agents' benefit. Within fifteen minutes, Slade was on Zeus, had the satchel containing the ransom strapped to his saddle and was riding out into the cold Wyoming morning.

Amanda tugged her scarf up over her nose when an icy breeze sent a chill rippling through her. Prince William snorted and shook his head, rattling his harness restlessly. She leaned forward in her saddle and patted his neck, whispering, "Shh. Easy boy. We gotta stay quiet."

Despite her calming words for PW, Amanda's nerves jangled like her horse's bit and reins. She'd ridden out with Gray, Stewie and one of the FBI agents to cover the east perimeter of the north pasture. Hidden behind a steep rise, they couldn't see any of what was transpiring in the frozen meadow beyond the hill where they waited. Slade had been gone for almost an hour. They'd maintained radio silence, concerned Mathilda could somehow hear the broadcast and balk. The waiting was killing her.

She idly rubbed her gloved thumb on her saddle's horn, lost in worrisome thoughts. Was Cheyenne cold? Had they fed her? What if Mathilda suspected a trap?

A large hand covered hers, and she jerked her head up to meet Gray's warm brown eyes. Before marrying Catherine and leaving the ranch for the police academy, Gray had been the ranch's foreman, and as a boy, he'd been his father's apprentice while his father served as the Coltons' foreman. Through the years, working side by side in the stable, riding fence and laughing together on sunny summer days, Amanda and Gray had formed a solid friendship. Now, his comforting gesture wrapped her in an invisible hug. He lifted one corner of his mouth and gave a silent nod. *Things will be okay.*

She drew a deep breath and managed a weak smile of thanks. When the radio crackled, her heartbeat scampered.

Slade's voice said, "Peters, you there?"

"Go ahead," Chief Peters's voice answered.

"Ms. Perkins has the satchel, and she's headed west, toward the woods. Everyone hold positions until I get her call, saying where Jared has Cheyenne."

"Roger that," Peters answered, and the radio fell silent again.

Gray squeezed her hand before he let go, then swung his attention to the top of the rise. "Here he comes."

Amanda shielded her eyes against the glare of the sun off the snow and spotted Slade, riding over the hill toward them. His expression hardened when he saw her.

"What are you—" Then jerking his gaze to Gray, "Why is she here?"

Amanda bristled. "I'm helping recover my daughter. What does it look like?"

The furrow in his brow deepened. "It could be dangerous. You should be back at the house—"

"Sitting on my hands, being a good little girl, waiting for word from the big tough men?" she finished for him with an edge in her tone. "If you think I could ever be satisfied being *that* person, you don't know me at all. Cheyenne is *my* daughter, and I *will* be part of her rescue."

Slade opened his mouth to respond, but the distant drone of an ATV engine drifted over the rise. Everyone stiffened. Whipping the radio to his mouth, Slade snarled, "I said hold positions! Whose ATV is that?"

A series of denials from the various hands and police officers followed before George's voice cut through the clutter. "It's Jared! He just left the woods, and he's cutting across the coulee about a quarter of a mile from where I am. He's got the baby with him!"

Adrenaline surged in Amanda's blood as her gaze clashed with Slade's, effectively saying, "No way will I stay back. This is my fight."

Begrudging resignation flashed over his face as he turned his horse and followed Gray and Stewie to the top of the ridge for a view of the long coulee below. A half mile or more from them, a lone ATV trekked through the thin layer of snow. Amanda could just make out Cheyenne's pink snowsuit in the baby carrier that was loaded precariously on the back of the ATV.

"Oh, chickpea!" Amanda whispered as she kicked Prince William to a run, following Slade, Gray and Stewie as they charged down the slope into the bowl of the coulee. Amanda raced forward, Slade at her side, matching her speed as their horses ate up the distance between them and Cheyenne. Amanda kept her sights locked on the ATV, desperate to reach her daughter.

Suddenly Jared's head snapped up, as if only then noticing the men on horseback closing in on him. He scanned the surrounding hills and cut the ATV hard to the right, attempting an escape. When he gunned the engine, the acceleration coupled with the change in direction made the ATV tip up on two wheels. The baby carrier was pitched off, into the snow.

A scream slipped from Amanda's throat. "No! Cheyenne!"

Jared righted the ATV, glanced back at the baby carrier on the ground behind him and forsook his hostage in order to expedite his escape.

Amanda's breath hung in her lungs as they rushed across the pasture toward the fallen baby carrier. *Please, God, let her not have been hurt in the fall!*

Amanda and the men gained ground on Jared, closing the distance between them to a couple football fields. When Slade pulled ahead, almost overtaking Jared, the panicked hand drew a gun. Turning, he fired two shots.

Amanda gasped as Prince William spooked, turning from their path, rearing up on his hind legs and throwing her to the ground.

"Amanda!" Gray reined his horse and swung down from his saddle. He knelt beside her, his brow creased with worry. "Are you hurt?"

Though the breath had been knocked from her and she'd hit the ground with a jarring impact, she dismissed her own aches. Her attention stayed locked on the fleeing kidnapper and the baby seat lying upside down in the snow. She was so close to her baby and still so far…

She waved Gray off, gasping, "I'm…okay. Help Cheyenne."

* * *

When Jared fired again, Slade felt the heat of the bullet as it whizzed past his ear, missing him by inches. He returned fire, aiming for the young ranch hand's leg. And hit his mark.

Jared howled in pain and clutched at his thigh.

Slade charged forward, then jumped from Zeus onto Jared's back. Together, they tumbled into the snow, and Slade wrestled for possession of the hand's gun. Stunned as he was by his leg injury and being tackled, Jared lost the weapon in seconds, but recovered his wits enough to head-butt Slade in the nose.

Pain blurred Slade's vision briefly, and he felt the warm seeping of blood from his injured nose. Rearing back with a fist, he smacked Jared across the jaw.

Stewie arrived and rushed toward the men tangled in combat.

"No!" Slade shouted, his focus on restraining Jared. "He's mine. Get Cheyenne!"

Stewie disappeared from his peripheral view, and Slade backed away enough to dodge a blow from Jared. But that distance gave the hand room to raise his good leg and kick out, planting his foot in Slade's chest.

Air whooshed from Slade's lungs as he stumbled back. Recovering his balance, he charged Jared again, knocking him flat. Slade struggled to pin down his opponent's shoulders, and Jared fumbled at his hip…and whipped out a buck knife. Slade saw a flash of metal, felt the tug on his sleeve then the sting of the blade slicing his arm.

Jared wielded the knife with deadly intent, swinging and thrusting it at Slade. Adrenaline and fury fueled Slade's fight. He blocked one strike, dodged another, then blocked a third before a shadow fell over them.

Gray pressed the muzzle of his gun to Jared's temple

and grated, "Drop the knife, Hansen, or I'll put a hole in your head."

Jared stilled.

Slade seized the opportunity to grab Jared's wrists, hook a foot around the young man's feet and take him to the ground.

Panting for a breath, he glared at the man who'd caused Amanda so much heartache and snarled, "You're under arrest, you bastard."

A muffled cry reached him, yanking his attention to Cheyenne. Stewie had the carrier turned over, but was fumbling with the straps that held Cheyenne.

"Take him," he told Gray, releasing his prisoner to Amanda's brother-in-law before racing over to Cheyenne. Swiping blood from his nose, he dropped to his knees and pushed Stewie aside. "Don't cry, baby girl. You're safe now."

Abandoning Prince William, who was still jittery and uncooperative, Amanda started running the remaining distance to her child. Her legs were weak and wobbly as emotions flooded her, and she staggered in the slick snow. Hot tears left tracks on her cheeks that quickly froze and stung her skin. But her focus was entirely on the scene before her.

Slade was locked in a hand-to-hand fight with Jared, and Stewie was at Cheyenne's carrier. Finally, Gray reached the scene and, having subdued Jared, Slade rushed over to her daughter and lifted her into his arms. A tiny wail drifted across the pasture, and a pure sweet relief that Cheyenne was alive and in safe hands flooded Amanda. Her legs buckled, and she collapsed on her knees in the snow, crying happy tears and shaking from spent adrenaline. As she watched, holding her breath,

Slade gave Cheyenne a quick once-over for injury, then clutched her baby to his chest.

I can't believe God would be cruel enough to let two babies I loved die. Slade's words from the day before echoed in her mind, and a pang lanced her heart. Slade loved Cheyenne.

He stood there for a long moment, simply cradling Cheyenne to his chest with his head bent over her, his body swaying in the age-old motion intended to soothe a baby. Stewie backed away, then turned to help Gray restrain Jared. From the opposite end of the coulee, more men on horseback and ATVs appeared and hurried toward the scene.

Icy dampness was soaking through the knees of Amanda's jeans, but she couldn't move. She stared, transfixed, as Slade raised his head and locked his gaze on her. With a long, sure strides, he crossed the snowy field toward her. He cut a striking image. His black cowboy hat and broad shoulders stood out against the wintry backdrop. His chiseled jaw was set, and his blue eyes were brighter than the Wyoming sky. All the air whooshed from her lungs as she drank in the breathtaking view of the man she loved.

A startled noise wheezed from her throat. She *loved* Slade. The truth spun a fresh wave of tender emotion through her, and tears filled her eyes. As he neared her, she could see his cheeks were damp and streaked with blood, his eyes rimmed in red.

Her pulse hitched. He'd been crying. Whether in relief, or joy...or remembering the daughter he'd lost far too soon, she didn't know. A little of each, she'd guess.

She trembled and hiccupped a half sob, half laugh as he dropped to his knees beside her and placed Cheyenne in her waiting arms.

"She's okay, Mom," he said, his voice cracking. "Your little girl's okay."

Amanda hugged Cheyenne close, kissing her head and rocking with her, side-to-side. Tipping her head up to meet Slade's eyes, she said, "*Our* little girl."

His expression reflected surprise first, then melted into a tender smile of gratitude that she understood his pain and his connection to Cheyenne. "Thank you."

She curled her hand around the back of his head and pulled him closer. "No, thank *you,*" she murmured before covering his mouth with a deep kiss.

A satisfied rumble purred in Slade's throat as he wrapped Cheyenne and Amanda in a bear hug and returned Amanda's kiss with unrestrained passion.

When Cheyenne wiggled and whined, Slade backed away just enough to stroke a finger over the baby's red cheek. "She's cold. You should get her back to the house and have Levi check her out."

Amanda nodded her agreement. "Are you coming with us?"

He shook his head as he pushed to his feet and checked the chamber on his service weapon. "My job out here's not done."

A spasm of fear and dread twisted her gut. Mathilda was still out there. Still a threat.

She noticed the blood on his sleeve then and gasped. "You're injured!"

He flicked a casual glance at his bleeding arm. "Not badly. Just a cut."

"You need a doctor."

"Not now. I have to finish this."

With one hand, she tugged her scarf from her neck. "At least wrap it with something to stop the bleeding." She held the scarf out. "Here."

With her help, he tied the scarf tightly around his injured arm.

Slade's radio crackled to life. "Agent Kent, we've got Hansen in custody. My officers are taking him back to the station," Chief Peters said.

Slade glanced back across the pasture where police officers were putting Jared on the back of an ATV, and he released a huge sigh. "Thank God." Then in the radio, "Roger that. What about Perkins?"

Amanda cuddled Cheyenne close as she listened to the radio exchange.

"FBI has a fix on her location. She appears to be on foot, nearing the county road through the woods north of you. Helo is en route but won't be able to set down in those trees."

"Damn," Slade muttered under his breath. "I'm on my way." He held a hand out to Amanda, which she took, and he pulled her close for a kiss. "Keep a sharp eye out going home." He shoved his service weapon in her coat pocket. "Do not hesitate to use this if you need to."

Her eyes widened. "What about you? What if you need it?"

He caught Prince William's reins and walked her horse to her. "I'll get a replacement from Peters or Agent Colby."

"But—"

He smacked another kiss on her lips and touched her cheek. "I'll be fine. I'll hold Cheyenne while you climb up."

After Amanda was settled in her saddle with Cheyenne securely zipped inside her coat, Slade tugged the brim of his Stetson. "I'll see you back at the house."

Before she could reply, before she could beg him to

be careful, he'd turned and was jogging back across the frozen coulee toward Zeus.

Cheyenne wiggled and whined, drawing Amanda's attention. "It's okay, chickpea. Mommy's got you."

With one arm around her daughter, Amanda flicked the reins and headed back to the house. But her thoughts were with Slade and the hunt for the heartless woman who had, for months, made her life a living hell.

Slade rode Zeus up beside Gray and Trevor, who were in a huddle with George and Stewie. "What'd I miss?"

"Mostly a lot of resistance and name-calling. Hansen's headed to the police station," Trevor said.

A few yards away, one of Chief Peters's officers talked with an FBI agent over a map spread on a large rock. Slade glanced back at Trevor and Gray. "Speaking of which, I gave Amanda my gun for the ride back to the house. Either of you have another piece on you? The FBI has a bead on Mathilda near the county road, and I want a part of her takedown. I can't imagine she'll give up without a fight."

Trevor reached under his coat and pulled out a pistol. "Take mine. Peters has asked me to follow his men to the station with Jared. Be present for his interrogation. I'm heading that way in a few minutes with Agent Colby." Slade took the proffered weapon. "It's got a full clip. Eight plus one."

"Thanks." Slade nodded to Trevor then turned to Gray. "Join me?"

The former foreman's eyes darkened, and his mouth drew into a tight line. "With pleasure."

The whoop of an approaching helicopter drew Slade's attention, and he tipped his head back, shading his eyes from the sun as the chopper passed overhead. "That's our cue."

Slade gave Zeus a kick and headed out at a run in the direction the helicopter flew. Gray and the hands followed until they reached the edge of the tree line. "Stewie, George, stay here and keep watch in case she gives us the slip and doubles back this way."

The hands looked genuinely disappointed not to be in on Mathilda's capture, but Slade couldn't have civilians in the line of fire in case of a volatile confrontation. As he rode into the woods where Mathilda had disappeared, his eyes needed a moment to adjust to the dappling of shadows and broken beams of sunlight. He and Gray proceeded at a trot, their gazes scanning, their weapons ready. A twig snapped loudly under Zeus's hoof, and Slade tensed. Exhaled. *Get it together. Focus!*

After a few minutes, Gray said quietly, "We're getting close to the county road. Maybe we should go the rest of the way on foot?"

Slade jerked a nod and swung down from Zeus's back. After quickly tying his reins to a low-hanging branch, he crept forward, keeping to the shadows and moving from tree to tree. In the distance, the sound of the helicopter rotor was punctuated occasionally by a male voice or the crackle of static. Slade kept the volume of his radio low but monitored the exchange of communication between Chief Peters and the FBI agents. Mathilda had not been spotted yet.

He gritted his teeth. He would stay out here, searching the frozen terrain until kingdom come if he had to, but he would *not* let Mathilda escape justice again. Today *would* be her day of reckoning, if he had to—

A blur of color and movement caught his eye, and Slade stilled.

Silently, Gray swung his gun up, aiming at the same spot. Motionless, they watched the shadows. Had it been a deer? An FBI agent?

A moment later, Mathilda ran from behind a fir toward a break in the trees and the county road beyond. An old model sedan sat parked on the shoulder of the road, and she made a beeline toward it.

With quick hand signals, Slade told Gray to swing wide and flank the fleeing woman. Gray suited orders to action, sprinting through the winter-dead undergrowth.

Slade charged forward, keeping Mathilda in sight. As she burst from the cover of the trees, headed toward the getaway vehicle, Chief Peters and one of his officers emerged from cover on the opposite side of the empty road.

"Stop!" Peters shouted.

Mathilda spun toward Peters, fired a shot at him and kept running. As she neared the car, an FBI agent rose from behind the vehicle where he'd been lying in wait and raised his weapon. "Drop your weapon and lie on the ground!"

Instead, Mathilda shot him in the chest, and the agent crumpled. Peters fired at Mathilda, and the rear window of the getaway car shattered. She darted to the far side of the sedan, and using the trunk as cover, returned fire.

"We have you surrounded, Ms. Perkins," Peters shouted. "It's over. Drop your weapon."

"No!" Mathilda screeched, her attention on the police and the weapons the officers had aimed at her. The helicopter made a low, noisy pass over.

Slade took advantage of her distraction and the din from the helo, which drowned out his footsteps, and eased from his cover. With his weapon poised, he crept up behind Mathilda. Gray surged forward, as well, just a few yards off Slade's progress.

Right before he reached Mathilda, she sensed his presence and swung around, her gun waving. "Stop!"

Slade lunged, knocking the muzzle skyward as she fired. Using his momentum, he tackled her, and they tumbled to the ground.

Mathilda thrashed, struggling to get free, but within seconds, Gray was next to Slade, grabbing her arms and helping restrain her.

"Give it up, Ms. Perkins. It's over. You're under arrest," Slade growled and wrested her gun away.

"No!" Lying on her back, she glared at him, her eyes wild. "It's not over until I have my revenge on Jethro Colton."

Chief Peters and his officers surrounded them, issuing her Miranda rights. The chief tried to drag her to her feet, but she crumbled to the ground, weeping and snarling with fury. "You can't take me! I need my revenge!"

Peters took out his handcuffs and clipped one shackle around Mathilda's left wrist, the other to the car door handle.

"Revenge? On Jethro Colton?" Slade glared at her, his feet braced in a wide stance, his fists clenched and shaking with adrenaline. "What did he do to you? He gave you a job and housing for the last thirty years."

"He never loved me like he should have!" she shouted back, her voice full of emotion. "I did everything for him, but I was always just a servant to him! Someone for the high and mighty lord of the manor to take to bed, then order around like a second-class citizen."

"If you love Jethro, why hurt him and his family?" Peters asked.

Mathilda turned back toward the police chief. "Because he got sick, and I knew I'd run out of time to change his mind and make him love me. I wasted my life waiting for him, taking care of him, keeping his bed warm whenever he crooked his finger." Her face puckered in a snarl. "He *used* me, and I refuse to see him die without exacting my pound of flesh."

Slade and Peters exchanged a look. The woman had been advised of her right to remain silent. If she chose to waive that right and spill her guts, they'd pump her for information before she changed her mind.

"So you devised a scheme to kidnap his granddaughter and extort a ransom from him?" Slade asked.

"He owed me! I stayed true to him through three worthless wives. But did he leave me anything in his will? No!"

Slade remembered a comment Amanda had made earlier about the former police chief. "What about Drucker? You had an affair with him."

Mathilda visibly stiffened. "That doesn't count. Drucker was an idiot. He believed he was in love with me and did anything I asked to keep me in his bed. He looked the other way when I told him to and covered up a truckload of evidence in the past months to keep me out of jail."

Chief Peters crouched in front of her and removed his sunglasses. "Did you kill Drucker?"

She hesitated. "Let's just say I helped him take the coward's way out. I couldn't risk him spilling his guts once he was found out."

"And Tom Brooks?" Slade asked.

Her eyes narrowed. "That was Jared. He'd been squeamish about killing anyone, but I told him to get the baby whatever it took or I'd frame him for everything, and he'd not see a penny of the money I'd promised him."

"So Jared's part in all this was about money?" Slade glanced at Gray, who, along with Catherine, had suffered plenty himself from the housekeeper's machinations. "How much did you promise him?"

"I promised him half of the ransom." She chuckled wryly. "But he'd never have gotten it. The fool boy would have been a loose end. I couldn't leave him alive and risk him talking to the wrong person."

A chill shimmied through Slade. Deep down, Mathilda's jealousy and hatred had spawned pure evil.

"How'd you convince him to work for you and do such hideous things?" Gray asked.

"Same way I did with Duke. And Misty Mayhew. I found his weak spot and used it to my advantage. Jared had gotten himself in a financial bind with some unsavory folks. Greed and fear are powerful motivators." Mathilda twisted her mouth in a smug smile. "Once I convinced him to kidnap Kate McCord and he assaulted Agnes in the process, I had the means to blackmail him to do my dirty work again. The deeper he got into things, the more influence I had over him to finish the job."

Down the road, the helicopter landed and a handful of FBI agents disembarked.

"Okay, let's take this to the station and process her," Chief Peters said, heading off to meet the FBI agents.

Slade knew he should feel some sense of satisfaction for having captured the mastermind behind all the horrors the Colton family and staff had suffered for months. Instead, studying Mathilda's smug expression, her defiance despite being in custody, a festering rage for her unrepentant arrogance burned in his chest.

He crouched in front of her and stuck his face in hers. "Don't you care how many lives you've ruined? How much pain you've caused? The innocent people you killed?" he growled.

Her eyes were cold and unemotional. "No. I only regret that I didn't cause Jethro more pain, that I didn't kill him months ago, so he'd know I was the one who had the last laugh." She took a slow breath and slowly raised one eyebrow. "And I regret that I didn't kill you when I had the chance. I'd be on my way to South America with Jethro's millions by now if not for you and your interference."

His hand itched to smack her, but his code of honor wouldn't allow him to hit a woman, even one as reprehensible as Mathilda. "Go to hell."

Slade Kent rose to his feet and strode away from her, and a ball of icy hatred expanded in Mathilda's gut. Defeat was a bitter pill to swallow. She refused to accept failure or a future in prison. If she was going down, she would take that cocky Kent down with her.

The police officer nearest her was in conversation with Gray Stark, another thorn in her side. Keeping still, she cast a surreptitious glance around her, calculating. Then she drew a deep breath. And sprung to action.

With a hard kick to the back of the officer's knees, she made the policeman topple backward, his hands reaching for the ground to catch himself. With the sidearm at his hip now in her reach, she snatched the gun with her free right hand. Swung it toward Kent's retreating back.

"Slade, look out!" Gray shouted.

Slade whipped around at the exact moment she fired. His body jerked as the bullet found its target, and he stumbled back. Fell.

A final victory, she thought, as multiple gunshots fired around her. The force of the bullets slamming into her was stunning but not surprising. Suicide by cop. Her vision dimmed, and she slumped over. *No prison...not for me.*

Chapter 23

Slade opened his eyes slowly and blinked the room into focus. His brain was fuzzy and confused as he made a quick assessment. Hospital room. A row of prickly stitches on his arm. Something stiff taped to his nose. An ungodly pain in his left flank.

He moved a hand there and groped the wad of bandages taped to his side.

A feminine gasp preceded a beautiful, if tired-looking, face with the sexiest gold eyes he'd ever seen moving into his field of vision. "Slade? Thank goodness! How do you feel?"

"Like I was kicked by a bull."

"I bet you do." Amanda stroked his cheek, and he tugged his dry lips in a lopsided smile.

A vague memory of Gray shouting at him wavered at the edges of his mind, then...nothing. "Why am I here? I'm kinda...fuzzy on what happened."

Her face creased with consternation. "Mathilda shot you."

"Mathilda?" The name spiked adrenaline through him. He flashed on a wintry road, officers surrounding the housekeeper who was handcuffed to a car. He tried to sit up, his heart thumping wildly. "But we had her in custody! Did she get away?"

Amanda put a hand in the center of his chest and guided him back down against the pillows. "Whoa, cowboy. Take it easy. You've just had surgery to remove a bullet from your side."

When he complied, settling back on the bed, she continued, "She's dead. After she shot you, the officers and agents at the scene fired at her."

Slade released a breath and curled his fingers around her hand. "And then?"

"You were in and out of consciousness. Losing blood fast. They flew you and an injured FBI agent here on the FBI helicopter, and you were rushed into surgery."

"Where's here?"

"The hospital in Cheyenne." A tired grin slanted across her lips, and she leaned closer, smoothing his hair with her fingers. "I had about forty heart attacks driving up here with Gabby and Trevor. I was so scared I was going to lose you!"

"No way. You can't get rid of me that easily." He caught her hand in his and kissed her palm. "Where's our girl?"

A wide grin spread across her face, telling him he'd remembered her gesture correctly. "She's back at the ranch with her aunt Catherine, getting spoiled rotten." Amanda paused and drew a deep breath. Released it. "You know, today was the first time in months I've felt truly safe leaving Cheyenne with someone else." Tears filled her eyes, and she flashed a melancholy smile. "It is such a relief to have the incidents and tragedies at the ranch solved at last and the people behind this nightmare captured or killed."

"Finally."

Her brow dented, and she frowned. "Although I wouldn't have wished for Mathilda to be killed, it does put a period on the whole ordeal, huh?"

A quiet knock sounded on the door, and Chief Peters stuck his head in the room. "How's the patient?"

"Awake," Amanda said, brightening for their visitor and waving him in. "And alive thanks to your fast action. I was just filling him in on some of what's happened."

"Yeah. It's been a busy day." The police chief stepped into the room and slid his hands in his pockets. "Thanks for your help."

Slade used the button on the railing to raise the head of the bed. "Do you have a report on the FBI agent who was shot?"

The police chief nodded. "He was wearing his Kevlar. The bullet broke a few ribs, but he was treated and released a little while ago."

"That's good to know." Slade wet his dry lips. "Is Jared talking?"

"Yep. When we told him Mathilda was pinning everything on him, he opened up and spilled the whole story of his involvement, what Mathilda had done, where evidence had been hidden—"

"Wait." Amanda gave Chief Peters a puzzled look. "I thought you told me earlier Mathilda had been killed."

"She was." The chief flashed a crooked smile. "But we haven't told Jared that yet. She did give him up and tell us a good bit of her story before she shot Slade, though, so that much is true. So far he's admitted to kidnapping your daughter, in addition to Kate McCord and your sister, Catherine, killing Tom Brooks and Jenny Burke, shooting at Jagger McKnight—"

"The reporter who let you all believe he was Cole back in September?" Slade asked, remembering reading the name in Peters's files.

"Yeah, he lied to us in order to get a story on the family," Amanda said, her tone reflecting disappointment, even hurt, at the man's deception. She turned to Chief Peters. "Mathilda's involvement explains how they got their hands on heirlooms like the scrap of Cole's blanket. That's what led us to think Jagger was Jethro's long-lost son to begin with. Mathilda had access to every part of the ranch house as the head housekeeper, and having worked for the family so long, she knew what bits of evidence would be most incriminating and influential."

"Jared has confirmed the entire plot. Every attack and kidnapping was orchestrated by Mathilda, either to advance her ultimate plan to extort a ransom in exchange for Cheyenne, or to cover her tracks and keep people off her trail."

Amanda shook her head sadly. "So many people were hurt trying to find the truth and protect Cheyenne." She jerked her head up, her expression hopeful. "What about Aurora and Dylan? Was Mathilda behind the attacks on them last month? I know our maid Misty Mayhew took the fall for most of what happened, but the rest…maybe it wasn't men sent by Aurora's ex-husband—"

"Sorry," Peters interrupted, shaking his head. "I know you'd love to have Dylan and your best friend back, but we're sure Aurora's ex has hitmen gunning for her. Mathilda may have been using Misty as her lackey, but Hope's—as she needs to be known now—situation hasn't changed. She needs to stay in Witness Protection."

"Oh." Amanda visibly wilted.

"Well…" Peters straightened and lifted a hand in a wave. "I should go. I have a lot of paperwork back at the station. In light of all the new information in the last forty-eight hours, I have open cases going back thirty years to tie up and close." He nodded toward Slade. "Good to see you're doing better."

"Thanks, chief." As Peters left the room, Slade shifted his attention to Amanda, whose eyes were cast down, her expression troubled. "Amanda?"

"You must hate my family. Especially my father." She lifted melancholy eyes to his. "I've done nothing but preach to you about being honest and open, but my father's lies have hurt you for years. I wouldn't blame you if you wanted nothing to do with me or the Coltons ever again."

He frowned at her. "Really? That's what you think?"

"Jethro murdered your father and covered it up for years! He gave his son away and told the world Cole was kidnapped in order to save face, and Dead River Ranch is crawling with liars, killers, manipulators, freeloaders, womanizers—"

"Amanda, I love you."

"—cheaters, fraud—" She stopped. Blinked. Stared at him. "What?"

He lifted the corner of his mouth. "I don't care about those other people. You and Cheyenne are the ones who matter to me."

"But my father—"

"Did a lot of terrible things in his life. Yes. And I resent the hell outta him for killing my dad. Under other circumstances, I'd see that he was prosecuted to the full extent of the law. But the man's dying." He paused and squeezed her hand. "He only confessed to me after learning I have feelings for you. He wanted me to tell you how I felt. He said you deserved to be happy."

Amanda frowned, anger flaring in her eyes. "And his idea of helping me be happy is to tell the man I love that he killed his father? Sounds more like he wanted to drive a wedge between us."

Slade held his breath and twitched a crooked smile. "You love me?"

She stilled. "I…I can't." Tears glittered in her eyes. "You're leaving. You have a life in Jackson."

"Not the life I want anymore, if you're not in it." Her expression reflected surprise and yearning, and he gave her a minute to absorb his words before adding, "And while I can't believe I'm defending your father, I also think he confessed what he'd done to me so we could start a life together with a clean slate. No hidden secrets that could hurt us later. No lies or deception between us." He pulled her closer and swiped away a tear on her cheek. "I won't hold your father's sins against you. I have what I came to the ranch looking for. The truth. Falling in love with you is a bonus."

She shook her head, confusion creasing her brow. "A few days ago, you pushed me away. You told me to find someone else to fall in love with."

He heaved a sigh. "I know. I'm sorry. I was scared."

"Of me?"

"Of my feelings for you. Losing my wife and daughter hurt…." He paused as the familiar pain swelled in his chest. "So much. I barely crawled out of the pit of my grief and learned to put one foot in front of the other. One day at a time. I didn't ever want to hurt that much again, and I thought that meant never investing my emotions in anyone again. I thought I could protect myself from that pain if I didn't let myself love anyone else the way I'd loved them."

He read hesitancy in her eyes, a trepidation to risk her heart because of past betrayals, and a tender ache gripped him. Curling his fingers against her scalp, he nudged her closer and held her gaze. With the appeal in his eyes, he opened his soul to her. "I know Cheyenne's father made you feel unwanted, unloved. From talking to your sisters, I know your father was cold and demanding toward his kids. I know why you are reluctant to risk your heart again. But...I love you, Amanda Colton. And I love Cheyenne."

She blinked rapidly, and tears rolled down her cheeks.

"The truth is," he continued, wiping her face with his thumb, "I tried not to fall in love with you, but Cheyenne's laughter and innocence snuck past my defenses. And once she opened that crack in my heart, you barreled in with your strength and integrity and fire. Your tremendous love for your daughter. Those sexy eyes and smokin' body..."

That earned a small grin.

"Maybe Cheyenne's father hurt you. Deeply. But I'm glad he's not in your life, because *I* want to be the one holding you at night and helping you raise Cheyenne and working beside you to save horses with colic. I want you, Amanda. In my bed. In my life. In my heart. For always."

She surged forward and caught his mouth in a tooth-clicking, lip-bruising kiss that shot straight to his soul. He angled his head, softening the kiss while amping up the heat. When she pulled back enough to catch her breath, she whispered, "See, I told you you had the soul of a poet. That was the most romantic thing anyone has ever said to me."

"Oh, yeah? How about this— Will you marry me?

I want you and Cheyenne to be my family and make a fresh start."

Her beautiful gold eyes widened, and she gaped for a moment before a slow teasing grin tugged her cheek. "Naw…"

Now he gaped. "You won't marry me?"

"Oh, I probably will." Humor lit her eyes. "But the other thing you said about wanting me for always in your life and your heart and how Cheyenne's laugh cracked your defenses. That's still the most romantic, I think."

He chuckled. "I see. But you'll marry me?"

"I have to check with Cheyenne first. This decision affects her, too. But if she's on board—and judging by the way her eyes light up when she sees you, I can't imagine she wouldn't be—then I'd say you have a deal, cowboy."

He smiled and smacked another kiss on her lips. "Perfect."

Epilogue

"**P**erfect," Catherine said as she put the finishing touches on Gabriella's hair, Christmas Eve morning. "Hit her, Amanda. Quick, before it falls."

Amanda, wearing a formfitting, Christmas-red bridesmaid dress, stepped forward. Armed with a can of hairspray, she liberally doused her sister's hairdo.

Gabby coughed and waved at the cloud that enveloped her. "Hey, whoa! That's enough!"

Amanda shrugged. "Sorry. I don't use this stuff, and Cath didn't want it to fall."

Gabby patted her stiff hair. "Well, it won't. I don't think a hurricane would muss it up now."

Amanda stepped back and studied her youngest sister. Gabby positively glowed as Cath, in her maternity version of the red bridesmaid gown, helped pin Gabby's ivory lace veil in place. "Gab, you look beautiful. Trevor is a lucky, lucky man."

"Thanks," Gabby said, meeting Amanda's gaze in the mirror and smiling broadly. "I'm lucky, too. Trevor and Avery are the world to me." She cocked her head, her expression speculative. "So when do we start planning your wedding?"

A warmth swelled inside Amanda, as she thought of her future with Slade. "Soon. Let's get you married today, and then we'll talk. But I'm thinking it'd be nice to be a June bride."

"Oh, good! I was afraid you'd want it earlier, and I'd be a blimp in all the pictures," Catherine said with a relieved sigh.

"Speaking of weddings, did I tell you all Jagger and Mia sent us a Christmas card?" Gabriella said. "They're planning a wedding in the next few months, too."

"How wonderful!" Cath smiled and rubbed her swollen belly.

Amanda returned her attention to the bride. Her sister's expression was pensive.

"Gabby, what's wrong?"

Gabriella perked a bit and flashed a sad smile. "Just… thinking. I always thought that on my wedding day, Dad would walk me down the aisle. And even knowing everything we do about his deception and crimes and ill-gotten gains, a small part of me still wishes he could escort me at the ceremony."

Silence fell in the room, and the sisters exchanged commiserating glances. Amanda had filled her sisters in on all she and Slade had discovered about Jethro's past, the murder he'd covered up, the kidnapping he'd faked… the whole sordid story. When all was said and done, Jethro was not the man they'd thought he was and was not a man whose legacy they wanted any part of.

Amanda spoke first. "I know it's probably bad form

to talk about such things before Dad's even dead, but…
I've decided to donate my inheritance to the Center for
Missing and Exploited Children. I've known the nightmare of having my baby missing, and if I can help even
one child be returned safely to his parent, I'm all in."

"Are you sure? All of it?" Gabby asked.

Amanda nodded confidently. "Slade wants to return
to ranching. His career as a lawman was largely to honor
his father and give him the means to find his father's
killer. He's done that now, and he says his time here has
reminded him how much ranching means to him."

Cath squeezed her sister's arm. "That's terrific. I know
you'll be happier on a ranch than living in the city."

Amanda set her shoulders, feeling more and more certain about the plans she and Slade had made together. "I
can set up a vet practice wherever we land and also help
out with our animals."

"I'm planning to give my inheritance away, too," Cath
said. "I could never spend money I knew Dad got through
such nefarious means. We can live off of Gray's salary
as a policeman until the baby is old enough for me to
go to work."

Amanda gave her sisters a serious look. "Along the
same lines…I think we should sell the ranch. Not dis-
mantle it. I don't want any of the staff to lose their jobs,
but sell it at a fair price to someone else. As is."

Her sisters nodded their agreement.

"But if we sell, the troubled teens I work with will
need a new place to meet." Gabby bit her lip in thought,
then her face brightened. "So I'll use my share of the
inheritance and sale of the ranch to build a teen center
in town and develop programming that will give kids
guidance, job training, family therapy when needed…
It will be great!"

"So all of Dad's money will go for good causes." Cath smiled her satisfaction. "I like it. It's the perfect solution."

Gabby frowned. "What about Levi and Dylan? They deserve a share of Dad's inheritance. They're his children as much as we are."

"Of course," Amanda said. "It's only fair."

"Levi has already rejected his share of the estate, but I think we should insist he get his cut." Cath divided a look between Amanda and Gabby. "He could use the money to pay for medical school bills or open a free medical clinic or throw it all in a river if he wants. But it should be his."

"Agreed," Amanda said, and Gabby nodded. "As far as Dylan goes…we have no way of getting it to him."

"Then we'll give his share away to a cause he'd have approved of. A horse rescue and rehabilitation center or a domestic violence shelter for women," Gabby said.

Catherine smiled her approval. "Yes. An even split. I think he'd like that."

Amanda grinned slyly. "I rather like giving all of Dad's millions away. After the way he's hoarded it and refused to use it to help others in need all these years, it's about time the money did some good."

"Oh!" Catherine gasped, putting a hand on her belly. "Judging by the dance the baby's doing on my kidneys, I'd say she agrees!"

A knock on the door interrupted their shared laugh.

Slade, looking especially delicious in his dark suit and holding Cheyenne on his hip, poked his head in the room. "Are you ladies ready? I was sent to tell you they're all set at the chapel."

Amanda rushed over to take Cheyenne from him. "Hey, now, you're not supposed to be lifting anything heavy. Doctor's orders."

He snorted and dodged her attempt to take Cheyenne.

"The princess is not heavy, and I feel fine. I told you, I'm a fast healer."

Gray appeared behind Slade, carrying Avery. "What's the verdict? The crowd's getting antsy."

Gabby did a final check in the mirror and faced the men. "Ready." Seeing the babies, who wore matching ivory dresses with red sashes, she cooed. "Aw, don't you two look precious!"

"Thanks, Gabby," Gray said, grinning. "But I'm a happily married man."

Cath play-punched his shoulder.

Levi arrived and wolf-whistled. "Ladies, you all look stunning."

"Why, thank you, sir." Gabby gathered her bouquet of Christmas greenery and poinsettia blossoms and held her arm out as she approached Levi. "Dr. Colton, would you do me the honor of walking me down the aisle?"

He blinked, clearly startled by her request. "Me?"

"You are my brother. I can't think of anyone better to give me away."

Emotion filled his face, and he cleared his throat. "I'd be honored." He took her arm and escorted her out of the room.

Gray and Catherine followed, and Slade held his arm out to Amanda. "Shall we?"

She hooked her arm with his and sighed contentedly. "Wow."

"What?"

"Just thinking." She smiled up at him. "Despite all the hell this family's been through in the last few months, we've been so blessed, too. I have two brothers now, Darla and her kids are out of our house, and all four of my siblings and I are starting new lives with someone they love dearly."

Slade gave her a kiss. "Sounds like Santa Claus came early to Dead River Ranch, and all the good boys and girls here got their deepest wish."

"Yes, he did, cowboy," Amanda said, tweaking Cheyenne's chin, then quoting, "But I heard him exclaim, 'ere he drove out of sight…'"

"Happy Christmas to all," Slade joined her, "and to all a good night!"

* * * * *

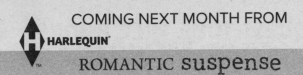

COMING NEXT MONTH FROM

HARLEQUIN®

ROMANTIC suspense

Available January 7, 2014

#1783 LETHAL LAWMAN
Men of Wolf Creek • Carla Cassidy
When heartbroken Marlene Marcoli is targeted by a
madman bent on revenge, Detective Frank Delaney vows
to protect her while breaking down the walls that shield
her heart from love.

#1784 THE RETURN OF CONNOR MANSFIELD
The Mansfield Brothers • Beth Cornelison
Connor Mansfield leaves witness protection to save his
daughter's life and reclaim the woman he loves, but to have
a future together, they must escape assassins and rebuild
lost trust.

#1785 DEADLY ENGAGEMENT
Elle James
Adventure diver Emma is soon in over her head when
undercover agent and former SEAL Creed Thomas
commandeers her boat, and her heart, in a race to stop a
terrorist plot.

#1786 SECRET AGENT SECRETARY
ICE: Black Ops Defenders • Melissa Cutler
Catapulted into the middle of an international manhunt,
secretary Avery has no one to rely on but herself...and Ryan,
the mysterious spy with a secret connection to the enemy.

**YOU CAN FIND MORE INFORMATION ON UPCOMING HARLEQUIN® TITLES,
FREE EXCERPTS AND MORE AT WWW.HARLEQUIN.COM.**

HRSCNM1213

REQUEST YOUR FREE BOOKS!
2 FREE NOVELS PLUS 2 FREE GIFTS!

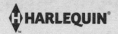

ROMANTIC suspense

Sparked by danger, fueled by passion

YES! Please send me 2 FREE Harlequin® Romantic Suspense novels and my 2 FREE gifts (gifts are worth about $10). After receiving them, if I don't wish to receive any more books, I can return the shipping statement marked "cancel." If I don't cancel, I will receive 4 brand-new novels every month and be billed just $4.74 per book in the U.S. or $5.24 per book in Canada. That's a savings of at least 14% off the cover price! It's quite a bargain! Shipping and handling is just 50¢ per book in the U.S. and 75¢ per book in Canada.* I understand that accepting the 2 free books and gifts places me under no obligation to buy anything. I can always return a shipment and cancel at any time. Even if I never buy another book, the two free books and gifts are mine to keep forever.

240/340 HDN F45N

Name _____ (PLEASE PRINT) _____

Address _____ Apt. # _____

City _____ State/Prov. _____ Zip/Postal Code _____

Signature (if under 18, a parent or guardian must sign) _____

Mail to the **Harlequin® Reader Service:**
IN U.S.A.: P.O. Box 1867, Buffalo, NY 14240-1867
IN CANADA: P.O. Box 609, Fort Erie, Ontario L2A 5X3

Want to try two free books from another line?
Call 1-800-873-8635 or visit www.ReaderService.com.

---

* Terms and prices subject to change without notice. Prices do not include applicable taxes. Sales tax applicable in N.Y. Canadian residents will be charged applicable taxes. Offer not valid in Quebec. This offer is limited to one order per household. Not valid for current subscribers to Harlequin Romantic Suspense books. All orders subject to credit approval. Credit or debit balances in a customer's account(s) may be offset by any other outstanding balance owed by or to the customer. Please allow 4 to 6 weeks for delivery. Offer available while quantities last.

Your Privacy—The Harlequin® Reader Service is committed to protecting your privacy. Our Privacy Policy is available online at www.ReaderService.com or upon request from the Harlequin Reader Service.

We make a portion of our mailing list available to reputable third parties that offer products we believe may interest you. If you prefer that we not exchange your name with third parties, or if you wish to clarify or modify your communication preferences, please visit us at www.ReaderService.com/consumerschoice or write to us at Harlequin Reader Service Preference Service, P.O. Box 9062, Buffalo, NY 14269. Include your complete name and address.

HRS13R

Connor Mansfield leaves witness protection to save
his daughter's life and reclaim the woman he loves,
but to have a future together, they must escape assassins
and rebuild lost trust.

Read on for a sneak peek of

THE RETURN OF CONNOR MANSFIELD

by Beth Cornelison, available January 2014 from
Harlequin® Romantic Suspense.

Darby's chin snapped up, her eyes widening. "That sounds
like a threat. What do you mean assure my silence? Connor,
what kind of thugs are you involved with?"

"Not thugs, ma'am," Jones said, pulling out his badge.
"U.S. Marshals. Connor Mansfield is under our protection as
part of WitSec, the Witness Security Program."

"U.S. Marshals?" Darby ignored Jones's badge and scowled
at him. "Since when is it okay for federal agents to kidnap
law-abiding citizens?"

Darby's stomach swirled sourly, and she held her breath,
wondering where she'd found the nerve to so openly challenge
these men. The bulges under their jackets were almost assuredly
guns. How far would these men go to *assure her silence*?

The man named Jones looked surprised. "You haven't been
kidnapped. You're free to go whenever you like."

Darby scoffed. "Childproof locks ring a bell?"

Jones smiled and sent Connor a side glance. "Feisty."

"Just one of her many attributes," he replied.

"Marshal Raleigh," Jones said, still smiling, "would you be so kind as to unlock Ms. Kent's door for her?"

"Roger that." Raleigh pushed a button on the driver's door, and the rear door locks clicked off.

Darby blinked, startled by the turn of events. Was she really free to go, or would they shoot her in the back if she tried to leave? She glanced from the door to Jones, narrowing her eyes as she decided whether Jones was pulling a trick. She tested the door release, and it popped open. Then she paused. *Connor.*

She jerked her gaze back to Connor, the man she'd once loved and conceived a child with, and her heart staggered. This wasn't about a standoff between her and two U.S. Marshals. The important issue was Connor. Who was alive. In Witness Security. And who'd contacted Dr. Reed.

He could well be a tissue match for Savannah's bone marrow transplant. *Connor.*

She exhaled a ragged breath, shifting her gaze from one man to another. And closed the car door. "I… All right. You have my attention."

Don't miss
THE RETURN OF CONNOR MANSFIELD
by Beth Cornelison, available January 2014 from
Harlequin® Romantic Suspense.

ROMANTIC suspense

LETHAL LAWMAN
by Carla Cassidy

Trust your love...

Marlene Marcoli made the mistake of falling
in love, and almost lost her life. Hoping to
put her abusive marriage behind her,
Marlene moves to Wolf Creek, Pennsylvania.
When targeted by a madman bent on revenge,
Detective Frank Delaney vows to protect Marlene
while threatening to break down the walls that
shield her heart from love.

Look for the next title in Carla Cassidy's
Men of Wolf Creek miniseries next month.

Wherever books and ebooks are sold.

Heart-racing romance, high-stakes suspense!

www.Harlequin.com

HRS27853